The Man in the Mirror

# The Man in the Mirror

Jim Dales

This first edition published in Great Britain in 2016 by
Yolk Publishing Limited

ISBN 978-1-910130-11-7



Available from www.yolkpublishing.co.uk
All major online retailers and available to order through all
UK bookshops

Or contact:
Books
Yolk Publishing Limited
145-157 St John Street
London EC1V 4PW

books@yolkpublishing.co.uk
www.yolkpublishing.co.uk

Printed in the UK by Yolk Publishing Ltd
Yolk's policy is to use papers that are natural, renewable and recyclable
products and made from wood grown in sustainable forests
wherever possible

My thanks to those friends whose advice, support and feedback made it possible for me to finish the book: Andy Baker, Matthew Dales, Jane Doonan, Miriam Elloway, Debby Holt, Ann Levick, Pat Scott, Jim Taylor and Julian Watson. Special thanks to my wife Caroline whose perseverance found me my publisher.

# 1

She heard him sigh softly as she entered his workshop, carefully balancing a hunk of bread, cheese, and a jug of beer in her hands. Seeing that he was preoccupied she placed her burdens carefully amongst the clutter on his painting table and, going quietly back to the door, slipped out of the room. She feared that one day she would find him in exactly the same place, in exactly the same pose only dead. But not today; today, he shifted in his chair, staring at the painting where it stood on the easel a few feet in front of him.

Too late, he sensed her presence, turned and smiled after her. He hadn't heard her. Was he deaf? No, not yet, and he wasn't blind either. He might need a lens and a bright light to read and write but, as he did little of either now, he didn't really care. In fact, for a man of his age his eyesight wasn't bad. True, it could be irritating sometimes to peer at a blurred edge and an out-of-focus area, but it simplified things and made him trust his senses more. Not that he didn't trust his intuition and now, in old age, with his technique imprinted in his hands, he didn't have to think about it too much. He got to his feet and stretched cautiously. At his time of life he was less concerned about what others thought of his work, it was enough that he satisfied himself.

He leant forward; smearing and scratching at the canvas with his fingers, trying to coax the paint to obey, to coalesce and coincide with the vision in his head, so that when he inspected it later, with his spectacles perched on the end of his nose, and it came into focus it had a simplicity, a directness; something he hadn't always achieved when he could see clearly. Executed loosely, the coat rendered in sombre dead colour, the paint dragged so that the forms, the outlines, dissolved in the light: it was good. It was very good.

There he stood, looking out, life-size, resigned, the hands barely indicated, clasped in front of him, his brushes abandoned, nowhere to be seen: the curly, grey hair springing out from beneath his cap, the coat with its moth-eaten fur collar pulled close around his neck. It was cold in Amsterdam this spring, in this studio, in this house; stripped bare by his creditors. He didn't really need the mirror. He might not see clearly, but his eyes were still bright and he knew that face: he had spent most of his life looking at it, charting its progress and now its decay; no longer the young, ambitious painter with his career before him. Now, he was an old man with a thickening nose, podgy skin, sagging creases, broken veins, open pores and that wisp of a moustache. Was it vanity that made him wear it even though it did make him look faintly ridiculous?

He scanned his workshop and picked at the paint embedded beneath his finger nails. The plain, plank floor spattered with colour, the canvases stacked against the wall: some finished, some awaiting his attention, others not yet primed. Dirty rags in piles, brushes upended in pots, worn out or stiff with dried pigments: lead white; red ochre; vermilion; red lake; lead tin yellow; azurite and smalt. Drawings scattered across his table or pinned up beside old palettes dangling from a nail bashed into the wall, a skinny neck through the noose on a gibbet. Like the debris and detritus on a beach after a shipwreck when the tide recedes, and there pushed against the wall at the back of the room was the trestle with the stone where he and his assistants ground their colours. Worn to a deep hollow in the centre, it had been with him all his career, scrounged from Van Swanenburg's when he first set up as an independent painter. There were other props from the days when he lived in a grand style on the Jodenbreestraat: books in ancient bindings; a skull; a scraggy lion's pelt; old shields and rusty swords; an easel crusted with paint, and hanging over everything the smell of linseed oil and turpentine, alchemical elixirs, the tools of his trade.

He rubbed the callous on the end joint of his middle finger. He was rather proud of it, even if it did itch on occasion. It was the mark of his years holding a brush. He had spent thousands of hours studying and painting his reflection. This half-length mirror in Venetian gilt, the frame chipped and worn showing the red bole beneath and, in places, the original oak, was a replacement for the great ebony-framed mirror that he had owned at the height of his career. He'd sent it to the pawnbrokers when things first went crash and had almost recovered it when his house was sold and he'd had a little money. But, as usual, fate was waiting on the bridge as he was bringing it home and it fell and smashed into pieces. He looked into the glass again, hoping to see himself alone, and not accompanied by that stranger, the stranger who he sometimes saw reflected in his eyes.

He nibbled at a piece of the cheese and stared at his image. Then, with his little finger, he delicately manoeuvred the paint around the eye, stepped back and absentmindedly sipped his beer. A frown crossed his face: he needed to piss, immediately, it was an urgent matter. He stood over the bucket in the corner of the room, behind the screen where his models used to undress, and waited. The days of his childhood, when he had competed with his friends to see who could piss the highest or played the game of push-piss, driving a twig along with a stream of urine to see who could cover the greatest distance: all that a distant memory. Now it was just a dribble, a few drops at a time, and he was lucky if he got complete relief. Having a shit was painful too. He shook himself vigorously and farted, a common occurrence these days. If this was old age he wouldn't mind getting out of it. On the other hand, he reminded himself, he could still manage an erection even though he hadn't had a fuck since Hendrickje's death.

He leant towards his painting table and picked up a brush. Using the end of the handle, he deftly scratched, onto the painting, the outline of his maul stick: a few more marks and his brushes appeared in his hand.

He must stink a little too. He couldn't tell: what was left of his sense of smell was disappearing along with his eyesight and hearing. It had been compromised long ago, working as an apprentice making paint, being inducted into all those dark secrets. Even now after all these years he still pondered on the miracle of those recipes. He could almost believe that someone might have seen the verdigris that forms a patina on copper when it was exposed to acid in the lees left from the fermentation of wine and tried to make a green paint from it. But how had anyone thought that dipping lead in vinegar and then burying it in rotting horseshit would produce a brilliant white? And what about vermillion - cinnabar mixed and heated with sulphur to make a dark substance that miraculously becomes a wonderful red when beaten under water. It was alchemy of course, magic, the by-product of centuries of messing about with chemicals, grinding rocks and pigments trying to make gold from base metals, and it was why painters like him were in a guild with the Apothecaries.

And what about those countless hours making etchings, pouring acid over copper plate, choking odours inhaled amongst the pipe smoke? Was it any wonder his nose looked like a desiccated tomato squashed on the front of his face? He put down his brushes and gazed up at the ceiling. They had been good times though, wonderful times: those days in Leiden when he was serving his apprenticeship with Van Swanenburg; struggling to stretch canvases, to make colours; when he and Jan had studios in the same street, using each other as models, painting each other's portraits: those had been productive days with lots of laughter. Of course they had been fiercely competitive, but that was the nature of the game; each thought they were the best. Jan had been wrong, of course, but then he had been wrong about lots of things: time had proved that. But he had to admit Jan had been a precocious talent, starting his apprenticeship at the tender age of eight: at that age he was still in Latin School. Jan Lievens worked with Lastman in Amsterdam by the time he was 10 and was an independent artist at 14 – the same age he had been when he began his apprenticeship. It was Lievens who had advised him to go to Amsterdam to study with Lastman. It had been a good move too, as things turned out, although he would probably have gone anyway. He had been far too ambitious to stay in Leiden.

Suddenly he was visited by another sensation. There had been a time when his memory had been under his command, something he could use at will, a source of images and ideas he drew upon to fuel his imagination. He had been able to bring back events, recapture their essence and savour them again. But lately this facility had become wilful and capricious as if it had gained its freedom and could not be denied, like a wayward clown it would, without warning, deliver a recollection he had not willed.

'Isn't he beautiful?' Saskia said as she held the boy. Although too weak to suckle him herself, she was immensely proud, so pleased with little Titus, joyful to have given birth to a healthy boy. Three times they had celebrated the birth of a child: two girls and a boy and three times they had mourned as each died before their first year was out. He'd learned a lot about death. So his pride had been tinged with apprehension when once again she presented him with a son and heir to the house on the Breestraat, a house worthy of Amsterdam's greatest artist who had risen from being the son of a miller to join the ranks of the city's finest. This time it was the child who survived and Saskia who died. His greatest joy lost at the height of his fame. So what had he gained from all these years of struggle? Now, the fine house with its furniture and servants were all gone too: they belonged in the past, but he'd kept his integrity, no one could deny that. True, he had occasionally put his signature to a work by a student. But that wasn't unusual, lots of painters did that. The students were grateful and in the old days his signature meant they could sell their work at a premium. He had been the best and everyone knew it, but not anymore, few people wanted his signature now. Perhaps it had been his confidence, his arrogance that had finally driven him to disaster?

No! It had been the death of Saskia: something beyond his control. That had been the turning point; the fracture; the split in the fabric that separated the certainty of the past from the chaos of the future. Although that future was now in the past and here he was again in front of this bloody mirror peering at himself, no longer the poet or philosopher but a man at the end of his life, the life he had lived the way he had wanted. But if it was he who had driven his life, then what about this other man, the man behind him in the mirror? When had he appeared? When Saskia died? He was sure that as a young man he hadn't seen him, but perhaps, even back in the days in Leiden, he'd been there. Perhaps he'd always been there. Was it this man, this stranger, he saw reflected in the mirror, who had wanted the things that fame and fortune brought with them? Was it he who had promised Saskia that one day they would own the house on the Breestraat? Surely not: it was all done with his skill and talent. It had been the house a painter at the height of his career should live in. Not only should, but must live in. So what if he had paid too much for it? He had had no intention of hiding his talent in some dingy backwater of Amsterdam. The rented house on the Vlooienburg had been a staging post before he crossed the canal and was out in the world. He had wanted to step from the street through his own front door, to look down and know that what was beneath his feet was his, his house, his property and to look up at the stone walls, solid, permanent, enduring, knowing he owned a piece of the city, a stake in the country, in its soil, in its water and in its history.

Leivens had assured him that both of them would become part of the history of the country, just like Titian in Italy and Rubens in the Low Countries. They were the ones who left something permanent behind, something that was part of the fabric of the place. After all, who would remember the admirals or the generals who fought the Spanish and the English if their portraits were not painted by the artists?

He moved over to where several canvases, covered with a sheet, were leaning together against the wall. He handled each one tenderly placing it gently, back to back before finding what he was looking for and lifting it out. Holding it at arm's length, he carried it across the room and placed it against the wall, opposite the window. He settled in his chair and leant back to squint at the picture from a distance as it stood in the light. No, it was not his greatest painting, but one in which he still took great pleasure: a portrait of Hendrickje standing in a stream, her breasts almost revealed as she bent forward and lifted her shift, a little too high, showing her thighs, knowing what lay between and might be reflected in the water into which she waded, sharing with him those secret places, a gift which he had celebrated in this picture, a testament to his craft and the woman he painted.

He went across the room and pressed his face close to the canvas as if he hoped to recapture the musky odour of her flesh. When other painters were adopting a smoother, slicker finish, hiding the painterly hand in the subject, he had made this daring tour de force, painted at speed with bravura brushstrokes. The ripples in the water indicated by tiny flicks of lead white; the reflection made with transparent ochre and red earth dragged in with a dry brush; the contrast between the, almost incoherent, left hand and the detail of the curl of her hair, flicked in as it fell on her shoulder just to the right of the earring: a stunning piece of painting exposing, rather than concealing, his handling of the paint. He had revelled in his skill knowing that the picture would be theirs to share; it was about their friendship, their love, their sexual attraction.

He knew his goddesses and Hendrickje hadn't been one, at least not in this painting. He had employed a subdued palette set off by the red and gold robe she had cast off as she proclaimed her reality, her physical presence, self-possessed, certainly an object for display: but for his eyes only. It was never meant for anyone else to see, only the two of them, the people involved. Hendrickje had suffered for her relationship with him, denied communion by the Calvinist Church and condemned as a fallen woman. She had remained loyal, given birth to their daughter Cornelia and, along with Titus, had protected him from the creditors who swarmed around after he was declared bankrupt. Had they known of its existence, those creditors would have loved to get their hands on this painting. But he had outwitted them, hiding it in the house of a trusted friend: it did not appear in any inventory of his possessions.

He replaced the canvas among the others in the stack and covered them over again. He returned to his chair and sank gingerly into it, resting for a few moments before he turned his attention to the portrait again. Wasn't this proof enough that his hand was still steady? He had been famous once, hadn't he? Even the odious Dircx woman would be remembered if he was remembered. She was another of those memories that came back unbidden. That woman had bothered him: the colour of her skin, pale but with the tint of someone brought up by the sea, her infectious laugh with a coarse edge. Her smell was as comforting as the odours of his house, combining cleanliness with food and paint, but she distracted him too, made him clumsy, breathless but also younger, more alive, attractive and virile.

It had started one evening in the summer. He was accustomed to working late while the light was good. Always alone, he would sit at his table beneath the high windows, a relief after standing in front of a canvas all day. He was making an etching: the copper plate had already been bitten twice in the acid and now needed the accuracy of the burin, the engraver's tool, which he had mastered as a young man.

'I have put the boy to bed.' She was standing by the open door.

'Thank you,' he said, still peering at the plate, turning it in his hands, holding it to the light to see if the cut was deep and clean enough. He leant back in his chair aware that she was still there.

'He is asleep. The wet nurse will be back in the morning.'

'Be sure to close the door as you leave.'

He resumed his examination of the plate even though he had already decided that he could do no more that night. He mustn't forget to dampen the paper so that it would be ready the next day when he proofed the image: pressing ink into the indentations made by the acid and burin, wiping the unmarked parts of the surface, polishing it with the side of his hand before running it through the press to transfer the drawing onto the paper.

'What are you doing?' She was still there, standing inside the closed door.

He looked down at the plate, irritated at being disturbed but answered, 'I'm working on an etching, a landscape I made a few days ago. I'm strengthening some of the lines.' He tried to concentrate. Why was she still here? Why didn't he tell her to leave?

'Is it difficult?' She came closer and leant over his shoulder.

'No. That is to say I don't find it difficult.' He tried to suppress the stirring in his stomach, feeling the warmth of her breath on his cheek. 'I have been doing it for a long time.' Saskia had been dead for months and he was lonely. 'You have to think in reverse.' He tried to overcome his exasperation, but still he didn't dismiss her. 'The drawing you make on the copper prints back to front, like in a mirror. I only know what I have done when it has been through the press.'

'You must be very clever.'

Was she really here to admire his skill, his hand and eye coordination? 'Look at this.' He made a last attempt to distract himself, drawing a sheet of paper from a large packet lying on the bench close to where he was working and held it towards her. 'This paper has come all the way from Japan; it is very strong and smooth and takes the ink well.'

'It seems like magic to me,' she said, gingerly feeling the paper between her finger and thumb.

'Yes, sometimes I think I am a magician working a kind of alchemy, using metal and acid to make something new. There is something thrilling about peeling back the damp paper to reveal the image. It's as if the lines were already there beneath the polished surface of the copper needing only my ingenuity and skill to find them and bring them to the surface.'

Why was he telling her this, she wasn't in the least interested: was she? 'Is there anything else?' He asked. Suddenly it happened. He raised his eyes and met hers as she looked down, her thoughts perfectly visible, exposed in the evening light that flooded in from the high windows.

'Well?' She said.

He reached out and put his arm round her thighs,

feeling the firm flesh beneath the material of her skirt. She hadn't moved away. He had dropped his hand lower, feeling under her hem and touching the skin just above her ankles. Then she'd stepped back, leaving him aroused and angry, but she didn't go. She stood with her hand on the door handle, as if undecided as to what to do, but she couldn't claim innocence, not now.

He would have her, it was his right, she was his servant, living under his roof, eating his food, wearing the clothes he had paid for. So he had taken her, there and then in haste, on the floor of the workshop, struggling to get out of his britches, to lift her skirts, pull her down. She had resisted at first but she must have wanted it to happen or else why had she come to the room, surely not just to tell him his son was asleep?

In those first few weeks, he had searched her out in the quiet corners of the house, his lust driving him to recklessness. She was compliant. Was it part of a plan to trap him? He didn't care: after a few weeks they'd settled into a routine, the fact that she was willing took the edge off his appetite and he became more circumspect. He would go to her room and occasionally she would share his bed, but if anyone had noticed they said nothing and, at the Marital Court, she had not been able to produce a single witness. He had been stupid but he hadn't been found out and he wasn't going to confess.

He still had moments of guilt, haunted by nightmares of his own making, a doubly heinous crime. He had never loved the woman, but he had been lonely in his bed at night listening to the creak of the wooden walls and floors as the building adjusted itself. So he had invited her in: bad enough but understandable. His greatest regret was the furtive copulation on the grass in places where he and Saskia had walked when he was trying to comfort her over the loss of their children. He shuddered, clenching his fists as he fought to deny the recollection access to his mind.

There was a story going around about a German astronomer and necromancer who had been so ambitious that he had sold his soul to the devil in exchange for all the wisdom of the world. Had this man in the mirror made a similar kind of pact without him knowing anything about it? Could that be possible?

What had that young Jew told him all those long years ago? He couldn't remember: couldn't even remember the man's name; something else he had forgotten. What had he told him? Along with his other faculties, his memory was unreliable now but he should remember. 'Cogito ergo sum', that was it. He knew how to translate it, after all he'd been to Latin school for seven years, but what did it mean? He couldn't be sure: that he was two substances, a brain and a body? Perhaps; these days it did seem that his crumbling body was in control, dictating what he could or couldn't do most of the time. Spinoza, now he remembered, that was the young man's name.

# 2

Leiden: summer almost over; not a breath of wind; barges stand marooned in the meadows, their sails hanging limp. Swallows, swifts and martins wheel high in the sky, skim the canal and the river as it seeps towards the sea, hunting their final feast before they leave these fertile flatlands for the south. It has been a hospitable home for the summer: the thatched cottages and hay-barns with their deep shady eaves and the wetlands offering an abundance of mud and insects.

The two mill buildings stand on either side of the miller's house, close to the city walls where they fall away towards a murky creek that joins the main river as it enters the town. Not a grand building with its narrow, three-storied brick façade beneath a steeply pitched roof, stepped gables and tall, leaded-windows, but solid, permanent, denoting an owner of substance, someone with roots.

The day is sultry; the mill almost silent; the only sounds the gentle creak of the wood as it adjusts to the heat of the sun and voices from below where someone checks the machinery. A young man is lying on his back, hands behind his head in the tiny space at the top of one of the mills. Beside him is a drawing scrawled in the dust on the floor, dust that coats the space here below the vane; swags of cobwebs festooned with the corpses of insects; a charnel house where even the dead are dusty. Our young man loves this dark interior, the atmosphere thick with the smell of barley, the sunlight glowing through the narrow windows and the cracks in the wooden walls as if they had been pierced with arrows, the dust in the air making light visible. It is this light shining in amongst the deafening din of the huge rotating stones when the mill is working, the creaking of the wooden spars of the sails harnessing the wind, driving the cogs and gears that he wants, one day, to invest in his paintings. Generations of his family have worked milling barley for beer, a superior craft according to his father, above the common grinding of wheat for bread even though in medieval Europe bread made from barley had been the staple food of the peasants.

And there are books: one lies open, leather-bound from the fifteenth century: 'De Pictura' enclosing the distilled wisdom of Florentine art, written in Latin and gathered together by Leon Battista Alberti: painter, sculptor and architect of that city. Is our young man using its accumulated wisdom to help conjure the recalcitrant dust into an image of the landscape seen through the tiny door that gives access to the sails of the mill? Or has he put it aside to dream of the future? A future where he plans to climb a very different ladder, not to a tiny space at the top of a windmill, but to the very pinnacle of success where his fame and fortune will outshine even those illustrious men commemorated in the venerable book beside him.

'So here you are. Your father said you'd be up here reading.' Another youthful head appears through the trapdoor.

As there is no room for two in the tiny space, our young man scuffs out his drawing and crawls to the opening, lowers himself onto the ladder and gathers the books beside him. He hands them to his companion below, and then drops to the floor himself, shaking the flour dust and cobwebs from his tousled hair as his friend helps brush his clothes with his hands.

'All ready to go? I've come to say goodbye. I know you're off tomorrow but before you leave, I thought you might like to see a place I've found that I reckon will make you a fine workshop.'

'What?' Our young painter stops dusting himself, 'Jan you're a marvel. Where is it?'

'It's in the same street as mine, across the river from Van Swanenburg's place. Have you time to come and look?'

'Certainly I've got time. You'd better show me straight away.' He gives his head another vigorous shake. 'On the way I can pick up a few things from the workshop.' He knocks more dust from his clothes, 'And I must return this.' He takes the leather bound book from his friend, blows the dust off the cover and polishes it with his sleeve before handing it back. 'Jacob doesn't know I've got it, yet.'

Jan examines the book, turning the pages delicately. 'You're taking a risk borrowing this without permission. It must be one of the few copies left in the country.'

'I know. It's one of his souvenirs from Italy, but I only took it for a few hours and, with luck, he'll never find out.'

The two friends descend to the ground floor.

The young man's father is floury white, his thick eyebrows acting as shelves for a layer of dust. His hair seems to have abandoned any attempt to grow on the top of his head and now searches for other places from which to sprout. He had told his son that, 'The white things growing out of my ears and nose are to keep the dust out of my brain.' And for a long time the boy had believed him, although it didn't explain the hairy fuzz on the back of his hands or his voluminous beard.

The old man lifts and sifts, plunging his hands deep into a sack, cupping and pulling them out overflowing with grain, sniffing, cracking and rubbing with his fingers as it cascades back into the sack. He holds out a handful and gestures towards his son. 'He's got a good nose for this job'. Then, allowing the grain to drain from his hands back into the sack, he added, 'But he's chosen a different profession.' He knocks his hands together releasing another halo of dust into the air, 'Just as well I suppose. There's not enough business to keep all our families going.'

The two young men set off towards the centre of the town.

'His eyesight isn't so good these days,' our young man tells his friend. 'Luckily my brother is still fit enough to take over.'

'Was that him in the yard; the man with a limp?'

'Yes, that was Gerrit.'

'What happened to him?'

'Milling can be a dangerous business. Apart from the risk of getting your limbs caught up in the machinery, there's a lot of heavy work. A few years ago, when he was removing some sacks from the hoist, he fell. It was a silly accident. I was down on the ground sweeping but I remember it clearly: the slow curve as he fell the twenty feet onto the cart below. The doctor who came told him he'd been lucky: the sacks had broken his fall.' He paused, 'They'd also broken both his legs. Still, they set well, but that's why he has a limp. The real luck, if you can call it that is he can't do military service and, as my father's sight is failing, he's free to take over the business.'

'I was talking to your father before I came to find you and he told me that years ago your grandmother carried the mill here piece by piece. Is that true?'

His companion smiled. 'That's the family tradition. She was a young woman when the war with Spain was at its height. The Spanish were about to lay siege to the town so the authorities ordered that all the mills outside the walls be destroyed and, as one of them belonged to her, she told them she wasn't having any of that.'

'So what did she do?'

'Well, first she pointed out to them that if the town wasn't to starve, someone had to grind wheat to make bread or at least what passed for bread.'

'Better than boiled grass, I suppose.'

'True. Anyway, she told them that whatever happened she wasn't standing by while they destroyed her property. But neither was she going to let it fall into enemy hands.'

'So she dismantled the mill and carried it single handed to where it is now, and saved the town from starvation?'

'That's what she told me when I was a boy, if you can believe the ramblings of an old woman. But I thought everyone knew that story. This area has been left open ever since, so the mills get the wind most of the time.' He pointed to the roofs of the houses beyond the walls. 'I can remember when all that was orchards and meadows.'

'And it's all below sea level.'

'Yes, but then so is most of the country around here and it had rained a lot too, or so my mother says. She was a child at that time. It is so low around here that after a year of the siege the city council ordered the sluices to be opened and the land flooded.'

'Not a strategy that would go down very well now that the town has grown so much.'

'No, but inside the city the houses are so close together that there's always a risk of fire, so later when they needed to expand, they had to build outside the walls.'

'So, it was a victory over the enemy using rain and a lot of dirty flood water.'

'You could say that. I think it's more likely that the Spaniards simply got fed up with the damp and wanted to go home to the sunshine. Don't forget that the plague was about too. But it makes a better story if you defeat your enemy in battle, rather than they just run away to avoid the wet weather.'

Jan, who was still carrying the book, returned it to his friend as they approached Van Swanenburg's studio. 'Can you read Latin?'

'Seven years at Latin school studying Ovid and Horace? Oh yes, I can read Latin.'

'And was it useful?' Jan pointed to the book.

'I haven't had time to read it all. There's a bit too much maths in it for me but the bits about story telling, what he calls "Istoria" I found very interesting. You must have done the same stuff with Lastman. Wasn't he in Italy like Jacob?'

'Pieter prefers Van Mander's "Schilderboeck" as his guide. He loves those southern painters too, but he's a man of business. He knows what his clients want and how to produce it. How long have you been with Van Swanenburg?'

'Three years.'

'You'll learn more from Pieter in six months than you've learned here in all that time.'

'So you say, and I hope you're right. Don't forget it's your idea that I should go.'

'Don't worry: it will be the making of you. It will be much better than going off to Italy. You'll come back ready to start in the business straight away.'

Jacob van Swanenburg's workshop was in one of the better areas of the town, part of an old style patrician's house but kept in such a way as not to flaunt its status; aware that grandeur counted far less in the new dispensation where zealous Calvinism held sway.

In the yard outside the workshop a young apprentice straightened up from planing a panel of oak, wiped the sweat from his face then nodded in recognition at the young painter, 'I thought you'd left us.'

'I'm off tomorrow but I need to collect a few things. Is Jacob about?'

'No, you've missed him. He's in town pricing a job. He won't be back for a while.' The apprentice spat on his hands and returned his attention to his plane.

The painter took the opportunity to slip into the

house and replace the book. When he came out Jan had disappeared into the workshop. The doors had been left wide open to increase the flow of air. It was a large space with high windows and hinged, cloth screens to control the light; closed now because of the sun.

He looked around, perhaps for the last time. He had spent many working days here and, despite Jan's reservations, he knew he'd picked up quite a lot. True, it would be an exaggeration to say he'd been taught very much about composition or the finer points of painting. What he had learned was that much of the painter's craft is dull and routine and that moments of insight are rare but when they arrive it is an experience like no other and it made him want to go on. He had done all the tasks required in the workshop: the jobs a master painter gave to his minions, the kind of thing he would, in his turn, hand to his apprentices. There, on the window sill where they received the sunlight to keep them bleached, were the glass jars containing the different oils: linseed, walnut, and poppy, each with their own character. Beside them, on the shelves above the benches were the pigments. Grinding pigment had been a daily task, done early in the morning so the paint would be fresh for the day. He had planed planks and prepared wooden panels, stretched and primed canvas. He had served his time. When he came back from Amsterdam it would be as an equal, in fact more than an equal because he knew he would surpass his master. He doubted that the workshop Jan had found would be as imposing as this but it would be a beginning.

Jan was watching a couple of the apprentices. They

seemed a little intimidated by his presence, his fame having gone before him. He watched as they primed a wooden panel, layering it with lead white, chalk and glue paste. Jan ran his hand over the surface. 'Good,' he told them as he squinted along the grain of the wood. 'Very good. I've lost count of the hours I've spent planing wooden panels. I was always told that if you have to ask if it's flat enough, then it isn't. We've all had to do it. Don't despise it. I dare say I'll have to do it again myself before too long.'

Later, they made their way through the narrow streets towards the more commercial sector of the town. Though it was cooler out of the sun the smell of lanolin from sheep's wool hung in the air. Imported Spanish and English fleeces were the base material from which the wealth of the town had been spun. Wool fluff lurked in every nook and cranny and hung on the breeze like thistledown. The painter, having rid himself of his coating of flour, brushed it away.

The workshop that Jan had found was on the first floor of an old warehouse up a wooden flight of stairs. There were cracks and patches of damp and in places the rough plaster on the walls had fallen away revealing the narrow brickwork beneath. That, and the worn plank floor, gave it a dilapidated but romantic air.

'It's going to be cold here in the winter,' the young painter remarked running his hand along the wall and examining the white lime paint that rubbed off on his palm. 'Even on a day like today there's a chill in the air.'

'Of course it's damp. No one has been in here for months.' Jan stamped hard on the floor. 'This is solid enough to take the weight of a press. You could make etchings up here.'

'Perhaps, but I'm still trying to master the technique. I've got plenty of ideas but there's a lot I don't know. Can we get the press up the stairs?'

'Of course we can get it up the stairs. I'll give you a hand. A couple of strong men like us will have no trouble. We could always rig up a hoist and bring it in through the window. We don't want you giving up and going back to the family milling business, now do we?' Jan paced out the length of the room, looked up at the windows set just below the eaves to let in the maximum daylight, 'It's well lit, like in the theatre: it will lend drama to your work.'

'The whole damned business of life is a drama,' the painter said. 'Thanks Jan, you've done well. This will do fine.' He looked up at the ceiling then at his friend, 'There's a lot of ill feeling about in the town. Are you worried it will boil up again, and we'll find this dislike of images will kill the market for paintings?'

'No, no, I don't think so, after all, this is a rich town. There's always someone wanting their portrait painted: lawyers, surgeons, not forgetting the theologians who, despite their railing against worldly goods and fame, want to be remembered too. Look at Van Swanenburg: he's not a great painter, with those weird paintings of Hell and Damnation but he makes a good living and Lastman has made a fortune. You've only got to look around to see there's plenty of material in these parts. Beggars and cripples will let you draw them for practically nothing in the winter, just to keep warm and we can use each other as models. I can't wait for you to get back from Amsterdam.'

'I thought you told me Lastman was a Catholic?'

Jan put a finger to his lips, 'Best keep quiet about that. He's a great painter and he's in Amsterdam. I'm a better painter than Van Swanenburg; even you have to admit that. I know I'm a year younger than you but I'm the better painter. Apart from Lastman, I don't believe there's a better painter in Germany or Holland; probably not even in the Seventeen Provinces.' Seeing the frown on his friend's face he added, 'I mean, we're both good, the best in fact. It's just that I've had the benefit of working since I was seven, whereas you've come to it a bit later. Your time with Lastman will be well worth it but I think we should forget about Amsterdam as a base for a few years. In Leiden, there's less competition and we can make a good living. We've got to be realistic; we need to establish ourselves; build a reputation then, I think we may do great things.'

As the young painter made his way home he pondered on the future. Jan Lievens, the embroiderer's son from Ghent, a celebrity by the time he was 12, a prodigious talent but also an arrogant bastard. Was he the best? Better than himself? He didn't think so. He was the one who was special. As for poverty, he wanted nothing to do with it. He could see that many of the people around were grotesque and ugly, beggars and children, insignificant and suffering but he had come to the conclusion that suffering made you weak and tamed your independence. He might use them as source material to populate his paintings but he saw nothing romantic about living in squalor. He accepted much of the teaching of the Calvinists' but not that the meek would inherit the earth or there was some grand purpose in poverty. He didn't believe that God favoured the downtrodden. He couldn't see it and in any case he intended to do his utmost to avoid it. Six months in Amsterdam should be enough. He would meet the right people, make contacts then get back to Leiden but he wouldn't stay long: fame and fortune lay in Amsterdam. Jan had said they 'might do great things.' There was no 'might' about it, he would do great things. He could learn a lot from Jan but that shouldn't take long and then he would be off.

He smiled to himself: he would sign his pictures RHL: Rembrandus Hermanni Leydensis.

# 3

So what was it like? That first time in the winter of 1624 as he wandered south from the Breestraat, over the bridge, past the brick houses facing the canal where the more prosperous merchants lived? Was Lastman his guide? Master and pupil strolling together; the precociously talented apprentice from Leiden walking with Amsterdam's greatest history painter Pieter Lastman, the epitome of success, a painter to rival Rubens with his gift for narrative; the expressive gesture and grimace; crowd scenes full of action; loafers, pedlars, snoopers, stragglers and conjurors; men in hats, men in turbans, men in the tattered remnants of their clothes; girls in satin, girls in silk; images that are not lost on a young man who wants more than success as a provincial artist. A visit to the Vloorienberg, the Jewish quarter in Amsterdam, is part of his training. To paint Histories you need to study the people of the Old Testament: and here they are.

The Dutch aren't stupid; they might be fighting a war to be rid of the Spanish but it's as much a war about keeping Spain's hands out of their pockets as a war for religious freedom. This isn't a ghetto: Jews don't have to live here, already the more successful have moved out. Some clip their beards and wear tall, black hats instead of skullcaps; dress in the sober fashion of the Gentile; wear black linen or felt, sometimes silk, so he might pass rabbi or pastor and see no difference. The Sephardim gave up many of their customs under the Inquisition. If you are commanded to remove your trousers, circumcision is difficult to conceal so some abandoned it. Many feasts go unobserved but not all their rituals are given up. Passover is still observed. More importantly Jews brought their wealth; trade with the Americas and the Indies diverted from Spain to Amsterdam: emeralds, diamonds, indigo and exotic timbers.

He must have noticed, as he went deeper, the sails that slipped across the vertical strips of daylight at the far end of the narrow alleys. Here, where the houses are poorer and made of wood is where the tailors, bakers and wig makers, gem cutters and lens grinders ply their trade and where physicians and surgeons, some of whom will become his clients, have their businesses. At night he might return to an inn and hear Jewish music but perhaps it was the smells and not the sights that impressed him more: the watery scents of mud, fish and salt air where the Binnen Amstel joined the Amstel proper.

Seagulls swirl overhead or swoop down for some discarded herring or oyster; quarrelsome and squabbling their cries in competition with the cacophony of the sawing, the hammering, and the shouting of the shipwrights who build the ships and barges that move the wealth about the city and the country. Here, the smells are pitch, hemp, canvas and rope, mingling with sawdust from the tiers of timber planks, each separated from the one below by wooden wedges to let the air flow through so they finish dry and straight. This is where he would find the quays and warehouses storing the imports of the Jewish merchants. The prosaic odours of the north: Baltic grain and timber can find no entry here, overwhelmed by the exotic fragrances of the Levant, the Mediterranean and the Americas: an intoxicating mixture of tobacco, spices, almonds, Spanish raisins, figs, candied fruit, and ginger, oriental carpets, and fabrics: the smell of history. He is intoxicated by the exotic. When he moves to Amsterdam, he will rent a house in this district close to the river. He will live by the Binnen Amstel for two years before, flush with success and confident in his talent, he will leave the Vloorienberg reversing his journey as a student, back over the bridge, and like Lastman, move into a grand house on the Breestraat, a new area of the city. All this the outward sign of his success and this is the area of the city where he will find his patrons, dealers and other painters.

On the day he moved there was a steady stream of students carrying his worldly goods: mysterious boxes; furniture; paintings and picture frames; sculptures; a printing press; all his painting paraphernalia, and his pregnant wife.

## 4

I knew his house. It faced the river and was a magnet for the curious because of the clamour, the comings and goings of students and clients, materials going in and paintings coming out. It was next door to the baker's so in the mornings the smell of bread and cakes spiced with cloves and candied ginger filled the air. Some older boys took me there: I was curious. They told me that to even look at his house was to risk the wrath of God because he made images of the Almighty and that was forbidden. One day they dared me go up to the front door and knock whilst they watched from a distance. When the maid opened the door they ran away leaving me alone on the doorstep. She was angry, but then the mistress of the house appeared and took me in and gave me a piece of cake. There were supposed to be naked men and women there but I didn't see any. I remember pictures on the wall but as for any graven images, I'm not sure I would have known what they were. I was more interested in the cake.

Although I was still a little afraid I went back another day to watch. Again, I waited a little way off and peered round the corner. Was he an alchemist and sorcerer as people claimed? Did he follow people about and draw their faces for use in his magic? Another rumour that circulated was that he conjured with acid and copper, wax and paper, oil paint and canvas. For a Jewish boy, that was both fascinating and blasphemous. I was intrigued by his house and went often until my father found me there and dragged me away. He wasn't angry, just perplexed but he made me promise never to go again and I obeyed. I was only six and my mother had recently died. Soon after that the painter moved away and faded from my memory. It wasn't until we were both in trouble that we met again.

## 5

Three men stand together in an imposing room: the great hall of the Kloveniersdoelen in Amsterdam. In the middle, beneath the high oak-beamed ceiling is the painter Rembrandt. He is now in his middle thirties, stocky, soberly but expensively dressed, his dark eyes set in a round face. He wears a goatee beard, a moustache and curly, shoulder-length hair topped by a beret. He has a slight swagger as he moves and gesticulates to his two companions as if to let them know that he is not in awe of them or their building. They are here to discuss a grand project: the commission to paint the district militia company of which they are the leading members.

He can remember the construction of the building: their splendid new headquarters overlooking the river Amstel. Built in the classical style to reflect the wealth and status of its members; its six tall windows on the ground floor set within seven pilasters, whilst above on the first floor they are separated by double, classical columns. Due to the leaden, winter skies of northern Europe, allowing light to penetrate the building is a major consideration.

Even as the building rose from the mud and sand, depositing dirt and dust into his studio adjacent to the site, Rembrandt was confident that when the construction was complete he would be amongst those commissioned to make the paintings that would decorate the very room in which they now stand. Like the building, he has risen in the world and now lives in a grand house on the Jodenbreestraat. He is highly regarded as one of the leading painters in the city but, for all his bravado and confidence in his ability to win the contract and complete the picture, he is nervous. His extravagant lifestyle means that in spite of his fame, and the wealth it has brought him, his finances are not good. It is important that he gets the work. He needs the money.

There were to be seven paintings in the great hall but he was there to bid for only one. But, he told himself as he surveyed the vast space allocated to the picture, it was by far the biggest and most important and it would certainly be the best. A little flattery and self-promotion should win the day. After all, these days the militia companies only fulfilled a ceremonial role in the life of the city

He was also aware that civic pride, independence and freedom were the values uppermost in the minds of the city's rulers, despite the more severe Calvinist culture that now dominated the country. The heroes of this newly won independence were the citizen soldiers and the most revered amongst them were the Kloveniers, the shooters. Their weapon, the Harquebus, was a long-barrelled flintlock, so long indeed that it needed a stick with a forked end to rest on whilst it was fired. Rembrandt smiled inwardly, they certainly needed the protection of their patron Saint Christopher because the gun was just as likely to blow the shooter's head off as send its lead ball into the enemy.

He knew, as all the inhabitants of the city knew, that here in Amsterdam there had been little opportunity for epic feats of courage. The sieges, massacres and battles had taken place in other parts of the country with foreign mercenaries doing most of the fighting. Nevertheless, the citizen soldiers and their militias had retained a civic role and encouraging them in the sense of their own importance would not go amiss.

'So, of the three paintings yet to be completed, ours will hang there,' Captain Banning Cocq stood with his back to the empty space on the left hand side of the wall facing the windows. 'Will the sunlight present a problem?'

Frans Banning Cocq was a tall, cultivated man, well educated with a doctorate in law from the University of Poitiers. He had married into money; his father-in-law had been a powerful man in the city, a founder member of the East India Company with a fleet of ships. When he died Banning Cocq inherited his daughter and with her his wealth. He was now the leader of the militia company and would be awarding the commission. 'I am told that it might be difficult to see it if the sun is full upon it.'

'No. It will not be a problem,' the painter replied. 'In fact, I believe we can take advantage of the light from the windows. I'm sure you gentleman can see that with the position you have been allocated in this splendid hall, you have been presented with a wonderful opportunity.'

'We want something grand; something monumental.'

'And you shall have it. I can guarantee that,' the painter told him. 'We live in historic time's gentlemen. The war with Spain cannot go on much longer. Soon we shall be victorious and your part in our victory must be celebrated.'

His companions looked at each other: Lieutenant Willem van Ruytenburgh was a rather puffed-up, little man; fond of fine clothes, somewhat at odds with the prevailing fashion. Not as wealthy as his Captain, though he still maintained a house in the city and a country estate. 'I am not as confident as you,' he said. 'The war is not yet over, and even when it is, I am not so sure the Provinces will hang together. What if they fall apart? The south has stayed loyal to the Spanish Crown and threatens us both politically and religiously. We must protect the freedom we have established for the Reformed Church. We Calvinists are the community of the elect, predestined for eternal life by the redemptive blood of Christ.' Then, as if suddenly remembering that he is here to discuss the painting, he shrugged his shoulders, 'But that is for the future, now to the business in hand. What do you propose?'

Rembrandt unfolded some sheets of rough sketches and spread them on the floor. The drawings were broadly made with pen and wash and gave only an approximate idea of his design. He needed to allow himself some latitude as the painting progressed but he also wanted to appear inclusive, to let them think they were involved in the planning of the audacious painting that he proposed. But it was also a gesture of contempt: he knew that his prospective clients' dignity would not allow them to stoop too low or get down on their hands and knees to take a closer look. He was certain that they, well-educated as they were, had no artistic sensibility of any kind.

With the end of his stick, he pushed one drawing clear of the others. 'I suggest we set our picture outside your headquarters. We can make use of the sunlight by imitating the light from the window so that you are seen coming out of the building across the bridge and into the sunshine.'

Banning Cocq was enthusiastic, 'You mean to make our painting a symbol of a nation emerging from the darkness of war into the light of true belief?'

'Yes, perhaps,' Rembrandt was less enthusiastic. It was not quite what he had in mind but if Banning Cocq wanted to put that interpretation on the picture why should he object? As long as he was paid, Banning Cocq could interpret the painting in any way he liked. The actual work would be as he, Rembrandt van Rijn, decided.

'It is a monstrous size,' Van Ruytenburgh added. 'But we have every confidence in you: your reputation speaks for itself.'

A feeling of resentment ran through the painter's head. Of course they should have every confidence in him. He was the best painter in the city; in the country for that matter and, if the paintings he saw passing through the Amsterdam salerooms were anything to go by, the best in Europe. He was unrivalled. Rubens and Titian might come close but they were both dead. 'It will be splendid,' he insisted. 'Simply splendid.'

# 6

He struggled to subdue his irritation as he walked back to his house. It wouldn't do for Amsterdam's leading painter and one of its foremost citizens to be seen with a black look on his face; but he was furious. He reckoned he was the equal of these men. True, he might be the son of a miller but Van Ruytenburgh's father had been just a grocer for God's sake! He was less confident about Banning Cocq: his father had been an apothecary; ostensibly in the same guild as himself but he had married into money and now occupied a place of some importance in the city's hierarchy. But what he found most galling was that they had dared to haggle over the price; forcing him to accept only 100 guilders for each of the 16 junior officers. True, Banning Cocq and that puffed-up little turd Van Ruytenburgh had agreed to pay more for their own portraits but only on condition he gave them prominent places. That was something he could cope with; but not the price! The painting would take him a year, at least. He supposed that some people would have considered it fair but it was a lot less than he had asked for, a lot less than he was worth, and a lot less than he needed. Now, to make matters worse, there was a bitter wind and it was beginning to rain.

There was some compensation in another line of thought running through his head. The Calvinists might see themselves as the community of the elect but they were not able to completely suppress ideas that were in opposition to them. Toleration continued to flourish, religious diversity and an intellectual climate were having profound implications for political, religious and scientific thought and there was nothing Banning Cocq or Van Ruytenburgh could do about it. He pulled his coat close about him; he wanted to be home in the warm.

## 7

The housemaid stopped sweeping the hall to take his coat then, pausing only to change into his indoor shoes, he ran up the stairs. He was anxious to tell Saskia of his success in winning the commission but when he looked into her room, she was asleep in the box bed with her maid dozing in the chair beside her. He decided it best not to disturb them.

They had been married for seven years and of all their children none had survived their first year. Their most recent daughter, Cornelia had died only a few months ago. Now Saskia was fretful and concerned about being pregnant again. He would use some of the money from the new commission to get the best medical advice possible. He would consult Dr Tulp. Claes Pieterz had been with him at Latin School in Leiden, then gone on to study medicine at the University and was now a leading member of the medical establishment. A doctor who diagnosed illness and recommended treatment, not as he insisted, when Rembrandt had painted his portrait, definitely not like the surgeons who were lumped in with the Guild of Tripe Cutters.

He went to his workshop at the back of the house and stood for a few moments amongst the litter and debris scattered about the floor. He crossed to his workbench, opened a folder of prints and leafed through the proofs and spoiled paper. There was one in particular that he was searching for: it was not an etching but a drypoint, a drawing made with a fine needle directly into the metal. It showed a young couple hand-in-hand before the dark entrance to a tomb where a skeleton stood waiting. The man was presenting the woman to Death and she was offering him a flower. What had he been thinking when he made that print? That his love for Saskia and her love for him could overcome even death? Now they had lost three children: Rombertus their son, and two daughters, both christened Cornelia neither of whom had lived more than two weeks. Death was no stranger to the Van Rijn household. Was this print in some way responsible for those events? Had he been tempting fate with this image; challenging death as he challenged life? He tore the print into pieces and scattered them across the floor.

In the centre of the room, on his painting table, were his palette and brushes. He had left instructions for some fresh colours to be prepared. There were some pictures to finish before he began work on the Militia piece but he wasn't ready yet; he needed some distraction.

Along one side of the room were some of the props he had collected for use in his paintings. He ran his hands through a long line of costumes, caressing them, fingering materials from China and the Orient. He replaced his beret with a gilt helmet and stood in front of the mirror beneath the high window, turning his head from side to side to catch the bouncing metallic glint of light. If things went wrong he might have to sell some of these items. He quickly dismissed the idea. He needed all of them: this helmet, and all the other pieces of armour, muskets, halberds, pikes and drums were all essential for the new commission. He wrapped himself in one of the heavy cloaks made of Indian cloth before picking up an oriental sabre and slashing at an imaginary foe.

He cast his mind back to the paintings already in the Kloviersdoelen. They had all the elements that he intended to challenge and confound. That 'horror' on the entry wall, above the fireplace, he remembered with particular vehemence. True, the space was long and narrow like a Flemish brick but what kind of excuse was that? He struck out vigorously. The painting had the stamp of that flashy painter Hals all over it; except it lacked his energy and bravura brushwork.

'Where's the imagination! Where's the vision?' He shouted out loud. 'All the figures arranged in a row!' He gave one long swing with the sabre, and in his mind's eye, watched the line of heads fall to the floor. 'And what is the point of that dog: another sop to the money?' Then, he rested the point of the sword on the floor and leant on it heavily, breathing deeply. 'Don't look at me like that,' he announced to his perspiring image in the mirror. 'I'm not to blame; you know I need all these things for my work.'

He gave a start. There was that shadowy figure again, beside his reflection, on the other side of the glass. 'Well don't blame me,' it seemed to reply. 'You're the one who can't resist buying things.'

He shook his head to regain control of his imagination. Yes, he must certainly keep all these treasures. The heaps of hats, turbans and scarves were absolutely essential, as was all the jewellery that spilled from the boxes stacked on and under the shelves. Slung across a chair was the indispensable lion skin; he couldn't do without that. He couldn't do without any of it, but where was he going to store it while he made the Militia painting?

He took off the helmet and cloak and sat down: all this bravura and bluster wasn't going to get him anywhere. Was this commission a turning point in his life? The room would have to be emptied, but even then would there be enough space? He glared at his image in the mirror, demanding an answer, but it seemed to be indifferent to his problem. Was the clearing of his workshop a clearing out of his past? Why was he clinging to all of this old stuff when everything he planned for in the new picture pointed to the future?

He paced across the space. Even if he hung the canvas on the back wall it would be so big he'd be unable to get far enough away to see it properly. He thought for a few moments then clicked his fingers as an audacious solution came to him. He would knock away part of the back wall and extend the studio out over the narrow yard at the rear of the house.

Saskia was awake when he looked in again, propped up against a pile of pillows. They slept in separate rooms during her pregnancy, she in this large room at the front of the house, he in their four-poster in the master bedroom. He didn't like it, but his habit of getting up in the night to see how his paintings were getting on disturbed her too much.

He dismissed the young maid who had been sitting with her, before embracing his wife and perching himself on the edge of the bed. He held her hand, drawing some comfort from the fact that her colour was better and she didn't look so drawn. But he thought he could still detect that fear skulking behind her cheerful, lopsided smile and were those hints of grey among the coppery curls struggling to get free from beneath her cap?

'I've done it,' he announced, his voice measured but confident. 'I'm going to paint the most important picture in the Great Hall of the Shooters, the most important picture in the history of the city, I shouldn't wonder.'

The look of delight and pride that suffused her face made him more confident. 'And they've agreed to my price: no haggling.'

She squeezed his hand, 'You must tell me all about it. Perhaps we can go out for a walk tomorrow if the weather is fine. I'm a lot stronger and the fresh air will do me good, besides once you start work I'll hardly see you.' Her words were cut short by a sharp intake of breath and a dry cough.

He hugged her again, and then moved over to the window. He didn't like the sound of that cough, but his news had cheered her up. There was no chance of their going out together, not in this weather. It was the cold and damp that brought on her cough. If it had been summer things might have been different. They could have gone outside the city walls where they had once roamed before they were married, towards the coast where the air coming from the sea was fresher. As a girl she had loved to stroll in the meadows and follow the streams through the lush countryside in her native Friesland. She had travelled to Amsterdam for the first time one summer and had paid a visit to her cousin's workshop where Rembrandt had been working as one of the assistant painters. He had invested money in the business and was busy teaching as well as overseeing the copying, restoring of old paintings and making new portraits and prints. It had been a hot summer's day and, because of her fair complexion, she was wearing a wide straw hat. They were introduced, and soon they were walking out together.

He turned away and leant against the sill, silhouetted against the grey light, gazing out into the leaden sky. It was there in Friesland, in her family home, that he had begun to love her. The freedom permitted by her parents, who had demanded no chaperones, allowed them to remain in each other's company at all hours. His pleasure at seeing her undress had disconcerted her at first, but over time she became accustomed to it, displaying herself to him in the narrow room at the top of the house, while her parents slept. Sometimes, he would stand at the foot of the stairs looking up to where she appeared naked beneath her shift, small, plump and voluptuous, flickering in the candle light against a piece of the night sky seen through the window. He had persuaded her to reveal herself to him and she had complied, perhaps out of love or pity, seeing it as compensation for her refusal to submit to a deeper intimacy. As she came down the stairs he climbed towards her, his stomach tightening as his eyes possessed her: her ankles, legs, her golden triangle, and each step bringing him closer until his head was level with her shoulders. She lifted her shift and allowed him to place his hands on her hips: run them up her sides and cup her breasts. He'd felt her heart race through her arched ribs as he pressed her against his coarse shirt, aroused by the silky touch of her skin. Then she'd turned and run back up to her room, shutting the door, leaving him damp and sticky on the stairs. His eyes might possess her, and his hands caress, but he knew that it was so far and no further. Try as he might she never allowed him to cross that line, not until they were married, only then did she reveal the secret of that promise, only then might he enter fully into the sacred place she guarded, and possess her completely. His pleasure in her body was overwhelming, but it was to be short-lived. She remained a willing partner in his exploits, but with the inevitable pregnancies and the deaths of their children her flesh became lumpy, sullen, as she was slowly worn down. Making love meant making children, pregnancy, and she was not good at pregnancy. Yet, he went on loving her, his love growing deeper, more intense, as she began to fade away before him.

He composed himself, then turned back to face her across the room. 'Do you remember the portrait of you I started when we were first married?'

'The one where I was wearing that big, red hat?'

'With the wide brim and the plume: yes, that's the one. I got as far as the drawing and putting on the dead colour.' He hesitated, 'dead colour' was a technical term not, he hoped, an omen. 'I've just had it out again, the hat I mean, bright red, stacked with the others on a shelf in the workshop. I'm going to finish the portrait. Would you like that?'

'Of course, but I've changed a lot since then.'

'Not to me.' He was determined to find time in the next few months to complete the portrait. She had changed, it was true, not that it mattered. He would paint her as he remembered her when he had begun it, pretty and serious at the same time.

He returned his thoughts to the new commission. 'You know the bridge outside the archway at the entrance to their new headquarters? I'm going to place them there.' He looked over his shoulder at the grey, slushy light falling across the building opposite, not the light he would use in the painting. 'It's a monster,' he told her. 'I'm going to make it look as though the whole damned Militia Company is about to break out of the picture and march straight into the room. 'Here,' he placed a chair against the wall, 'is the door into the room, and where that chest is standing opposite the window, there's a fireplace. There are six windows; you'll just have to imagine the other five.' He kissed her on the forehead. 'The main fireplace is there, in the middle of the end wall, just like ours.' He pointed to the short wall opposite her bed, then went over and placed a log onto the fire. 'On the end wall here, where your bed is, there's a painting by Govert Flinck. Do you remember him? He was a student of mine only a few years ago. He's done the Governors of the Militia Guild and he's got another painting on the other end wall, to one side of the fireplace.'

He returned to the window, trying to hide the tide of irritation that flooded over him again. That must have been a good commission, he told himself, the Company of the Bas Clan. Dirck Bas was a leading member of

Amsterdam society: but why Flinck? He knew of course. They'd gone for the safe option: putting the picture in the hands of someone they could trust to produce a conventional arrangement.

'Go on,' she said.

He turned back to her, 'The Company of Cornelis Bicker is on the other side of the fireplace, that's by Von Sandrart. You know, he was an old friend of Rubens's.'

He remembered the theatrical display in his workshop: the Bicker Clan, one of the most powerful groups in the city and he'd chopped the heads off the lot of them. He began to laugh and threw himself into the chair beside her bed. She stretched out and stroked the top of his head. He reached up taking her hand in his, looking at her, not in distress so much as quiet forgiveness. She was very frail and they both knew another pregnancy might kill her, and yet it was what they both wanted: she a child and he ambitious for an heir to set the seal on his fame and fortune.

'And will you be well paid for this important commission?'

He went over to the window again, intent on ignoring her question. She managed the household and, so far, he had been able to hide financial problems from her, but it was becoming more and more difficult. Naturally, she knew about the debts he had incurred in buying this house: understood that he needed it to match his status. But running a big house didn't come cheap; he had only made a down payment and was paying interest on the balance. 'Yes of course I will get paid: Banning Cocq and Van Ruytenburch will see to that.'

'What about the other pictures? Will yours fit with them?'

'Ah,' he turned to her and grinned, 'Fit with them? What do you think?'

She looked at him warily, recognising this mood of defiance. 'No, I don't suppose it will.'

It was what had first attracted him to her: a young painter, rough hewn but learning fast, and daring, with a real gift for story telling. He was confident too, with that streak of obstinacy in the face of convention: essential in a young artist finding his way, eager to make his mark. It had served them well, but it mustn't go on, not now he was established. He had to be more careful. But she knew him well enough to know that he wouldn't compromise; not this time. She gazed at him lovingly, watching as he began moving the chairs to the side of the room, hoping she could see the painting when it was finished, but fearful that she wouldn't live that long.

She lay back against the pillows, and watched as he gazed out of the window, lost to her for the moment, 'There is one thing I want to discuss with you before you go.'

He looked at her a little alarmed. 'There's nothing's wrong is there?'

'No. No, of course not. It's just that one of the women you use as a model asked to see me this morning.'

'One of the models wanted to see you? Why? What could she want to see you about?'

'It's alright; there is no need to worry. She asked if I should want a nurse for the baby, when it arrives.'

'I thought you were going to feed him yourself.'

'I am, but I will need some help, I'm not very strong and it will be a comfort to know that there is someone on hand.'

'What's her name?'

'Geertje: she seems quite a respectable person.'

'Geertje Dircx, the bugler's widow. Do you think she knows much about children? She has none of her own.'

'You don't object do you?'

'No, no of course not. You know I leave those decisions to you. You shall have whatever you need. But now I will leave you to rest. I must speak with Carel. I've just had an idea about how I might accommodate this big, new canvas.'

# 8

Back in his workshop, he stood in front of the mirror again. Who was this figure looking back at him? It wasn't the face that others knew; it was its mirror image, the face he saw every day as he washed and dressed. What others saw was the reverse. He often had to remind his sitters that their view of themselves was not his. Sometimes, by manipulating two mirrors he could show them the stranger that was themselves.

He had been making images of himself ever since his career began. He had drawn himself grinning, leering and smirking. He had once thought he knew this figure well. He had been sure it was him, always him, whatever the fine clothes, the extravagant postures, the man who strutted and swaggered behind the surface of the glass was him. But now he wasn't so certain. Now, when he looked in the mirror he sometimes saw a stranger behind his eyes. Was the character that inhabited this other world real? As real as he was, or was it just a mannequin he had clad with his imagination?

This figure beyond the mirror, looking back into the world on his side of the glass, had the same face, but he seemed to be more an observer, watching him, scrutinising him and independent of the body he inhabited. Who could this other self be? Was it free of the past, the past that clung to his body, the physical reality of his everyday existence with its demands and desires? How much did he know about this other Rembrandt? There were ideas being discussed around Amsterdam about the limits of knowledge. How much was it possible to really know? Could it be true that his brain made decisions independently, and his body merely carried them out? He had come to realise that the world was an odd place, and so he shouldn't be surprised if the truth about it was also pretty odd.

In Leiden, he had developed the skills to make paint, stretch canvas and to improve his eye and hand coordination. During the time spent with Lastman in Amsterdam he had learnt to trust his imagination and use his mind's eye. He had honed those skills to such a peak that he had ceased to think about the physical act of painting: the process of mixing colours and drawing with the paint. He worked intuitively; disappearing into the world of his imagination, another reality behind the one that lay before him to find the essence of the emotion that surged through his body; to step into the past, to witness a drama as the events unfolded and bring back a visual record. He had been at Christ's crucifixion, helped take down the body from the cross and carried it to the cave. He had stood in Danaë's luxurious chamber admiring her plump sensuality as she welcomed Jupiter to her golden bed. How did he do that? It was a mystery. But had there always been someone else with him? Who did he argue with when he was trying to persuade himself to make corrections, and if things went wrong, who did he blame? Who did he call a fool?

When he was painting a portrait he had no difficulty in seeing behind the face, the outward mask of the sitter, revealing their emotions, what they believed and why they believed it. He could show them what they thought of themselves and the image they wished to convey. Often his clients would find, in the finished painting, a side to their character of which they had little or no knowledge, but could he do that for himself? Was there something about this man in the mirror that was him, but who he refused to acknowledge? Could he ever know more about himself than what lay beyond this physical appearance? Could he record his own changing moods, his own thoughts and emotions? Could he really see beyond the surface, beyond the figure staring back at him?

There was an Italian who had been locked up for saying that the earth circled the sun and not the other way round. And there was a Frenchman loose in the country questioning what humans could and could not know. Should he be concerned about these things? He was certain that there was a physical world out there, he could see it, touch it, smell it. He believed the act of drawing and painting was a way of thinking about the physical world, and that in order to paint he had to move and to think. Reality had a surface that he could sense at the end of his brush, the paint was a physical fact: a texture he could alter and manipulate. But there was something else, something he could only guess at, as if there was another reality beyond what he could see. He knew he existed, his works proved that. They were a palpable presence in the world and he had made them. Was he really a sorcerer, conjuring things into existence, an alchemist who could turn base materials like oil and pigment into recognisable objects? No, 'objects' was wrong; they were only images of objects but for him they had a reality of their own. They couldn't exist without his collusion, but now he wondered if, perhaps, unwittingly, he had conspired with another to bring them into being? Sometimes it was as if someone else was guiding his hand, bringing elements into his paintings that he couldn't explain. When it had first happened he had found it terrifying but now he found a kind of elation in the experience knowing that later he might be surprised, but understand what he had done. It hadn't always been like this. As a young man he had scarcely a doubt about his ability; it all came so naturally to him. True, he worked hard, but that was because there was so much to learn. His parents had sent him to Latin School in Leiden which was then the most prestigious place of learning in the Low Countries. At the age of 14 he had been offered a place at the University but had chosen instead to be apprenticed to a painter. It had puzzled his parents although they could see that he had talent, and trusted he could make a good living. He had, he'd made a very good living, so why after all this time should these doubts appear? This man in the mirror, who was he? Was it really his reflection or someone else, someone with a will of their own?

# 9

My brother Barent and I had started in his workshop a couple of years earlier. Part of our training had been to do the preparatory work: grinding pigments, mixing colours, preparing canvases and, as we progressed, copying paintings as well as teaching other students. Along with Sam Hoogstraten, we worked on the big Militia piece with him.

Some parts of his technique weren't too difficult to master: contrasting dramatic light with more obscure areas; sometimes creating different light effects with lamps and shades. He showed us how to use subtle interlocking colours to model rather than define shapes. We could all paint faces and the body pretty well. The difficulty came with trying to show the inner and outward expression of emotion. He had a gift for that, and it was impossible to fake. You had to try to feel it the same way he did. But it was his freedom with the brush that was quite magical: it made your hair stand on end to watch him at work.

Geertje wasn't what you'd call bright: she hadn't got the first idea about art, but then not many people have. She seemed a good sort but there was a coarse side to her nature, which I suppose was to be expected, given her background. She was from a village near Edam up in the Waterland where she'd worked in an inn. She'd married a ship's bugler, a friend of her brother's. When he died, she'd stayed on in Amsterdam and there were rumours that she'd been a bit free with her favours before she came into the workshop on the Breestraat to earn some money, modelling. I was never sure of her motives, but she was willing to share a joke with the rest of us. I always found her straightforward enough. He was lucky to find her.

Everything changed when Saskia died and Geertje took over the responsibility for the domestic side of running the house. I'm not sure what arrangements they made between them because the boss was mostly out of sight in his workshop or off on long walks in the countryside. You couldn't blame him, he'd buried three children and now he'd lost the love of his life. He took it hard. Children die all the time, but it seemed to affect him more than most so, when he did put in an appearance, he was usually in a bad mood.

Geertje was an efficient housekeeper, although she made a lot of fuss about being in charge. I think she quite enjoyed it. Even before Saskia died, she'd begun to order people about. At first, it seemed that she was only doing her job, making sure people kept quiet while Saskia was resting, seeing that the wet nurse was clean and up to the job, but slowly she took over more and more responsibility. I don't think she started with a plan to take over running the house, but as Saskia sank lower and lower it was natural that she should do more. Gradually, the idea must have drifted into her head that she might replace her. After all, it was a good position for someone like her: housekeeper to Amsterdam's leading painter and one of its most prestigious residents. It must have been a dream come true: a huge leap up the social scale, even if he was only the son of a miller made good. She became more proprietorial towards him as time passed and she did have a kind of low cunning that became more apparent as the years went by. But it all began to go wrong when they started sleeping together. It was a mistake, for both of them. She always maintained that he made the first move, which could be true of course. I don't really know, but I doubt it. It was mutual need, I should think. He needed physical comfort and pleasure, and for her it was a way to a secure future: or so it must have seemed.

He had always been gentle and affectionate with Saskia. He liked to buy her things. I remember when he got the commission for the big Militia piece he bought her a ring with a diamond cluster. Something else I remember happening was just after we'd had Van Ruytenburch in for a sitting and I was cleaning up: one of his habits was to stand looking at the picture, squinting and peering at it, occasionally turning his back and walking away before suddenly turning round as if to catch it off guard. I could see something was bothering him.

'The man's family were grocers.' He'd been brimming with irritation, 'Just because he owns a house on the Herengracht doesn't give him the right to act like a minor aristocrat.'

I didn't think it would have improved his mood to remind him that Van Ruytenburch also owned a large property in Vlaardingen, bought from a family with connections in the court at Brussels.

'Look at this uniform!' He'd lifted Van Ruytenburch's heavy, bright yellow coat which was draped over the mannequin. It was made from the finest hide, decorated with French bows and elaborately patterned at the edges. Standing next to the outfit was a pair of thigh-length, cavalier boots and planted on top was a broad-brimmed hat in the same colour and material, sporting a huge white feather. He'd placed the hat on his head, swung the coat across his shoulders and then stood in front of a tall mirror. 'I suppose I should be grateful,' he'd said in a slightly calmer tone. 'It's going to help make the painting more interesting, give it some focus, but it must have cost a fortune. He's making sure we all know how important he is. But whether he likes it or not, he's going to be behind Banning Cocq.'

I think the boss got on better with Banning Cocq, even though he wasn't a self-made man either. His father had grown very rich as an apothecary and married into the Banning family. Frans Banning Cocq had been well educated, studied law in France then married into money like his father, his wife being the daughter of a ship owner and trader. Her father owned a spectacular house called The Dolphin. He had built himself a manor house so he could play at being the country squire. When he died, Banning Cocq and his wife inherited the lot.

Even though his outfit for the painting was black, it reeked of money. I'm no expert on tailoring but I've been told that the way the cloth was cut showed how much material they could afford to waste so that everyone could see they didn't have to worry about the cost.

We all knew that the boss wanted to be part of the same elite, to share in the wealth and prosperity of the city, but then I think we all did. Things were on the move: his two heroes, Titian and Rubens had made vast fortunes. But in Calvinist Amsterdam, he was supposed to distain such venal considerations.

Then Hendrickje had come into the household. It was strange in a way, ironic really, because it was Geertje who brought her in. After Saskia died, she had taken over the running of the place and could engage or dismiss servants. When she was asked to take on Hendrickje as a housemaid by an old friend of her late husband's, she agreed. Hendrickje's father had been a sergeant in the army so Geertje must have thought she would be used to rough company and hard work.

Hendrickje could have been about 16, quite pretty, dark haired and fair skinned. She was shy at first, and unassuming. Whether Geertje was jealous right from the start, I don't know. She'd always been a stickler for order; things being in their right place and that kind of thing. Saskia had kept the house clean and tidy but the place had a friendly lived-in feel to it. After Saskia died something changed and slowly Geertje began to turn it into a shrine to cleanliness. She became fiercer and fiercer with the cleaning of the house. Scouring, scrubbing and washing the walls, wiping the beams, polishing the heads of the nails in the front door. I think it began to drive the boss out of his mind.

He was growing more cantankerous and eccentric as time went by and a bit less tolerant of bad behaviour. Part of the workshop routine was that once a week we'd gather together in the painting studio to draw the nude. Sometimes he left the teaching to us older students, but on this particular occasion he took the class himself. There were two models, and we worked for a couple of hours, then the models took a break to have a smoke with the rest of us. When we started again one of the models was missing and so, it appeared, was one of the students. I don't remember his name but he must have been one of the newcomers or he would have known how seriously the boss took drawing. The floor above the big painting studio had been divided into small cubicles so that each student had his own separate workspace. Sometimes they'd be making their own paintings, sometimes copying the boss's, to learn his manner, so they could sell them later. Occasionally, if they were good enough, he could pass them off as his own work. He didn't take beginners; some came from a long distance – even Germany. They had to have a recommendation from their own master and be pretty well-off to afford his fees. He was very conscious of the importance of his craft skills, the things he could show us. Although he played down his time in Leiden, where he served his apprenticeship with Van Swanenburg, he'd learned the basics of his craft there, the skills he could pass on to others: how to grind and mix colours; stretching and putting the ground on canvases and drawing, always drawing. He believed in 'disegno', drawing as a way of thinking. 'Draw,' he used to shout, 'draw, draw you have no time to lose.'

Anyway, this model and the student were missing; so he told us to carry on while he went looking for them. Most of us guessed where they might be. Some of our models came from the red light district, so were not everything they should be, but they were good company and on the occasions a few of us went down to the musicos and taverns, we might meet them practicing their other trade. But when Rembrandt went in search of the two, we stopped work and followed, expecting a very interesting outcome. We were not disappointed. We crowded onto the landing while a couple of braver souls tiptoed gently up the stairs behind him. It was a tight spiral staircase so they had to stand one behind the other. Even the maids appeared, standing at the bottom by the front door, sensing that something was afoot.

For a few moments it went very quiet, and then there was a huge bellow and a loud crash. The two students, who had followed, reappeared scuttling down the stairs in great haste. Then they pressed themselves against the wall of the landing just as a violent row broke out above our heads and a couple of boots came flying down the stairs, followed by a pair of trousers and a jacket. The commotion above us continued with various items of women's clothing joining the pile at the bottom of the stairs. Almost immediately the missing student and the model came after them. The girl first, clutching her shift, her hair in disarray, shouting defiance at their tormentor while he continued to hurl a stream of invective. The student, who was naked from the waist down, stumbled after her struggling into his shirt – one arm in the sleeve, his head still buried. He made the mistake of trying to grab his trousers. The delay allowed the boss to descend in time to give him a hearty boot on his bare backside and send him tumbling down the stairs to the hall below. One of the maids was convulsed with laughter but managed to open the front door, precipitating him into the street.

His partner in passion stood for a few moments by the door, still clutching her clothes, and faced the enraged painter as he stood at the top of the stairs between two lines of grinning spectators. Then, having decided that discretion was the better part of valour, she turned on her heels and, with as much dignity as she could muster and a naked behind, she made her way down the steps to the street. For a few moments, those of us who had watched all this didn't make a move. Then there was a rush to the windows overlooking the street to watch Rembrandt standing by the open door, shouting and waving a maulstick in the air, aiming a torrent of abuse at the hapless pair, as they struggled into their clothes on the pavement outside, much to the amazement of passers-by.

There was a look of anger mingled with suppressed amusement on the boss's face when he returned to the workshop. We couldn't work out whether his anger was real or an elaborate charade. After all, he was no prude: since Saskia's death he hadn't led a blameless life. No one spoke of it out loud, but it was no secret that he had been sleeping with Geertje. Perhaps he'd put on this act of outrage for our benefit, to show us we shouldn't mix work with pleasure. The lesson had been taught; we knew that he disapproved of us bringing our baser instincts into his house and the workshop.

Although we never saw that particular model again, the student did sneak back into our company the next day. But he kept away from the boss, hiding in his cubicle most of the time, only gradually re-joining our collective ventures. He'd come here to learn from this particular master, so he was careful not to transgress again. It appeared that Rembrandt had put the incident behind him too, although his forgiveness may have had something to do with the 100 florins in fees that the student paid him.

# 10

When we'd finished the big Militia piece and installed it, he gave me a few days off. I went to visit my parents in Beemster, about 20 miles up north. It was while I was there that I heard of a whale coming ashore on the coast near Beverwijk. I thought I'd go and take a look. There had been quite a few of these enormous fishes coming ashore over the years. I'd seen engravings of them, but I was curious to see what they really looked like. This one was supposed to be a spectacular size, although I was told that one twice as big had been stranded on a beach further south. All the whales that come ashore are males and it was the size of this one's enormous penis that seemed to attract the most attention. Someone told me it was a metre long but, by the time I arrived, someone had cut it off and taken it away. I had intended to make a few drawings because whales are popular subjects and it would be useful information if we ever had to make a picture of Jonah. By the time I got there it was too hacked about and rotten to be of much use. I was warned not to go up too close to the corpse because by then he was several days old and likely to explode at any minute. I didn't need telling because the stench was horrendous; enough to make you vomit. Some people believe that whales bring bad luck, that they are a warning not to disobey God's law. I don't believe that kind of nonsense, and neither do the burghers of the city. They nip their noses and pat their purses; whales bring in a lot of money.

When I got back to Amsterdam they told me Saskia

had died. The house was deserted: everyone was at the funeral. It was a warm day with that, all too familiar, stink wafting in on the air from the whale factory out on Marken Island. At first, I went to the Zuiderkerk because that was where they'd buried their children but it was the wrong church. He had arranged to put Saskia in the Oude Kerk. Later, we found out that he had struck a deal with the predikant there. He was Saskia's brother-in-law and he'd found a cheap grave for her. Looking back, I suppose that was one of the first signs that things weren't going too well financially, because if he'd had the funds he would have given her a more suitable send-off but at the time it didn't occur to me that anything was wrong and no one else seemed to notice either.

I had known she was going to die: we all did. It was obvious, she had the consumption. At first, he tried to put a brave face on it, telling us to keep away from that part of the house because she was pregnant and needed to rest. We understood of course, they'd lost three children by then, so her having peace and quiet was sensible, but not after the baby was born. Titus they called him, after Saskia's sister Titia who had died the previous June.

Now, he said it was because she was nursing the baby, which we all knew couldn't be true because she was too weak. She had been about the house a few days after the birth, but she looked awful: pale and drawn but very sweet and trying hard. The baby howled a good deal so in the end they called in a wet nurse. Then things went from bad to worse. Sometimes when you went past her room you could hear her gasping for breath: it was horrible. She was worn out with child bearing and easy meat for the consumption. So I wasn't surprised when they told me she was dead. It was a shame because we were all fond of her, the students and everyone one who knew her.

Trying to make out that everything was alright was foolish, really. If it had been, he would have been as pleased as anything and showing off all over the place. He was like that, full of his own success and importance. Not that I blame him, he was a great man and we were all pleased to have him for a teacher. By then, I'd finished my training and was helping him as his assistant and doing some teaching myself.

We'd only delivered Banning Cocq's Shooters ten days before. It had been a major headache, a nerve-wracking business. Just getting it out of the studio and onto a cart took some doing. It was a big canvas: three and a half metres high and four and a half long. We had to wait for a day when there was no wind otherwise it would have taken off like a sail. When we got it there, we had to manhandle it across the courtyard and up the stairs. It looked wonderful when it was in place. It made all the other pictures look as flat and dead as playing cards.

I remember talking to him just after he got the job to do the big Militia piece. That was early in 1641 and he told me that because of its enormous size he needed more space. The third floor of the house had been divided into cubicles so that each student could have their own bit of space. He had plenty of students, being so well known, and they brought in a lot of money. It was because he was also busy with commissions that he paid some of us, who had been there the longest, to help with the teaching. There was a large studio where we got together to draw and paint from the figure. And on the ground floor there was a room set aside for his etching press. Lots of the houses in the street had yards behind them. There was a privy out there and a sand tray for pissing in, also a lean-to shed against the back wall with the roof at the first floor level. It was where we mixed the acid and, in the summer, we used to bite the etching plates out there.

I'd served my apprenticeship as a carpenter before I took up painting. So when he came up with the idea to extend his studio over the yard by knocking a hole through the back wall of the house and putting a floor where the old roof had been, he asked me to do the woodwork. We raised the roof to the second floor level, put in a door, and when we boxed in the sides, we included a window. The extension gave him a wall big enough to accommodate the painting. When it was finished, we just took out part of the floor and lowered the picture to the ground. We'd put a lot of effort into that picture so, once it was delivered, I cleared off for a few days.

When I got back to the house on the Breestraat, on the day of the funeral, he'd sent everyone away except for a few servants who were getting ready for when the mourners got back. I didn't think to ask where she was being buried; I just assumed it would be near the children. So I went straight to the Zuiderkerk where Rombertus, their first little boy, who'd only survived a few months and the two girls both called Cornelia: neither of them had lived more than a couple of weeks, had their graves. It was shocking to think that now Saskia had produced a healthy little boy, she was dead too, her lungs ragged with the effort of breathing.

But she'd been taken to the Oude Kerk, even though he must have known she would have preferred to be buried near her children. I was out of breath when I finally arrived just as they were coming out of the church. I couldn't help noticing that Geertje was there and she was carrying the baby. Titus must have been about ten months old by then and was beginning to be weaned off the wet nurse.

I was a bit surprised, Geertje had only been taken on as a nurse a few weeks before he was born, when even he couldn't pretend Saskia was going to last much longer. But I suppose it was only natural. She had the reputation, among the students, of being a good sort, enjoying a little flattery and bawdy humour, no doubt gained among her late husband's, the ships bugler's, nautical friends. But I never trusted her, I don't know quite why. There was something of the shrew about her, and she had a sharp tongue. Still she was what he needed at the time, a diligent nurse and housekeeper.

Looking back, it seems obvious that she was going to be trouble. I mean, I don't think she was after him at first, although you could see why she might have been. She was young, not particularly attractive but with a tidy figure. He was a rich, successful painter, a leading citizen and recently bereaved himself, perhaps a bit lonely, and with a baby boy to care for. I daresay he was not unwilling to be seduced, probably not above a bit of seduction himself. Who knows? He enjoyed the good things in life and liked the idea of being the grand patrician. He had a high opinion of himself and thought he was the greatest painter of his time. He wanted the recognition and material things that went with that status even though in Amsterdam it didn't do to flaunt your success. You had to be more subtle than that, your rewards were supposed to waiting for you in the next life, but he wasn't too good at being subtle, except in his paintings.

## 11

A dinner is being prepared at a house on the Sint Anthonisbreestraat, Amsterdam. Or it might be more accurate to say that the meal has been in preparation for several days. It is not that it involves some grand plan or a complicated menu but because here, in Calvinist Amsterdam, there is a moral dimension to all aspects of life, even the seemingly everyday activity of eating. The expenditure might be lavish, but it must be discreet. Ostentatious displays of wealth are frowned upon. The tracts on food and diet in circulation around the city censure over-indulgence both in gluttony and asceticism. The civic authorities favour moderation in all things culinary in order to control the passions.

Most of the houses on the street are occupied by merchants and traders of various kinds. This one is narrow and deep with four floors and a basement, a brick front ornamented by classical details, stone steps leading from the street to a front door set in a stone arch, the whole façade being topped by a decorative pediment. Previously owned by Flemish merchants, it is now occupied by the painter Rembrandt van Rijn.

For himself, Rembrandt favours a more personal self-regulating system, to include the occasional bout of intemperance. But in the case of this particular meal, these considerations are tempered by the need to give the impression to his guests that they are sharing in his success whilst, at the same time, concealing the fact that this success is not as secure as he might like it to be. He must also deal with Geertje Dircx his housekeeper, who is in charge of preparing the food. Lately, she has been proving less tractable so he feels the need to impose his authority. Together they must negotiate all these written and unwritten conventions.

It is summer and so the windows have been opened and the house aired. The furniture has been rearranged in the grand saal which, for this occasion, is to act as a dining room. The cedar, linen press has been pushed into the corner, the floors swept and scrubbed, and the table and chairs dusted and polished. The frames of the paintings, of which there are a good number, have been checked to see that no cobwebs are lurking behind them, and wiped clean. The dining table is covered with a starched linen cloth and places set with napkins beside the house's finest cutlery. The painter's collection of plaster casts, antique busts of the Caesars, has been brought from upstairs and displayed. Geertje has brought them down herself, unwilling to trust anyone else.

She must also deal with the financial constraints of a household spiralling into financial chaos. It is particularly galling as she is aware that her master has lately been casting lustful eyes over Hendrickje Stoffels, the live-in maid, who she herself has employed. As it is Geertje who, at present, shares his bed she is faced with a dilemma. The meal offers her an excellent opportunity to assert her authority and see off the opposition, but she must be careful: it involves some risk.

These days, the painter rarely visits the kitchens. It was different in the months following his wife's death, when he came in search of Geertje: not to suggest what food she might prepare, nor to check the quality of the meat or the freshness of the fish. No, the appetite he sought to assuage was of a more carnal nature. But today he has made an exception; as the final preparations for this meal are being made he wants to be sure that everything is as it should be.

'I trust that no expense has been spared and you have chosen well. All the food must be of the best quality. These are important people, influential men, who have commissions in their gift. We need to impress them.'

Geertje turns on him, 'Of course I can make a success of it. I know what to do, but how do you expect me to do it without money? That is what I want to know. You have exhausted our credit.'

'What! How can that be?' He is indignant, 'Does my name count for nothing in this city?'

'No, not anymore it doesn't. These days your reputation is worthless. You can't even pay what you owe on this house. You seem to think that it is a secret but everyone knows. And amongst the trade's people, you have become a laughing stock.'

'I must live amongst fools. Did you not tell them we are entertaining influential people who move in important circles? These tradesmen should see it as an investment. If we succeed in this venture we will pay them what we owe. We have always paid in the past.'

Now it is Geertje's turn to be indignant, 'Do you take me for a fool, of course I told them. I have had to humiliate myself yet again and beg them to extend our credit. Do you want your guests to eat yesterday's fish? Do you? You have no idea what is involved, not only is there the food and drink to buy but I must also hire extra servants.'

'What! Why do we need extra servants? Why don't you get some of the students to help prepare the food?'

'They are not to be trusted, and I have no time to watch over them. Besides, they are here to be taught how to paint. That's what they pay you for, not to work in your kitchen.'

'It will do them good. Let them see that being a painter involves things other than putting paint on canvas.'

'And do you ever come down here to help prepare the food?' She asks scornfully. 'No! Of course you don't. You're too busy with other things. If you hadn't come home from the auctions last week laden with another load of junk, you might have been able to finance this evening's dinner. Would that have been too much to ask?'

He raises his eyes, and puts his head in his hands in exasperation. 'Six years, six years you have been in this house and still you have no idea of what it takes to make paintings. Do you think what I do is easy? Well do you? How many times must I tell you that it is not? It is hard, laborious, sometimes tedious and often terrifying. But you will never understand. How many times must I tell you, that what you call junk is absolutely essential to my work?' He turns to leave the room. 'There will be no extra servants, do you understand? You and Hendrickje can wait on the table.'

Geertje is angry. 'So, I am not to join you for the meal?'

'Certainly not, it is too important. It would not be appropriate, and you said yourself that your place is in the kitchen, making sure everything goes smoothly.'

Geertje is almost in tears with rage and frustration, 'How dare you? How dare you? It is my right. You cannot treat me like some petty servant who waits on you at table. I have done everything to make sure that it will all be ready. Hendrickje can organise the kitchen and serve the food.'

'That's not what I want.' He waves his hand as if to dismiss her. 'Hendrickje does not have the experience. But if, as you say, you are too proud to shop and ask for credit you should have sent her.' He turns to leave, 'At least she seems to have an inkling of what I am trying to achieve. That's all over your head. Now I've got work to do, and who knows I may need some of "that junk" I bought last week.'

## 12

Hendrickje heard raised voices as she went down the stairs into the kitchen. She knew her master had been down earlier to see that all the preparations for the meal were in hand, but had thought nothing of it. Geertje had been in the house since before his wife's death. She was an excellent housekeeper and cook so everything would be in place. But Hendrickje also knew, as did everyone else in the house, that recently things had not been going well between master and housekeeper.

In all the years she had been there, Geertje had not shown the slightest interest in changing the arrangements for the running of the house. She had seemed content to leave things as they were during Saskia's lifetime. That suited the master, he wanted things to be as straight-forward as possible in his domestic life, leaving him free to concentrate on his work. Now, for some reason, Geertje had decided to change things, to impose her own taste on the house and make it the way she wanted. The master didn't like it and there was bound to be trouble.

If any of the other servants suspected that Geertje was more than just a housekeeper they said nothing. Such things were, after all, not unusual at their level of society. For all the talk of freedom and equality in the new Republic some things had not changed. Here, in the city, lip service might have been paid to the new dispensation; but if a servant girl refused the demands of her master and was dismissed, it was difficult for her to find another place. She could find herself marked out as unreliable, or worse, a thief. Even if the authorities knew she had been wronged they could still turn a blind eye to the matter. So here, in the Van Rijn household, no one was going to admit to knowledge of any affair. They did not want to be the one who lost their place.

Hendrickje didn't want to be accused of eavesdropping so she quickly retraced her steps, just as Rembrandt swept from the room. Halfway to the top of the stairs she leant aside to let him pass, but to her consternation, he paused and placed a hand on her shoulder. A brief gesture, but one she knew would not go unnoticed by Geertje who she saw standing below. She was a little alarmed at this turn of events. He had been showing her more attention over the last few weeks and she didn't know whether to be flattered or not. She had no wish to offend Geertje who had given her a place in the house. Now she found herself in a situation over which she had little control; what should she do? She decided to pretend that she had seen and heard nothing.

As Hendrickje entered the room, Geertje rounded on her, 'So now he wants you to go and charm the local tradesmen does he? Well it's too late I've already done it.' She retreated behind the table in the middle of the kitchen, as if this were the place where she still felt in charge while her authority in the rest of the house slipped from her grasp. 'Don't you forget I'm still the one who gives the orders in this house? The bread dough needs to be prepared: you can see to that.'

'Do we have cheese and butter?' Hendrickje asked, anxious to placate her.

On the table were the vegetables she had helped prepare earlier: peeled, diced and now covered with a muslin cloth to keep them clean and protect them from insects. Hanging from hooks in the ceiling were the fowl, plucked and drawn.

'Yes, of course. I'm not a fool, and I've arranged for the delivery of the fish. They were caught and landed this morning. They will be here soon, still alive so they will need to be dealt with quickly. They must be killed, gutted and cleaned ready to cook just before the guests arrive. That's another job for you.'

Recovering her domestic role seemed to help her regain her composure whilst Hendrickje felt she was being challenged; preparing fish was something Geertje usually did herself.

'Must I, Geertje? You know how particular you are. Are you sure I can do it well enough?'

'I'll have none of that nonsense. You know what to do. Just be quick about it.'

'The meat is already wrapped and stored in the cool place and we have plenty of fruit?' Hendrickje said.

'Yes, and before you ask, it is good quality.'

For a few moments they looked at each other uneasily.

'I know you wouldn't buy anything less Geertje. I'm sure everything will be excellent as usual and all the guests will be impressed.' Hendrickje took several deep breathes as Geertje began to busy herself around the kitchen.

'Geertje are you really not interested in his work?

Does it mean nothing to you to be in the house of such a famous man?'

Geertje, briefly caught off guard by this unanticipated change in the conversation, was silent for a few moments. Then placing her fingertips deliberately on the table, to take her weight, she leant towards Hendrickje. 'No, and I never have been. Famous: do you really think so? Perhaps he is, but he's still the son of a miller, no better than the rest of us. What gives him the idea that he's so special? Don't let him sell you the line that his family's type of milling is something superior. Being a barley miller is no different from any other kind of miller. He would still be successful if he'd taken my advice. When I came here six years ago to nurse Titus, he had plenty of work. There was money to spare, lots of students and we could count on credit. That's all changed. Now, I must twist and turn to find tradesmen who are willing to wait for payment. He can't or won't admit that although he may have been well thought of once, that's all in the past. Why has he changed the way he paints? Why? It makes no sense. His clients don't like it and other painters get the commissions he used to win.'

Hendrickje tried again, remembering something Van Rijn had told her. 'Don't you see he is looking for a sign that somewhere in this infinitely varied world there is the essence of The Creator's design?'

Geertje took off her apron and sat down looking fiercely at Hendrickje. 'That's a lot of nonsense. I'm not interested if it doesn't pay the bills.'

'But he wants to be remembered for himself as a

great artist. Is it so wrong to want to be remembered, even honoured? Look at us; we are two tiny people about whom nothing will ever be known. We could live our lives, die and be forgotten. Don't you want more than that? Perhaps because of him you will be remembered? Perhaps we all will. Aren't you grateful to him for that?'

'Grateful?' Geertje was scornful, 'Why should I be grateful? You may be satisfied with this "being remembered" nonsense, but not me. I don't much care to be remembered as his housekeeper. I've done a lot for him during these six years and I think I deserve more. It's the here and now that concerns me. You should keep your eyes to yourself. Don't get any ideas about your place in this house. I've seen the way you flatter him, hang on his every word. I got you your job here and I'm the one who decides when you go.'

Hendrickje was taken aback, 'I don't want to make any trouble between us Geertje. I don't want to offend you.'

But it was too late. Geertje came over and put her face close to hers, 'I've had enough. Tonight will be the last you spend under this roof. Tomorrow you can pack your things and go. And don't go pleading with him. I still have some say as to what goes on in this house. He'll do as I say.'

## 13

I knew something was wrong when I saw Hendrickje standing with the boss to greet the guests in the entrance hall. Usually, it was Geertje who helped with the hats and capes. I managed a brief word with Hendrickje, and she told me that Geertje had been ordered to stay in the kitchen. I shouldn't have been surprised. You know how it is: the emotional turmoil between two people souring the whole atmosphere in a house, so that even the most casual visitor can sense something is wrong.

One of Geertje's jobs was to make sure there was peace and quiet around the place. But instead, she had become the cause of trouble and that made for bad feeling between her and the boss. Once upon a time, he'd have trusted her to do things but now he seemed off-hand, and ordered her about. Obviously, things couldn't go on that way, but when the final break came it was a shock to us all.

Geertje had been with him a long time. She'd started off as one of our models. We shared a few jokes and became quite friendly. When Saskia was ill and needed help she volunteered to take over as housekeeper. She was especially kind to Titus. When, eventually, Saskia died she looked after the boy as if he were her own. Van Rijn appreciated that and realised he'd been lucky to find her. But there was always a shrewish side to her and gradually towards the end of her time in the house it became more obvious. You know, little things: she would not allow wet clothes in the hall or mucky marks on the floor which was difficult in the winter. And anyway, the maid soon mopped things up. We had to hang our coats in the proper place, not on the backs of the chairs. She started doing fewer of the ordinary chores herself and made the girls work harder. Even then she would still find fault. Some left because of Geertje's attitude, others because he couldn't always pay them. I think she would have liked to be rid of Hendrickje too, even though it was she who had taken her on in the first place. Hendrickje was a good worker but it was clear that Van Rijn had developed a soft spot for her and she in her way seemed to understand him. I think Geertje was jealous but she was also worried that he'd be angry if Hendrickje left. As time went on, the situation became more and more difficult.

Geertje told us she didn't like the smell of paint and complained that the students were bringing it from the workshop into the living quarters on their hands and clothes. What did she expect? She'd never complained when she was a model. The students were learning to mix pigments with oil to make paint and ink: it's a messy business. Paint has a habit of crawling onto you when you're not looking. I've had paint in my hair, of a colour that I didn't even remember using and when we were printing it was inevitable that ink got about the place.

Once, when we were outside taking a break and having a smoke she appeared at the door shouting in a fury, 'Who's brought ink into the parlour?'

As far as we knew nobody had been into the house recently, but we all held up our hands including the boss, and all of them were black.

'Come and look at this!' She demanded.

Van Rijn smiled wearily, 'You get back to work. I'll deal with it.'

When he came back to the press he was annoyed. 'I can't see any marks. Whatever it is, it's invisible to me, but I suppose one of you had better make an attempt to clean it off.'

Patience wasn't his strong suit and he got more and more frustrated with her pernickety ways. She started moving things without consulting him, rearranging his paintings and his collection of objects. One of the problems was that he was a voracious collector. It was an obsession, though he'd never admit it. He'd come back from the salerooms with all sorts of paraphernalia, some of it useful. We needed props for paintings, but some of the clothes he bought, so it seemed to me, were simply for him to enjoy dressing up. I never knew him to come back empty-handed. He always brought something 'useful' or 'necessary'. At first, his collection occupied the studio and some of the rooms at the top of the house where the students slept but gradually it crept out into other places. True, some of the art works he bought were good: Flemish and Italian paintings that were properly displayed. Other bits just cluttered up the place and were real dust collectors. He bought bits of armour, stuffed birds with exotic plumage, hats and headgear of all kinds. There were exotic sea shells, some unusual examples and all, in their own way, rather beautiful. There was even a lion skin.

It drove Geertje wild: she was forever tapping or

shaking the stuff, moving things outdoors and dusting them. Sometimes, she was quite distraught, but she never seemed to understand that he liked to have these things about the place, as if somehow he needed them.

Saskia had indulged him and accommodated his fancies. Hendrickje too, seemed to have sympathy with his weird imagination. I think that was one of the reasons he was attracted to her. Saskia had worshipped him and knew him so well. She could sense what he wanted almost before he knew it himself and she thought her role in life was to provide whatever he wanted, when he wanted it, including time to himself. She placed herself between him and the world outside for as long as she could.

At first, Geertje tried to do the same. She'd seen how Saskia managed him and tried to copy her, but it didn't come naturally. The position of housekeeper was a good billet: more than she could have hoped for. But either she wasn't bright enough to realise that she needed to be more subtle, or she didn't care. I tried to advise her when things started to go wrong. I told her it was a game she had to play. She needed to be a bit more circumspect and accommodating. It was useless to take him on directly. It was never going to work because he held all the best cards. No doubt she had right on her side and he should have treated her better but she would wear those jewels, that night at the dinner: that was her big mistake.

He once told me that in the early days of his career, when he and Saskia were first married, they did a lot of entertaining. It was the way you got to know your clients. Due to his background, he was a bit uncomfortable with the business of manners and etiquette, but Saskia had known about these formalities. She was brought up in Friesland and her family were well-to-do. With Calvinism, form is everything: the way you dress, what you eat, as well as attendance at church, which could be several times on the Sabbath. Saskia knew that outward show was important and she had the knack of making things go smoothly.

Since she died, he hadn't done much entertaining and on the few occasions when he did, Geertje was by his side. She had to be discrete but she was in charge of the house so it wasn't out of the question that she should be there to meet people and help them with their coats.

Perhaps he thought they suspected Geertje was more than just his housekeeper and he wanted to put them off the scent. I don't think they would have cared. Most of them had known him a long time and he was their idea of a genius, so they were tolerant of his more bizarre behaviour. In any case, he had been very clever at hiding his closeness to Geertje: even I wasn't sure what was really going on. I suspected she shared his bed occasionally but such a situation wasn't unusual. You might even say it was expected and they didn't lack opportunity. I don't think that after Saskia's death he cared too much about being respectable, at least not in the way that most people do. Certainly, he wanted to be famous and rich and he'd succeeded, but the way he went about it wasn't the conventional way. It was as if he was on a mission, driven by some inner demon. I often heard him talking to himself when he was on his own in the workshop and it sounded like a conversation, as if there was someone else in the room with him. Some of the students found it a bit creepy. Saskia's death had almost destroyed him, and his work had changed quite a lot. I still thought he was the greatest painter in the country but a good few people believed his best work lay behind him. He had become less popular, less sought after. There were still those who had a real understanding of his painting: his endeavours to take his work into new areas. They knew the work of the Italians and wanted our new country to match the best of them. Van Rijn was up to the challenge as far as they were concerned. So what if he did have a few peccadilloes: who doesn't?

## 14

I was invited to the dinner because I knew some of the guests, or at least that's what he told me. I think the real reason he wanted me there was so I could testify that working with him was a privilege. That he was a master craftsman whose name gave credibility to his students whenever they'd set up as independent painters. Govert Flinck had only studied with him for a year but already sold his paintings, saying he had the brushwork of Van Rijn.

I was also pleased because I hadn't been paid for weeks and, as I usually ate in the kitchen and money being short, it wasn't always the best quality. The prospect of eating with his guests was an offer I wasn't going to refuse. Geertje would have seen to everything. She was a good housekeeper and an excellent cook. This dinner was important so she would spare no effort.

Jan Six, Constantijn Huygens, Jan Vos and Jeremias de Decker were a distinguished group, part of Amsterdam's intellectual elite. They were collectors of paintings; men of letters; poets; playwrights and polemicists, as interested in the written word as the visual language. There were no painters because Van Rijn had little to do with other artists, seeing them as rivals out to steal his ideas.

Jan Six was the one I knew best. He was ten years younger than Van Rijn but they had become good friends. His family had made a fortune from weaving and dying silk. He was a handsome poet and playwrite, with a country estate where they often went walking together. Van Rijn was painting his widowed mother's portrait when they first met. Six was just back from Italy and later he had come to the workshop several times when Van Rijn was working on an etching of him. He'd also been to Leiden University to study the liberal arts so they were both familiar with the classical literature and read Latin. Six also spoke Spanish, French and Italian.

I suppose Van Rijn wanted to cultivate his company and, although they were from different social backgrounds, they did at least share an aesthetic culture. Van Rijn had few friends so I'm sure he was honoured by the patronage of a rich, energetic, educated and cultivated young man of leisure whose tastes had been formed on the Grand Tour of Italy.

Six boasted that he had rubbed shoulders with cardinals, painters, poets and sculptors. He had certainly acquired a passion for Italian poetry and paintings, a passion shared by Van Rijn. Six already owned several of his works and I'm sure that part of the plan for the evening's event was founded on the hope that he would buy more.

I've always thought the etching flattered Six. I was never sure what he made of it. I know Van Rijn took great pains, making several preliminary drawings for his approval, which was unusual. Generally clients got what he gave them, they didn't have a lot of say in the matter but with Six it was different. They must have agreed to compromise. I think he wanted to be seen as an elegant, young intellectual, reading a learned tome. In the end he got something a bit more informal, with him standing against a window, without his coat, examining a manuscript with another pile of papers on a chair in front of him. Although he's looking thoughtful, there is a suggestion of activity because there's a sword, a dagger and a cape in the room. One of the proofs for the portrait was on display in the workshop that night for the other guests to see the quality of the work.

In the days when Six first met Van Rijn, we had a lot of students. Now, there were fewer of them and only me to assist. He was becoming more eccentric and difficult. I think I was one of the few people who could deal with him, mostly because I still admired his work and what he had taught me. I was grateful for the insights he had given me into the deeper nature of what we were trying to do. Like Hendrickje, I thought he was a great artist and put up with his weird ways but unlike her, I knew things couldn't go on much longer.

This great dinner was one of the last throws of the dice. He couldn't pay me and, increasingly, I had to rely on selling my own work to make some money. As I worked slowly and produced very little it was difficult. To help me out sometimes, as a favour, he would sign one of my paintings which meant I might get a better price. But even that was becoming more problematical as his work grew increasingly out of favour. I knew I'd have to leave soon because, now that he had pretty much given up having students, there was very little work for me. I wasn't sure what I was going to do. We had discussed the possibility of me moving to Delft to set up on my own but nothing had been decided yet.

Constantijn Huygens was someone I knew only by

reputation. He and Van Rijn had both lost their wives when they were young. Now in his early fifties, he had a peculiar appearance with bulging eyes and, although he made out that he was a strict Calvinist, he wore his hair long and had a cavalier moustache: affectations that were an anathema to the church. Van Rijn seemed a little in awe of him having known him since the beginning of his career in Leiden when Huygens bought some of his work. I've often wondered if that was why Van Rijn also wore a moustache, though his was not so successful. With Huygens present we'd have prayers before the meal, something that Van Rijn usually dispensed with.

That evening, Van Rijn seemed on edge. He asked me to take the guests and show them the work we had prepared for them. I knew he needed their support because even he could not deny that tastes were changing and that he was not as fashionable as he had once been. Whilst I took them upstairs to the big studio, he went down to the kitchen to make sure everything was going to plan with the preparations for the dinner.

We had cleared space in his workshop that morning and I'd arranged some of the painting we had in hand on the easels: portraits and histories. I'd also put out some proofs of etchings he was working on at the time, mostly scenes from the Bible, especially the Life of Christ.

Six had written a play called 'Medea' which had been performed in one of Amsterdam's best theatres and Van Rijn had been among his guests at the opening. Six was intending to publish the text and had commissioned Van Rijn to make the illustration for the frontispiece. Van Rijn had recently acquired some Japanese paper and made several unsigned, loose impressions illustrating scenes from the drama. These were on display with another etching showing the wedding of Jason and Creusa, a scene which, strangely, doesn't appear in the play.

Jeremias de Decker, I only knew by reputation. He was a poet, a firm friend and a great admirer of Van Rijn's work. De Decker talked about shadow friendships: people who were only friends in the good times, when the sun shone, but disappeared when it was replaced by rain and damp. He also wrote a lot about death and the vanity of the world, something that seemed to strike a chord with Van Rijn.

It was Jan Vos who asked Huygens when he had first met Van Rijn and whether it was true that he had tried to persuade him to go to Italy. Vos was another poet given to writing long eulogies praising the achievements of the Republic. He saw the Dutch as God's chosen people, taking over from the Jews.

'Yes,' Huygens replied. 'But that was almost twenty years ago. I was living in The Hague at the time. Let me see, it must have been around 1626 or '27. I tried to persuade him and his friend Jan Leivens to go south.'

'Are you a collector?' Vos asked.

'I have my own collection, yes. I already knew the work of Leivens. I'd commissioned him to paint my portrait. At that time, I wasn't seeking work for myself: I had been commissioned to buy paintings for the Court in The Hague.'

'Were you working for the Stadtholder?'

'Yes, exactly that. Frederik Hendrick was Stadtholder at the time and wanted our finest artists represented in the Court collection. Lievens told me about his friend in Leiden and, as I was on the lookout for young talent, I went there especially to see him. I'm sure you would agree that our Republic can equal any monarchy, even the Habsburgs and the Stuarts.'

'Indeed, but I'm curious to know why you thought they should study in Italy?'

'It was quite common then. It was seen as part of the training. Both Six,' he indicated his colleague, who was examining a painting, 'and myself have been to Italy to study the art of the great Italian masters: painters, sculptors and to see the ancient architecture of Rome. Van Rijn's first masters, Van Swanenburg in Leiden and Pieter Lastman in Amsterdam, both studied in Italy. I am still a believer in the idea that artists are more than just craftsmen. Like poets, they need a rounded education, to read, listen to music, to take an interest in the theatre.'

'But he didn't take your advice.'

'No. He claimed he couldn't spare the time. None of his family had been great travellers and he was too busy. It would have meant being away from his work for the best part of a year, longer if he had spent time working in Rome. It's a pity because studying the great painters at first hand and making copies of their work would have been valuable experience.' Huygens paused, looked closely at a small print then continued, 'But now I know that being stubborn is just part of his nature.'

'I wasn't being stubborn. It was a purely practical decision.' Van Rijn was back from the kitchen and must have been listening at the door because at this point he joined us. 'I was beginning to make a name for myself and I wasn't going to risk being away for a year. People's memories are too short: besides, I could see plenty of Italian paintings in Amsterdam at the auction rooms.'

He moved over to one of the tables and began to leaf through a pile of prints. 'I admit that in the beginning I saw myself as having to match, or even surpass, the Italians. Like them, I was interested in Greek mythology as a source of imagery but as time went on I was less and less interested in their sort of painting.'

Jan Vos interrupted again, 'Weren't you interested in the classical idea of beauty?'

'No, I wanted something more down-to-earth, more real, to explore the possibility of smaller paintings, to hang in ordinary houses. It was the same for Leivens although he was more the traveller. He went to London the same year I moved here; three years later he was in Antwerp.'

'Have you had any contact with him since?' Huygens asked.

Van Rijn replied with scarcely veiled contempt, 'No, and from what I've heard I wouldn't like the work he's doing now. He's following the fashion: it's too elegant, too smooth.'

Vos turned to Huygens again, 'But who did you admire most of the two?'

'I thought they were a match for each other.'

'But you had commissioned Leivens to paint your

portrait. Does that mean you preferred his work?'

Huygens thought carefully for a few moments. 'No, that was before I'd met Van Rijn. To say they were both great talents would be to underestimate their merits. I venture to suggest that our host,' he smiled towards Van Rijn, 'is superior in his touch and liveliness of emotions. Conversely, at that time, I thought that Lievens was the greater in respect of inventiveness and his audacious themes and forms. They shared certain techniques and there was another complication. Did you know that they worked on each other's paintings? Perhaps I can show you. We passed a couple Leivens's works as we came in.'

He led Vos back down the stairs to the entrance hall which was hung with Van Rijn's collection of small paintings. Van Rijn followed, a little annoyed that the focus had shifted from him to the work of a rival. He stood at the foot of the stairs listening while Huygens, undaunted, explained, 'Can you see?' He pointed to a small genre painting, 'This is by Lievens from that time and I imagine it must have been done quickly. If you look closely you can see how he has drawn in the basic elements of the composition and the distribution of light in what they call dead colour: it's probably Cologne earth. There are some traces left here and here.' He pointed with his finger, his face close to the surface of the painting.

'I see what you mean,' Vos said, standing by his side. 'Not so much a sketch as a painting in one colour.' He turned to Rembrandt. 'And did you both work in this way?'

'It's a technique developed by Titian in Venice, working from dark to light.' Van Rijn seemed anxious to regain their attention. 'You sketch in the large areas using a very thin mix of pigment and turpentine which dries quickly then you can apply the body colour. You have to wait until that dries before you add the finishing touches.'

Vos turned to Huygens again. 'But you must have taken a view as to who had the greater skill?'

Huygens was non-committal, 'As I told you earlier, it was complicated.'

Then Vos turned to Rembrandt. 'But you have retained some of his paintings. Is this one of those that you worked on together?'

'No, those have long disappeared. I keep these because they are a reminder of my younger days. I can't deny we shared ideas and had some good times together.'

By now Van Rijn wanted to end the conversation. 'It's time we went in to eat.' He led them to the dining table. As he helped Huygens to his seat he said, 'You know you preferred my work from the first. Jan was good, confident but stubborn. He hated to be criticised. The few times he'd had to accept that he was wrong: he took it badly.'

'I think you exaggerate.' Huygens was not so easily silenced. He cast a quizzical look at Van Rijn. 'You know you both had that arrogance of youth, perhaps Leivens more so because he already had a formidable reputation. But you cannot claim to be wholly innocent. I admit that, at first, I did prefer Leivens. I thought his work had more grandeur. It seemed bolder and more inventive.'

Before Huygens could continue, Van Rijn interrupted again and there was a note of irritation in his voice, 'What you really mean is, that they were bigger.'

Huygens took no notice. Fortunately by this time we were all assembled so Van Rijn asked Huygens to lead us all in the grace, which he did, using a prayer he had composed himself.

I knew I'd made the right decision to come to the meal when Hendrickje began to serve the food. It seemed that Geertje was still in the kitchen. The first course was dried fish with bread served on pewter plates, beer in stoneware mugs; suitably modest fare. Next was fresh fish, cooked perfectly. Then we had meat: mutton, beef and poultry all accompanied by root vegetables served on porcelain plates with Rhenish wine in the best, tall, flute glasses.

The dinner was going well, although Van Rijn didn't look too happy. If he'd been hoping for an offer from someone to buy something or come up with a commission he had been disappointed. There was the usual exchange of gossip but soon the subject returned to the early days of Van Rijn's career and his, assumed, rivalry with Jan Lievens.

Huygens was once again, asked about his preference. 'You forget that I was already familiar with Leivens's work.' He hesitated, a vague smile crossing his face then, holding his glass in one hand, he pointed towards Rembrandt where he sat at the head of the table. 'But it is true that the more I saw of your paintings,' he paused again, 'and yes, they were smaller, but the more I saw of your work the more I understood that you had the superior imagination and particularly an ability to represent your subject's deeper emotions. You were more versatile than many of your contemporaries and interested in how to use the medium. Even in those early days you were experimenting with what you could do with paint. There was that early self-portrait where you used the wrong end of the brush to scratch away the paint and describe your hair.'

'I had more of it in those days and it was a better colour.' Rembrandt, pleased by the compliment, smiled and tugged at his grey locks.

'But surely there are many good painters in the country,' Vos suggested, not to be diverted.

'True.' Huygens leant back, wiped his mouth and drew his chair closer to the table. 'We have many fine artists who can paint everyday life, what we wear, what we eat, the landscape with the canals and rivers.'

Jan Six interrupted, 'And don't forget pub scenes: brawling; puking; militiamen showing off their fine clothes; women flaunting themselves; seductions; procuring; eating and drinking to excess. We're certainly good at all those subjects.' He wiped his plate with a piece of bread.

Huygens turned to him, 'And you must agree we have the finest landscape painters in the whole of Europe. Their ability to show the warmth of the sun and the play of the wind is second to none.'

'Of course we all agree on that.' It was de Decker's turn to add to the conversation. 'But is that enough? Surely we should also seek the art of the ancients:

rhetoric, poetry and the theatre, where we can explore the finer elements of man's nature, pure thought and reason, ideas about the state of man and how he can advance himself?'

Jan Six leant forward, broke off another piece of bread and looked across the table at de Decker. 'So you think that Homer's Iliad, for instance, can be seen as an allegory for each person's quest for a spiritual home?'

Before de Decker could reply, Huygens intervened. He was one of those who, at least on the surface, believed in the literal truth of the Gospels. 'Let me add another question on the same theme,' he said, addressing Six. 'What do you make of the Parable of the Prodigal Son in St Luke's Gospel? Do you believe it to be a report of a real incident or an allegory representing a series of spiritual episodes of sin and repentance in human life?'

Six didn't reply immediately but when he did he said, 'Perhaps it can be seen as an example of both. The story of a man who, leaves home and family, goes away and wastes his substance with riotous living, ending up starving and penitent and has to return home humiliated. We have all heard stories like that, about people who fall on hard times, sometimes through their own stupidity but often through no fault of their own.' He looked around the table. 'Perhaps it has happened to people close to us? But how often are they welcomed back by a father who greets them saying, "This is my son who was dead and who is alive again, who we thought was lost but is now returned."

That is when it turns into a parable, a sign of God's forgiveness.'

'And you are suggesting that, over time, this parable was assimilated into other biblical narratives and used to represent the totality of human history; like the Fall and Expulsion out of Eden to a coming redemption at the end of time?'

'Yes. The story of the prodigal can be seen as an allegory for the spiritual journey of humanity; a journey that ends at the point of departure; birth leading to death: a circular journey ending in the same place as it began.'

There was silence around the table for a few seconds before Jan Vos added, 'It was Augustine who established the Christian theme of the figure of the fallen man, the individual who wanders as an exile in an alien land. The goal of this laborious and dangerous quest is to find a land, a city where one truly belongs but when it is discovered it turns out to be home.'

'And which frequently, is also the dwelling place of a woman of irresistible sexual attractiveness,' added Six mischievously.

Perhaps Van Rijn saw the conversation slipping away and wanted to bring it back to painting because he interrupted and turning towards me said, 'That's all very interesting but in Amsterdam we have to be more down-to-earth and practical. There are not too many grand commissions; we have no cardinals or nobility. There are few opportunities to receive commissions to make religious or allegorical paintings or to paint the great and the good of the Church, which was part of

Rubens's repertoire. Why not ask Fabritius?' He pointed to where I sat at the opposite end of the table. 'He's trying to make a name for himself and knows the difficulties of finding ones way in the world these days.'

I was a little embarrassed to be suddenly thrown into the conversation like this, but he had identified the problem I'd wrestled with much of the time. And he had given me a chance to make an impression so I gave the best reply I could, 'It's true we have to cultivate a more domestic clientele: doctors, lawyers, merchants, who all lead a more restrained, less ostentatious way of life.' I'd hardly got this sentence out before Van Rijn cut me off, as if he didn't want me to take centre stage.

'We have to rely on our friends.' He looked pointedly around the table then gestured in the direction of Huygens. 'That was why Constantijn was so important in opening up the way for me to gain access to those rich members of the society who wanted their portraits painted. True, they might have preferred a Rubens or a Van Dyck but they were both Catholics and worked for the enemy. He did advise me to go south to Italy but I knew that if I wanted to make anything of myself I had to come here to Amsterdam.' Having gained the attention of his guests Van Rijn went on, 'Now I have arrived at this period in my life, I cannot deny my history. It is what has made me. I cannot renounce my past, it is impossible. You must see that the work I am doing now is important.'

De Decker interrupted, smiling broadly; his admiration for Van Rijn was such that he would support him whatever happened. 'Why is it that most people expect originality from artists but resent it when they see it? Where others need several brushstrokes, he uses only one and I personally like the freedom that it gives.'

Jan Six joined in and spoke almost as if Rembrandt was no longer in the room, 'Does it worry you that because of this, some people think his work unfinished?'

De Decker looked around at his fellow guests, 'No, not for me. I think he has replaced imitation by suggestion. He works with a limited palette and through his use of light and shade he gives the impression of rich colour.'

Rembrandt broke into the conversation, 'What I am doing is right. In endorsing me you are committing yourselves to the future, to immortality. I cannot change my path so you must support me. It is your duty, to me and to the Republic.'

I wondered what Huygens would make of this exchange. Being a Calvinist, he would not appreciate any kind of arrogance: modesty in all things was his maxim. But whatever his feelings he didn't have long to think about it because it was then that the disaster occurred. Hendrickje had been waiting on the table, bringing in the food and serving the guests. There had been no sign of Geertje, but now she appeared carrying a bowl of fruit. She placed it on the table, dismissed Hendrickje and, without any prompting, began talking to the guests. She was no great beauty and lately she had adopted a more severe style which I didn't think suited her. That evening I could see that she had spent a lot of time on her appearance. Her hair was washed and tied back. She was wearing a dress made from a dark material with a high, lace collar. Provocatively, around her neck, she wore a pearl necklace and on her wrists, two gold bracelets.

There was a perceptible change in the atmosphere, although none of the guests, including myself, was sure what was wrong. At first no one took much notice. Van Rijn looked angry. I suspected it might be something to do with the jewellery. Perhaps Van Rijn was worried that such an ostentatious display would offend Huygens. Did he see it as some kind of threat or was it because Geertje had gone to so much trouble over her appearance in order to please him? If so, she was to be disappointed. Whatever it was, he seemed barely able to suppress his fury. Nothing was said but seeing the black looks directed at her, Geertje quickly left the room.

I've given it a lot of thought since then, but I'm still not sure what she was trying to achieve. Was she wearing the jewels as an act of defiance, in revenge for being relegated to the kitchen? Was it to show she was someone to be reckoned with and not merely the cook and housekeeper? Or was it that being the mistress of the house and producing all this fine food she calculated it was time she made an entrance and received some praise from the guests. Whatever the reason: she got it badly wrong.

We finished the meal in silence: and even if Van Rijn had wanted his guests to stay on after the meal to discuss his work, he had changed his mind. He made some excuse about having a lot to do. I knew that couldn't be the real reason because by now it was far too late and dark. We had worked by lamplight in the past but he'd said nothing to me earlier, so that seemed unlikely.

Hendrickje reappeared to help with the coats and to wish them all a safe journey home.

I should have gone to my room at the top of the house but I was curious to know what the other guests made of the evening. I stood outside with them while they waited for their transport, speculated on what was amiss, and what would happen next.

'What on earth is going on?' It was Huygens who broke the silence, 'Why have we been bundled out so early? What was his housekeeper doing wearing such an expensive necklace and bracelets?'

'Not to mention the gold ring with the diamonds,' I said. 'But surely you've seen them before? I think they belonged to Saskia. I haven't seen them in years but you knew her and you might have seen her wearing them?'

'I knew her in the early days. But I don't remember seeing those jewels before, however, you could be right. Saskia did receive some pieces of jewellery with her dowry, but she was much too discrete to flaunt them in public. I don't remember her ever wearing anything as ostentatious as that.'

Jan Six joined in, 'If they belonged to his wife, what was he thinking of, letting his housekeeper wear them?' He looked up at the house. 'It really is most inappropriate.'

Huygens agreed, 'Yes it is, but judging by the look on his face, he didn't give her permission. He's not best pleased, that's certain. There is going to be trouble, no doubt.'

I was sure he was right and curious to see what would happen next. But as it was a warm evening, when they had dispersed, I decided to take a short stroll before I went back inside.

## 15

He was furious when the guests had gone. Hendrickje and Geertje were down in the kitchen starting to clear things away when they heard him.

'How dare you, how dare you?' He raged, almost falling down the stairs in his haste and anger.

They had both seen him angry before, but not like this. Geertje, still wearing the necklace, stood behind the table laden with the debris from the meal.

He was a man possessed. 'What do you think you are doing? Do you want to humiliate me in public? How could you do that when I have fed, clothed and lodged you in my house? Why do you seek to subvert me, to demand things I cannot give?'

'You told me it was important, this meal, this evening.' She sobbed, 'I only wanted to please you and to impress your friends. I tried so hard.'

He was implacable. 'Give it to me!' He pointed to the necklace, thrusting out his hand and moving around the table towards her.

By now she had removed the other jewels and holding them firmly in her hand, she retreated.

He raised his fist and brought it crashing down on the table.

Hendrickje took refuge in a corner, not knowing what to do.

'Do you dare to defy me? Give them to me.'

Geertje recovered herself a little. She was incensed by this affront to her dignity, seeing it as the final blow that would rob her of any hope of a secure future, a betrayal of her hard work and sacrifice. 'No. Why shouldn't I wear them? They're mine, you gave them to me.'

'Liar! I did no such thing. They were never a gift, they were meant only as a loan.'

'So that is why you only allowed me to wear them when we were alone together?' She sneered at him. 'But you did make a painting of me wearing them.'

For a moment he seemed taken aback. 'I did what? When was that?'

'You can't have forgotten? I posed for Sam van Hoogstraten in the doorway, but you did nearly as much work on it as he did.'

'I may have put in a few of the finishing touches, no more. As for the jewels I've used them in paintings. I need to know what they look like in their natural setting, the way the light reflects from them, the contrast with skin: that's all.'

'And when you made me stand naked, wearing only those pearls and bracelets? Was that to help with your painting too?'

His anger subsided a little and he looked confused. He glanced towards Hendrickje as if they were venturing into territory he wanted kept secret. But he was also determined to be obeyed. He advanced towards Geertje, his voice low and menacing, 'You were here as a model before Saskia died. You know that I have seen many naked women, that I have painted them as goddesses with all sorts of trappings.'

There was something pathetic in the way he looked towards Hendrickje as if he needed her help but she had no idea what to do. He turned to Geertje again, 'I expressly forbade you to wear them in public.'

'And if they are not mine, why did you insist that I leave them to Titus in the will you made me sign?' Geertje seemed to be taunting him now.

The mention of Titus brought on his rage again. 'Are you mad? That has nothing to do with it.'

'And how do you explain this?' She drew, from inside her dress, a silver medallion.

It was a mistake, because now he was close enough to make a grab for it and tear it from around her neck. He brandished it in front of her feigning to examine it closely knowing he had the upper hand. 'Do you take me for a fool? This trinket is worthless. Why, it's not even engraved.' He flung it across the room, scattering some glasses from a side table and sending them crashing to the floor.

As Geertje gazed in horror at this violence he took the chance to grab the house keys. 'Give them to me. I've had enough. Hand them over to Hendrickje! She can take charge here.'

Geertje tried to hold onto the keys while at the same time keeping the necklace and bracelets out of his reach.

Finally he wrenched the keys free, breaking the clasp which attached them to the belt around her waist.

Geertje clung onto the jewels but suddenly the strength went out of her.

Van Rijn, breathing heavily, turned to where Hendrickje was standing. 'Here, take them.'

He tossed the keys towards her but, taken by surprise, she let them drop to the floor at her feet.

She stood looking down at them. 'But sir, I am dismissed. Geertje told me to leave first thing in the morning.'

Rembrandt seemed calm again, but his voice retained that note of cruelty, 'Out!' He pointed towards the door glaring at Geertje, 'The only person leaving this house is you.'

Geertje knelt on the floor, trying to retrieve the medallion from amongst the shards of broken glass. She looked up sobbing pitifully, 'When I first came here you thought a lot of me, petted me, and taught me to appreciate fine food, clothes and other things. Why do you bear me so much malice after all I have done for you? Now I am your slave, at your mercy, treated like a pig and denied my rights, rights that you promised.'

'You are mistaken, I promised you nothing. I gave you a home here in my house. Now you want to destroy my peace of mind, my tranquillity. You made no attempt to understand me or my work.'

'Your tranquillity!' Geertje was on her feet again, laughing almost hysterically, 'You blame me because your tranquillity has been destroyed? It is you who have the debts, the creditors. It is your extravagance that has destroyed your tranquillity: your peace of mind. Not me!'

'Will you never learn? God I have tried. I pitied you.' He paused in exasperation, 'Stupid, stupid as I was. I tried to teach you about the good things in life, what makes it worthwhile, but nothing stuck, nothing stayed in your head for long. Get out of my sight.' He pointed to the door again, 'Get out of my house. Tonight! Now! Pack your things and go.'

Geertje scuttled from the room, all her courage gone.

He turned to Hendrickje again, 'Pick them up.'

She bent to retrieve the keys, they felt heavy and substantial and holding them spurred her on. 'You can't just throw her out in the middle of the night,' she said, surprised by her own boldness.

'Why not? She has betrayed me and sullied the memory of Saskia.'

'She might do something foolish: she is desperate and you are partly to blame. You shouldn't be so cruel. Let me go and tell she can stay, at least, until the morning.'

He looked at her wearily, 'Very well, go. Tell her she can remain until the morning, no longer. Now you have the keys: you must see to the house.'

Hendrickje knocked gently on Geertje's door but, receiving no reply, pushed it open slowly. Geertje was sitting on the bed talking to herself. Hendrickje, not sure what to do, stood silently by the entrance to the room.

'This house is as much mine as his. He promised I would be secure here. Now he wants me gone. He throws me out and replaces me with another woman. I should warn her how dangerous he is. He is a liar, a bully and a cheat. When I first came here he taught me many things, different things and then I loved him.' She stopped, 'No I never loved him. He used me, abused me and now rejects me. I cleaned, cooked, ran the house and saw to the needs of his son, who I still love. I curse myself for my stupidity in trusting him. What a fool I was. He taught me to speak better and now I have the language to curse him. All the plagues of Egypt alight on him. I am at his mercy but I have my rights, rights that he promised.' She lapsed into silence.

Hendrickje closed the door and went back down the stairs.

## 16

When I got back to the kitchen he was still sitting with his head in his hands. I told him what I had seen. 'She is too upset to speak to me but she is quiet now. I'm sure she will not cause any more trouble and, as it is so late, you should leave things until morning.'

He looked up, 'You must help me Hendrickje. The situation is intolerable. She must go. I cannot work with her in the house. You understand I need peace and quiet not this constant turmoil. I cannot be involved in the running of the house. I have always left that to her and up until now she's done it well but lately she has become bitter and shrewish.'

'Did you promise her anything?' I asked.

He looked up at me cautiously. 'If you mean, did I promise her marriage? No, of course I didn't. It's all her fantasy. There was never any talk of marriage. I promised her nothing. I could not marry her even if I'd wanted to.'

I knew I shouldn't believe him because I suspected, like most of the household, that Geértje was sharing his bed but I had no proof. I had seen nothing even though I had lived under the same roof for two years. In any case it was not the place of servants like me to know such things. Even if I had proof what could I do? It is just way the things are. But if I was to help him as he wished I needed to know something of the truth or at least as much as was useful.

He remained slumped in his chair with his head in his hands breathing deeply. At last he looked up at me warily and said, 'I cannot marry because of the conditions in Saskia's will.'

'Conditions?' I asked. 'What conditions?'

'It is of no consequence.'

'If you want my help, you must tell me.'

He was silent for a few moments then he went on, 'If I remarry I have to pay Titus his portion of Saskia's estate.'

'And you do not have the money?'

He looked at me again. 'I've told you, it is of no consequence. It's true I do not have the money at the moment. But the boy is only a child and he has no need of his inheritance. When my finances improve, as they will, I shall be able to pay.' He paused, 'The only thing that can change is if Titus were to die, and God forbid that should happen.'

'Does his portion include the jewels?'

'You are very perceptive Hendrickje.'

'And Geertje knows nothing of this?'

He clasped his head in his hands again and I realised that he hadn't told her.

'No.' He was defiant like a child, 'Of course not; do you think it would make any difference? She would not understand, it would simply add to her bitterness.'

'But you let her think they were hers.'

His expression darkened as he swung round in the chair to face me, 'How often must I tell you? I did not give them to her. They were not a gift. In a moment of weakness I might have said she could wear them. It seemed a pity that they should be locked away. But she was only to wear them in this house, in private, not flaunt them in public like tonight. That was inexcusable.'

'And is she telling the truth when she says it was your

idea that she should make a will leaving them to Titus?'

'She told you that?' He got to his feet and paced around the table as I waited for his answer. At last he stopped in front of me. 'No, no, I told her she could leave her possessions to whoever she liked. She doesn't have much, a few clothes and one or two trinkets. It was her idea to leave most of what she has to Titus, but there was nothing said about the jewels. How can her possessions include the jewels when they don't belong to her?' He looked at me as if he wanted my approval. 'It was stupid of me, but I thought it might make her more amenable. I can't deny she was very good to Titus. She has been his nurse and companion for these six years and the boy is very attached to her.'

Now it was my turn to be irritated, 'Why do you keep insisting that the will doesn't include the jewels and that you didn't give them to her, when clearly you did, and because of that, of course, she thinks they belong to her? Were you afraid she would leave and take them with her and you wanted some means of redress? Perhaps, if you want her to leave peacefully, you will have to let her take them.'

He stared at me again realising that I was not so easily taken in. 'Impossible. She is not to be trusted. She twists my generosity for her own ends.'

I could see that he was reluctant to act sympathetically towards Geertje and realised that he had been planning to be rid of her for some time. This night's episode had given him the excuse he needed. He had come to think of Geertje as stupid: that she had attempted to get the better of him; deceived him and was trying to destroy his creativity. I began to see how I could take advantage of Geertje's departure, but unlike him I was conscious that it must be done in such a way as to avoid trouble in the future. I put another idea to him. 'Surely you can attach conditions, like those in Saskia's will. You must make it clear that she cannot count the jewels as part of her possessions. Make her understand they are a loan, not a gift. You gave them to her for safe-keeping. That way you can be sure they remain in the family. Didn't she promise not to dispose of them, to sell or pawn them?'

'She would not dare to sell or pawn them.'

'She might not be clever but she is cunning. If she becomes desperate no one can predict what she might do. You said yourself that she had devoted six years to you and Titus. She does deserve some form of compensation.'

He sat at the table looking weary and dejected. 'So you won't help me. You take it upon yourself to admonish me, to take her part against mine. What I need is loyalty. I can dismiss you as easily as I can dismiss her. Why do you think I should keep you here?'

He gave me a searching look but by now I knew that this was all bluster, even a little pathetic. I hesitated, almost breathless by the thought that had been forming in my head, realising that it was an opportunity I must not miss. 'You could dismiss me, but you won't because I can give you something she cannot. I can give you a child. That's what you want, isn't it?'

He stared at me. 'Do you realise what you are saying? You would come to me willingly?'

'My submission would only be in the cause of your

work. I believe in your greatness; in your art.' I rushed on amazed by my own candour and audacity. 'I can see you are bent on removing Geertje, so I will help. I can and will take her place.' I took another deep breath. 'She can prove nothing can she, you said so yourself. She is not pregnant is she? It will be your word against hers.'

He seemed to take this as encouragement. 'The bitch has tried to get the better of me. She will not stop. She's mad. She must be crushed. We must find a way to destroy her.'

This outburst frightened me. I didn't want things to get out of control. I tried to make him see reason. 'Don't you see you are as much to blame as her? But the situation is not impossible. She is not mad: she is hurt and humiliated so she lashes out at those she believes responsible. And you shouldn't be so cruel.'

I could see from his face that he knew I was right. He had created this monster; brought this catastrophe on himself, but he wasn't going to admit it.

'Once again, you take her side,' he said. 'If I go to court she will say she was my mistress: that she only slept with me because I promised her marriage or that I bribed her with the jewels.'

'And what will you bribe me with?' I asked, 'The offer of a better life?'

He gave me a quizzical look. 'I can see I must be careful with you Hendrickje. I don't think I can promise you anything. It may be just the opposite. It may cost you dearly. If you have a child, it will be impossible to pretend you are not my mistress, my whore. You will be condemned by the Church and you know now

I cannot remarry. What if they call you to give evidence? Will you refuse?'

I replied as best I could, realising I would be entering into a dark conspiracy. 'I cannot give evidence against you. All I could say was that I saw nothing. That you must have been very clever, very discrete, because no one ever guessed that anything was going on. There is a lot of talk about us all being equal before God, but I will have none of that. You men still have the upper hand. Your word will carry the day; I am not so naïve as to believe that a court made up of men of the Church, who are no better than you, will find in her favour. They might make you pay but they will not condemn you. How could they? To condemn you would be to condemn themselves.'

To my surprise, he didn't seem angry. Perhaps he saw the truth in what I was saying so I went on, 'I think, if you want her to go peacefully and not fall into debt, you should give her an allowance. Why are you so vindictive towards her, why this bitterness? You must try to deal gently with her. Be generous for your own sake.'

His mood seemed to soften as he took hold of my hands. 'I will try for all are sakes. You must console me Hendrickje. That evil woman has wronged me but perhaps, with you by my side, we can make some sense of this mess.'

He kissed me gently on the forehead and, putting his arm around my shoulders, led me from the room.

## 17

The house was quiet when I got back, the doors not locked and some of the lamps still lit so I assumed that Geertje was still clearing up. When I went down to the kitchen it was in darkness, so something was wrong. I went back to the entrance hall and was wondering what to do when Hendrickje appeared on the stairs carrying a candle and looking a little flustered. She blushed when she saw me and stopped to compose herself. She was carrying the house keys and told me she had been waiting for me to come back before she locked the door.

'But where's Geertje?' I asked. 'I wanted to congratulate her on the meal.' There was no reply. 'Isn't it her job to lock up the house?'

Hendrickje didn't look at me and there was an awkward silence before she pushed past and began to bolt the front door.

'She's in her room,' she said curtly. 'She's been dismissed. She's leaving in the morning. You can speak to her before she goes.'

Then she was gone: down the stairs to the kitchen. I suppose I shouldn't have been surprised, after all, I'd gone for a walk to avoid being involved in any trouble. But I hadn't expected this: it was going to make things very awkward.

I was up early the next morning but tried to keep out of the way. Whatever had happened during the night, Van Rijn would be around as usual. One of the things I admired about him was his commitment to his work.

In spite of all the tantrums, the cursing and commotion around him, painting was his business and there was a work routine that had to be followed, so I got on with preparing the studio for the business of the day. If Geertje had been dismissed it would fall to Hendrickje to unlock the house so she would have to be up and about too. I wanted to avoid meeting her until I had said goodbye to Geertje, and wished her well before she left. I didn't see why there should be any hard feelings between us. It was going to be difficult because I didn't want her to think I was taking sides. In the event I didn't get the opportunity.

I was up in the workshop preparing paint when he came in and asked me to go downstairs with him. Geertje was waiting in the side chamber off the entrance hall. She looked dreadful. I tried to smile at her but she was distracted; crushed; as if surprised by the way things had turned out. There was no sign of Hendrickje. I was to be a witness to what Van Rijn was offering her. He would have a document prepared that she was required to return in a few days to sign. It was an uncomfortable experience because, in spite of our past friendship, it was obvious that Geertje had decided I too had betrayed her. But what was much worse was to witness the animosity between them. He seemed determined not to look at her, not to see her, even though she was there in front of him. He had come to hate her and that hatred reflected back from her onto him. That's what hate does: in order to keep the hatred polished and hard you must narrow what you want to see. I could feel it there between them.

Geertje saw how he didn't see her and hated him more because of it.

And so she left with her few belongings in a cart. There was not much to show for almost six years of service but it did include a portrait he had made of her. I heard later that she found a place on the Rapenburg; a much poorer district than she was used to. I don't think any of us believed that was the end of things but we had no idea just how bad things would get.

# 18

It was a cold October day; an ill omen for the months to come. The water in the canals snapped at the heels of the bridges and leaves scuttled for shelter in corners and under steps. The bitter wind from the north-east gusted from the Zuiderzee splattering the rain against the two figures as they manoeuvred between the puddles that lay in wait among the cobbles.

The woman's face was hidden inside the hood of her cloak. Bowed against the weather, she seemed in no hurry to get out of the wet but advanced reluctantly towards her destination. The man, wearing a broad-brimmed, waterproof hat and cape, had her by the arm, propelling her forward whilst at the same time instructing her as if for some important part in a drama.

They turned into a street between two canals and crossed a market square. It was almost deserted, the rain and wind confounding even the hardiest customers from their usual round of gossip with the stallholders. The few customers there were, clustered beneath the canvas awnings as the couple scurried past hugging the shelter of the stalls. Crossing the square was not without its perils. As the awnings became heavy with rain, their owners poked the sagging canvas with a broom handle sending cascades of water crashing down. The passers-by needed to be ready to leap aside or receive a soaking.

Beyond the market, the couple reached a bridge where they parted, but not before the man made one last plea for her cooperation. He stood in front of her trying to make her look him in the face, his hands on her shoulders, once more repeating his instructions. He made a rather comical figure with the rain dripping off his hat and flattening his wisp of a moustache against his skin. She refused to return his gaze as if apprehensive about what he was asking her to do.

Finally, he let her go and she went slowly over the bridge holding onto the stone parapet to steady herself over the treacherous cobbles. She paused under a tree and watched as he strode away, turned a corner and was out of sight. She gathered her cloak around her and walked along a street of tall, narrow, brick houses. Looking up at the entrances, she stopped in front of one where the plaque announced the offices of the Notary Laurens Lamberti. She climbed the wide steps flanked by ornate iron railings and knocked gently on the door. She was expected.

## 19

I was awake as usual just before dawn, on that first day of October. Looking out of the window I could see nothing but the fog coming in from the sea. It engulfed everything as if the city had vanished in the night: canals, bridges, buildings devoured and buried in silence. I was nervous about what the day might bring and hoped that this weather was not an omen of disaster.

He was already up and in his workshop so I tried to put all thought of what lay ahead of me out of my mind and concentrated on seeing that everything was as it should be. I unlocked the house, made sure the fires were lit and the front steps scoured, then I got Titus ready and together we set off for school. The fog was so dense that, although we knew the way, we were like two blind insects groping our way through a foreign city peopled by ghostly shadows. There was one good thing: the fog kept Geertje away so we did not have to run the gauntlet of her abuse. I still found it difficult to understand why Geertje, who had cared for Titus for so long, did not realise that her behaviour was frightening. It was not the way to win him to her side.

That short journey changed my mood and, although when I returned home, I was still apprehensive about the day ahead, I knew that Titus trusted me, that Geertje was gone from the house for good, and her shadow would soon be lifted, at least from over me and the boy.

I made a list of things to buy on the way back from the notary so that if anything went amiss I would have time to prepare what I should tell him. Slowly the fog began to clear and a thin grey light crawled over the rooftops. It began to rain.

As I was leaving the house again, he appeared, dressed for the weather and said he would go with me, at least part of the way. I had been summoned to the notary's to swear that Geertje had understood the terms of the agreement when she had signed with her mark in June. I was a little concerned that I might be seen with him. When we had discussed the visit earlier he had told me that he too had been summoned but intended to defy them on the grounds that he had done everything possible to make Geertje's departure from the house as easy as possible.

'Didn't I give her an allowance of one hundred and sixty guilders a year when it was within my rights to dismiss her without any compensation,' he told me. 'Didn't I take your advice and let her keep the jewels? Oh I know what you will say, that there were conditions but of course there were conditions, which was my right. If she dies before Titus they will come back to my estate. She should have known they were meant only as a loan, put into her hands for safe-keeping. And what has been my reward? She has dared to pawn the jewels. And now she claims I have cheated her because she was unable to read or understand the document and that I bullied her into making her mark.' He was furious, 'It's all nonsense. She can go to hell before I revoke one word of that agreement.' He held me by the shoulders, 'Are you on my side? That's what I really want to know.'

I never meant any harm to Geertje. We both understood how important it was to get a good place and keep it. Geertje had taken me on as a favour to a friend. She had been in charge of the house but was also caring for Titus and needed more help. At first, things had gone smoothly. We were not close but got on as well as possible given that Geertje was in charge and I had to obey her orders. She had been kind to me, but she made it clear that she had done me a favour and expected something in return. I didn't blame her. We were both from untutored backgrounds and felt the same insecurity with our positions. We could be dismissed at any time and for any reason. If we were refused a recommendation, finding somewhere else to work would be almost impossible.

I felt very nervous about going to the notary's and swearing an oath. It was all very complicated, but I knew that if we were to have any peace it was necessary. The situation was intolerable. I consoled myself with the thought that Geertje had broken the agreement and, someone like him, a great artist, should not have to be bothered with such matters. He needed to be protected so that he could get on with his work.

'All you have to do is remember what is said as accurately as you can, so when you get home, you can tell me everything, exactly.' He was clear about that. 'Exactly, mind you, in every detail: everything.'

All the way to the notary's, through the pouring rain, he kept telling me how to behave and what to say. 'Don't worry,' he'd assured me, 'everything will be alright. This interview is a mere formality. Don't let them intimidate you. Part of their game is to make you feel nervous, to put you off your guard, so you'll say things you might regret later. Geertje is not in her right mind but she knew what she was signing in June.'

'But I didn't actually see her put pen to paper and make her mark,' I reminded him.

'Do you doubt my word?' He said, 'I tell you that she did. The document was read to her and she made her cross. That is what happened, whether you actually saw her do it is of no consequence.'

'But it is. Don't you see that it all depends on the questions they ask me? I am happy to confirm it is Geertje's cross beside the witnesses' signatures. You told me she signed and I believe you. But what if they ask me to swear that I actually saw her do it?'

He tried to reassure me, 'I trust you to do what is right. But remember this is important for both of us. Be discreet; don't let me down. Success in this venture will benefit you as much as me.'

When I got inside Lamberti's house and out of the rain, I began to take off my hat and cloak, wiping my feet on the mat so as not to leave a trail of water across the tiled floor. It was then that I noticed the maid giving me a strange look and realised that she had been expecting a person of some importance who would require to be helped with her things. By my actions I had shown that I too was a servant and of little consequence. I stood in the hall, holding my cloak and hat, unsure what to do next. Eventually, she took them from me and went to hang them up. When she returned, she showed me into an anteroom where there was a fire and told me to wait until I was called. As she left, she gave me a sour look and I realised that I had been condemned: thought of only as one of those servants who seduce their master.

I was still trying to get used to the idea that I had responsibilities; that Geertje had gone and he had given the keys of the house into my hands. I had never imagined that I would be in such a situation: in charge of a big house and taking care of such an important man. I was still not sure that it was what I wanted. I had learnt a lot from Geertje who was the practical sort, cooking and keeping the house clean and in good order, was what she did best.

Making a house that reflected the status of her master was something she knew nothing about, but it was what I felt was important and needed to be done. I was curious to see if I might get some idea as to how other well-off people lived, here in this notary's house.

It was dark in the room even though the shutters were open and the heavy drapes had been drawn back, the sky outside was still black with rain. The room was furnished very much like the side chamber in the house on the Breestraat, except it was more formal with several straight, leatherback chairs of the sort that are not meant to make the client feel comfortable or relaxed, but more to keep them upright and awake. Like the other room, this one had a tiled floor, the lower portion of the walls was oak panelled and the space above was crowded with paintings. I recognised some of the blooms in the flower pieces: tulips, peonies, cornflowers and aquilegia, but others were more exotic and unknown to me. But the object that impressed me most was a huge globe standing on top of a cabinet which, if the sun had been shining, would have been in the full light. I had been told the world was like a ball and that men had sailed all the way round but I didn't really believe it. Now, seeing it like this for the first time, I realised how it could be true. I listened to make sure that no one was about to come into the room before I dared reach up and touch it very gently making it turn slowly to show all the different lands spread out across its surface. Just as it was coming to rest I heard the door behind me being opened, I stepped back quickly as the clerk came into the room and invited me into the notary's office.

I didn't really have time to take in this room except that it was warm, with a fire burning in the grate, and had the smell of learning. There was a huge map on one wall and shelves with old law books and lots of files tied with ribbon leaning against each other.

The notary Lamberti and his junior were both dressed in black with white, starched collars and wore their hair long, which surprised me because such immoderate appearance was frowned upon by the Church. There was another person in the room, the clerk from the office who had shown me in. I guessed he was there to act as a witness. He was also dressed in black but had short hair and a skullcap.

Lamberti went over to the fire, warmed his hands and rubbed them together. He indicated a chair in front of his desk and the young clerk held it for me.

'Sit down, Miss—?'

'Stoffels,' I told him and, because I wasn't sure, I

added, 'Sir.'

Lamberti returned to the chair behind his desk and turned over the pages of a file then looked up, smiling as if to put me at my ease. 'And what is your first name?' He peered at me again over his glasses.

'Hendrickje, Sir.'

'Hendrickje. Good. And how old are you Hendrickje?'

'Twenty-three, Sir, I think.'

Lamberti waved away my hesitation. 'It is not important. You live in the house of the painter Rembrandt Harmenszoon van Rijn on the Sint-Anthonisbreestraat. You are his housekeeper, are you not?'

'Yes, Sir.'

'And how long have you been employed by the painter, Rembrandt van Rijn?'

'A little more than two years, Sir.' I had decided to answer questions like these as simply as possible.

Lamberti got to his feet and warmed his hands again in front of the fire. He continued, still with his back to me, 'And why has your master not come himself to swear this oath?'

I stared at the books on the shelf. This was one of the questions I had dreaded. 'He is very busy, Sir.'

'Busy!' Lamberti turned back to face the room, and came to stand between me and the desk, leaning back and resting his fingers on the edge. With his glasses perched on the end of his nose, he looked directly into my eyes, 'I should explain the matter to you Hendrickje: failing to appear before us is a serious offence and will incur punishment.'

I took a deep breath. The temptation to look away

was almost unbearable, but I was determined to hold his glaze, 'He is aware of the court's impatience, Sir, but he is very busy at the moment. He has a lot of work and many new students.'

Lamberti walked slowly round to the other side of the desk, looked down at the papers and turned them over. 'You will inform your master that it important he appears before us. This is the last time he will ignore the summons. Even he cannot hold the law in contempt. Is that clear?'

'I will tell him, Sir'

'Be sure that you do.' He picked up one of the sheets of paper, 'Where are you from Hendrickje?'

'I was born in Bredervoort, Sir.'

'That is in Gelderland is it not?'

'Yes, Sir.'

'You are from a military family?'

'Yes Sir. I am the youngest of six: two of my brothers are in the army and my sister Martina is married to a soldier.'

'So you know the ways of the military?'

'I do, Sir and I don't much like them.'

The lawyer looked puzzled, so I told him, 'I don't like the drinking, the carousing and rough ways. My brothers used to tease me because I preferred my dolls and books, but they were good and protective of me.'

'Did you go to school?'

'I had some schooling, Sir, and I can read and write, but most of the time I stayed at home and took care of the house. I was very good at organising things, keeping the house clean and tidy.

'So what brought you to Amsterdam?'

'My father took care of me. I think I was his favourite, but then there was a terrible accident when the gunpowder tower blew up.' I hesitated: it was a cruel memory. 'He was killed, Sir, blown to pieces. Later, my mother remarried. Her new husband already had three daughters so there was no longer a place for me, Sir.'

'I'm sorry to hear that Hendrickje.' He smiled at me, 'And you do not need to keep addressing me as, Sir. You are acquainted with the woman Geertje Dircx?'

'I am, that is I was, Sir.'

The notary remained silent, looking at me expectantly.

I guessed what the next question might be so I went on, 'She was my predecessor, Sir. I worked under her when I first came to the house.'

'She gave you the position as a live-in maid?'

'She did.'

'So you have reason to be grateful to her?'

'Yes.'

'Do you recognise this document?' He turned the page towards me.

'I do.'

'Have you read or been told its contents?'

'I have read it, yes.'

'And the woman, Geertje Dircx agreed to the terms contained here in this document, and this is her mark here?' He turned the page and pointed to a small cross at the bottom, below the writing. 'You will affirm that under oath?'

'Yes Sir.' I tried to make my voice sound confident. 'I am ready to sign.'

# 20

Lamberti got to his feet and moved over to the window, watching as the young woman hastened away, buffeted by the strong wind from the sea. The sky leant heavily against the steep roofs of the houses opposite as the rain continued to cascade down and the surface of the canal appeared to simmer. For a few minutes he stood, with his hands clasped firmly behind his back, deep in thought. He turned to where his young colleague was leafing through the papers on the desk before tying the bundle together and handing it to the clerk with instructions to make copies. When the two lawyers were alone, Lamberti returned to the fireplace to warm his hands.

His junior stood by the desk, 'Do you believe her? Will she perjure herself?'

Lamberti shrugged his shoulders still staring into the flames, 'It's of no matter. She's obviously the painter's mistress and the other woman is the cast-off. I am sure that the mark on the document is genuine and was made by the Dircx woman. Whether our young Hendrickje actually saw her do it, I have no idea. That wasn't the question I asked. I've heard it all before. It is a clear case of a man shitting in his hat then placing it firmly on his head. Unfortunately, any fine we can impose on him for non-appearance will not make him more compliant to the court.'

'And what about the Dircx woman's claim that he promised to marry her?'

'I dare say he did, if it was necessary to get her into

his bed. But can she prove it? She was in his house for several years yet she didn't fall pregnant and as far as I know she had no witnesses for her version of the story. She hasn't helped her case by pawning the jewels when she agreed not to. Her defence that she did not understand what she was signing won't stand up against the testimony of the Stoffels girl.'

He took the young man by the arm and led him to a painting hanging on the wall. It was a still life showing a tabletop with a plain cloth on which lay an overturned wine glass, alongside an ancient book with battered covers and tattered pages. Perched on top of the book was a human skull and in the foreground a glazed pottery oil lamp guttering towards its final moments of life. An open pocket watch, with its key on a chain, lay close by. 'You've seen this painting before. Have you ever thought why I have it hanging in this particular place?'

'Well it's opposite the window so I suppose it receives the best light.'

'That's certainly part of the reason.'

'And you can see it from your desk.'

'That's also true and part of the purpose for putting it there, but look at it carefully, what does it say?'

His junior thought for a few moments before replying, 'That everything in human existence is transitory?'

'Exactly so. When I have a particularly difficult client I can focus on this picture behind his or her head and know that however awkward they may be, however intransigent, they will eventually die, and that they are terrified at the thought. I can reassure myself that they, just like me, are mere mortals and represent no threat to the deeper, more profound, order of things.'

Lamberti went back to the window and peered into the street. He could hear the gurgle of the water in the gutters on the roof above, the hiss of the rain as the storm moved away. The sky was still grey but ragged windows of blue fluttered through the clouds. 'Have you ever thought that you and I,' he said, still looking out of the window, 'are part of a collective hypocrisy?'

'I'm not sure I understand?'

'Come, come,' Lamberti protested turning back into the room, 'you are not so naïve.'

He sat down at his desk, drew another file towards him, and began to untie the ribbon. 'The common people believe that the law we uphold is there to suppress immoral behaviour, and that you and I, and others like us, are struggling to eliminate vice from our society. Whereas you know, as well as I, that we do no such thing. In reality we accept it as a necessary evil.'

His junior looked puzzled as Lamberti asked him another question. 'Tell me what is the common opinion concerning maidservants and women of their class?'

The younger man seemed unsure how to answer.

Lamberti prompted him, 'Are you not aware of the opinion of the so called well-to-do sections of the city?'

'Oh,' the other smiled, 'I understand. Well let me see: that they are certainly in league with the devil, are lazy, garrulous, insubordinate, have an insatiable appetite for food and drink. They go against the wishes of their masters persuading their wives to buy expensive clothes and finery.'

Lamberti raised his hand to silence his junior and

then continued in the same ironic tone, 'Of course we both know their sexual appetites are insatiable. They go to great lengths to make themselves alluring, pretending to work while wearing low cut bodices to expose their bosoms and lift their skirts to show their ankles. They wear flimsy clothes and in the middle of the night hear frightening noises so that their master has to come and comfort them.' Lamberti smiled. 'You are young and newly married yourself: surely you were warned against such cunning ploys?'

'And of course none of this true?'

'Certainly there are some women who behave in that way. How could it not be so? There is some connection between domestic service, petty crime and sexual misdemeanour, but the truth is that maidservants are more often the victims not the instigators of these crimes and usually have no defence against being accused of trapping men into unlawful sexual acts.'

'Then you do not agree with those people who demand a more vigorous prosecution of immoral behaviour?'

'No, no, it's stupid, stupid. If they had their way and the whores and strumpets were imprisoned, we should have to lock away our wives and daughters too. Amsterdam is a seaport. If we did not have areas like Haarlemmerstraat and Haringpakkerssteeg with their taverns, brothels and the musicos to control the licentious appetites of the men from the ships, no woman would be safe. Sailors would be rampaging in the streets and rape would become a common crime.' Lamberti resumed his seat at his desk, 'No, no, better to turn a blind eye to some of this moral turpitude, to confine it to specific areas of the city. Virtue needs vice to mop up unsavoury and repugnant acts that might otherwise contaminate the unsullied parts of our community. How else would decent people know where it is safe to walk?'

By now his junior had taken Lamberti's place by the window and was looking out at the clearing sky. 'So occasionally, we are obliged to hand out an exemplary punishment in order to keep the good opinion of the people?'

Lamberti turned and looked up at him, 'Quite so, and to maintain the prisons and have certain areas of the city patrolled. We rule this city with the Bible in one hand and the rod in the other.' He leafed through the bundle of papers in front of him, then reached over and dipped his quill in the ink and began to write. The lesson for the day was over.

## 21

None of the household was invited to be present when Geertje came back to the Breestraat, a week later, to make her mark. She is shown into the side chamber just off the entrance hall, a room which once had felt so familiar when she had been secure and in command. Now she senses that she is caught in a trap. She is seething with resentment and looking around to find something on which to focus, to attach some hope. But everything has been changed, no doubt to intimidate her, to make her feel uncomfortable, uneasy. The room is empty except for the witnesses who sit impassively waiting for her to sign away her rights. Is she to be humiliated before two of her ex-neighbours: Cornelia Jans and Octaeff Octaeffsz. What reliance can she place on a butcher's wife and a shoemaker? She trusts neither.

Do I deserve this? She asks herself, fighting back the tide of self-loathing and the impulse to say, 'Yes.' To confess to her own inadequacies, to accept that she should have tried harder to understand what he wanted, what he needed. She takes a deep breath, no, no! Whatever she had done she doesn't deserve this, to be treated in this way, in the house she had kept for so many years. She had done her best but now she knows she is on her own.

The side chamber is a small room with a chair and table at one end on which are arranged a quill pen, ink, and the legal documents. Also on the table is a glass paperweight, that she recognises as one of the few objects that came into the house amongst the cascades of trivia he had bought at auction. She had thought it both ornamental and useful and had always taken great care about its position, insisting it be placed at the side closest to the window where it received the best light. So what was it doing in the middle of the table; that couldn't be right? She moves it back to its proper place.

'Don't you dare to touch anything in this house.'

The two witnesses are on their feet as Rembrandt sweeps imperiously across the room, seizes the offending article and very deliberately returns it to its original position.

'Why are you shouting? It was always there when I was in charge of the house.' Geertje tries not to be intimidated. This outburst only serves to deepen her sense of betrayal. 'You left those things to me. If my choice was good enough then, why are you complaining now?'

For a few moments he is silent, taken aback by her defiance.

She reaches for the paperweight again but, before she can move it, he seizes her by the wrist. For a brief moment there is a battle of wills until he forces her to let go.

'Why are you so unjust?' She asks, rubbing her wrist.

'Unjust? You are no longer in charge of this house. Keep your hands to yourself. Touch nothing.' His voice is quieter now but with an icy edge. 'You have been dismissed.'

'Where is Titus? Where is the boy? Why do you keep him from me?'

'Leave him out of this. He has nothing to do with the

matter. This is to be settled between you and me.'

'You are cruel. He may only be a child, but he would tell of my kindness, my care, over the years. But I expect you will have already poisoned his mind against me.' Geertje shakes her head knowing that her persecutor is probably already sleeping with the Stoffels woman. No doubt, in time, she will bear him a child. She knows this is what he wants desperately and where she has failed. She suspects that he will use her failure as evidence that he was never intimate with her. Well, he is a liar. He no longer wants anything to do with her. She also knows that, although he has arranged this meeting, he would have done almost anything not to be here, not to face her or be in the same room with her. She is being asked to make her mark on a document she cannot read, before witnesses who have been chosen because they can.

She sits sullenly while Rembrandt reads the document to her. 'It is agreed that you shall have, and hold in safekeeping, the jewellery listed here. You will also retain possession of the blank, silver, marriage medallion. You agree you will not sell or pawn any of these items, nor dispose of them in any manner. In addition, you agree not to change the will in which you have bequeathed them to Titus. As long as you keep to these conditions you will receive a stipend, an annual allowance of one hundred and sixty guilders a year.'

He turns the document round and indicates where she should make her mark.

Geertje gets to her feet and pushes it aside. She does not intend to sign without a protest. 'This whole thing is a sham and a charade. How can I trust you or anyone in this room?' She speaks to the witnesses, 'He has made me homeless, and betrayed me in the most painful way. All I ever asked for was the certainty of marriage. Is that too much to expect after I had shared his bed and served him for nearly six years? He let me believe he would marry me. How can I be sure what you tell me is true, that what is actually written on this piece of paper is as you say?' She points at Cornelia Jans the butcher's wife, 'She can read. You can all read. I cannot so I must trust you, but you are all in this together. You are all against me. Even the lawyers will be willing to perjure themselves for the good word of Amsterdam's greatest painter.'

She stops, knowing her words are useless: it is too late. What had she hoped for? A safe and secure existence is now a distant fantasy. It had been within her grasp only to be snatched from her. Now she can look forward to none of those things; only curses and dishonour. As for this agreement, it matters little to her whether she agrees to his terms or not. She is sure he will not keep his side of the bargain and sees no reason to abide by hers either. She is being betrayed, she can trust no one and even the witnesses are traitors. He need give her nothing and yet he has given her the jewels, so they will think she has received a generous settlement.

'You agree?' He holds the pen at arm's length towards her as if trying to avoid contamination.

She takes it from him with hands trembling not from fear but from rage. The final words of the document mean that if she breaks the agreement, he will be able to recover not only the jewellery but any money he has advanced. He has won this round in the battle but she will not be cowed, not yet. She takes the pen and makes her cross, then waits as the witnesses sign. Let's see if he has given her a means to gain some power over him? She needs money so she will take this chance to gain something from the wreckage of her relationship with her persecutor.

# 22

October: early autumn, the nights are drawing in, the mornings chilly and full of mists: the canals now patrolled by herons, the summer visitors have already flown south.

Geertje is visiting her home town of Edam. She is here because as a girl she heard rumours of a barge skipper's wife who lent money against the surety of goods. She hopes the old woman is still in business because she is in possession of some suitable goods: jewels she was allowed to take with her when she left the house on the Breestraat. She has taken great pains to keep her visit a secret, hoping that by using this informal moneylender the painter will not discover that she has broken their agreement. Her years in his house have given her a taste for things which she needs to satisfy. Already in debt, she is driven in part by the need for money. But it is also an act of defiance; she feels she has nothing to lose. If he does discover her perfidy, she has already decided on her course of action. If he makes trouble she will sue him for breach of promise. In the months since she left his house, not one of the 160 guilders allowance has materialised so she feels she has right on her side.

The barge skipper's wife is indeed still in business, but she drives a hard bargain.

'Two hundred guilders, surely you can make a better offer than that?' Geertje is feeling rather queasy and is anxious to get the business over with, and escape from the stuffy space below the deck of the barge with its smell of tar, grain, tobacco and charcoal. She finds the woman a little unsavoury: she has come to feel superior to this kind of person.

The woman turns over the rings in her palm and peers at them through an eye glass.

'That one has a diamond cluster.' Geertje leans forward attempting to retrieve the most elaborate of the three.

The woman's hand snaps shut, and she looks up at Geertje, her face distorted by the lens still screwed into her eye socket. 'Most people who come to me do so because they need money quickly or because they want to be discrete. How did you hear about me?' Her hand opens but she does not give the jewels back. She holds them up to the thin shaft of light that penetrates the close confines of the living quarters on the barge. Finally, she places them on the table between them.

Geertje holds a handkerchief to her nose and fights back the feeling of nausea. 'When I was a girl I worked in an inn at Hoorn. I heard about you from some of the customers.'

'Hoorn is a good way north. I did not know my reputation had spread so far. How did you come by these?'

'It is not important,' replies Geertje. Then, as the woman raises the brow of the unoccupied eye, adds, 'They were a gift.'

The woman wraps the rings in the cloth they came in and pushes them towards Geertje. She leans back as if she knows her offer will be accepted. 'A rather fine gift for a servant. You must be very good at your job?' The huge eye peers quizzically at Geertje, 'But that is not my business. You are welcome to try elsewhere, but I think you will find two hundred guilders is a generous offer.'

Geertje surveys the bundle on the table between them. Should she pick it up and try elsewhere? But the woman sitting opposite, with the claw-like hands and huge eye behind the lens, is so intimidating she feels that the jewels are already lost.

The moneylender counts out the coins and although Geertje is sure that the jewels are worth more than a paltry 200 guilders, the need for secrecy means she cannot seek a better offer. She climbs the narrow steps and clambers out through the hatch into the cold morning air. She had hoped for more but if that is all she is offered, 200 guilders is still 200 guilders.

# 23

Rembrandt has ordered that all the fires be lit in the house except in the grand saal where the company will assemble. There is to be a trial, not in an official court of law but in his house on the Breestraat, so perhaps 'trial' is the wrong word. Certainly there will be a notary present, witnesses will be called and evidence taken, but there will be no oaths sworn, just a presumption that the truth will be told. The presence of a higher authority is implicit, and the fact that one day all those present will have to answer to that authority is assumed to be all that is required.

Rembrandt is in an almost uncontrollable rage. This very morning he had received another summons to appear before the Marital Court to answer the charge that he promised to marry the woman who has betrayed him, and who is the centre of today's proceedings. He knows, eventually, he will have to attend but it is intolerable that he, Amsterdam's most important artist, should have to defend his actions before a group of men, of the class from which he draws his clients.

At one end of the room are several chairs to accommodate the participants. They have been placed to the right of a desk with another chair behind it for the notary. Other furniture has been cleared to make a space where the witnesses will stand. To the left there is a single chair for the central character, 'the accused', the former housekeeper. It is clear that the purpose of this arrangement is to intimidate, to make the event uncomfortable for his opponent, someone who must be crushed.

Geertje is brought in. On her way through the house she had glanced into the other rooms on the ground floor. Things have continued to change since her last visit: the paintings are different, the furniture, over which she had lavished such care, has been moved or disappeared. When she made those arrangements he had not objected to what she had regarded as convenient placing. He had not even voiced an opinion, so why make it different now? Of course, it wasn't him, it was that Stoffels woman. These changes were her doing, her way of erasing any sign of her predecessor. But where is she, why is she not here to witness her humiliation? Is it because he does not want her to hear what will be said? How he is a liar, a lecher and reprobate. What conditions has she demanded for giving in to his lust, for sharing his bed? Or has she accepted her place as the submissive mistress. He will demand that she bears him a child: will she consent to that?

In spite of her precautions, somehow, he has discovered her trip to Edam to pawn the jewels. But she consoles herself with the thought that she has won a small victory. Now he realises that if she dies while the jewels are with the barge skipper's wife, and he cannot redeem them, they will be lost to him forever. So he has to make her a better offer, although it may be a pyrrhic victory. Her position may be no better. She has been brought back to this house to be held accountable for her actions and to accept new terms or he will revoke their previous agreement and she will be destitute. This time, not only will there be witnesses present, but also a notary who has drawn up the new agreement and will read it out: the notary who, in theory, she must trust. Does it matter that she cannot read that she must put her faith in others and believe what they read to her? She is tired and frightened and believes the document to be irrelevant. Rembrandt has lied before, made false promises and will do so again. So why should she not do likewise? If he can cheat so can she. She has been robbed of what is rightfully hers. Here, in this room, he might be all reason and benevolence but he is not to be trusted.

'You have been summoned here to sign this new agreement.' The notary holds a document in his hand. 'The terms are the same as before, terms that you have already agreed. Do you deny signing this paper?'

'I do not deny it. I cannot deny it.' Geertje looks around the room and glares at Rembrandt. 'He knows I cannot read. How do I know that he has not altered that piece of paper? I must take his word for it.'

'Not my word, but the word of the lawyer who drew it up,' Rembrandt insists.

The notary takes over and speaks to Geertje. He taps his finger on the sheaf of papers laid out on the desk. 'I have here an affidavit from Hendrickje Stoffels, the woman who replaced you as housekeeper, affirming that this is your mark here on this document.'

Geertje is white with fury, 'She is a liar. She was not even in the room, so how could she see me make my mark on anything?'

The notary shrugs his shoulders but goes on, 'There were other witnesses who will also attest that you signed this paper. You agreed before them these terms so why have you changed your mind?'

'I will not sign. That document also contains his promise to give me an allowance, but I have not received a single guilder. Why does he not dare to appear before the Marital Court? Is it because he fears they will discover the truth? I do not believe he will keep to his side of the bargain.' She looks around the room. 'But what difference does it make? You are all against me. I cannot read so how do I know you are not cheating me? You can read out whatever you liked, I cannot tell if it is what is written there.'

'I am sorry that you have such a low opinion of the law. These are generous terms.' The notary leans back and taps the tips of his fingers slowly against each other.

'I will not sign,' Geertje repeats sullenly.

The notary casts a cautious glance at Rembrandt. 'Van Rijn is prepared to make you a better offer. He will give you the two hundred guilders to redeem the jewels and clear your debts and you will continue to receive the yearly allowance of one hundred and sixty guilders.'

Geertje points an accusing finger at Rembrandt. 'His promises are worthless. So far I have received nothing. What if I fall ill and need money for medicine?

There is a whispered consultation between Rembrandt and the notary. 'He is also prepared to make an undertaking that should your circumstances change you may receive additional funds. A clause to that effect can soon be added to the document. Is that not generous?'

Geertje points an accusing finger at Rembrandt, 'I suppose these additional funds will be at his discretion?'

Rembrandt is on his feet again, 'Of course, at my

discretion, what more do you expect? I need give you nothing, after all my generosity you still want more?'

'How can I believe you? I know you will not keep your part of the bargain.'

Once again the notary seeks to calm things. 'The witnesses here will attest that the contents of the new agreement are as I stated. I will read it out, before you make your mark. You must trust someone. You must decide: will you agree to the terms set out in this new document or not? I must warn you that this is his final offer. Once you have recovered the jewellery you must make no further demands. If you do, the whole arrangement will be null and void and he will seek to recover the money he has given you.'

'No never.' She makes a gesture around the room, then through her tears, 'Shame on you all for siding with him. Fools the lot of you. You are all under his spell. Don't believe a word he says. Let the court decide who is in the right. Let him appear there, they will see through his lies. I will submit to this humiliation no longer.' She pulls her cape around her shoulders, 'Who will show me out?' She waits a few seconds but as no one moves, she wheels on her heel and is gone.

Only two people remain in the room. The notary sits behind the desk slowly putting the papers into order before slipping them into the file and Rembrandt slumps in his chair choking with fury and frustration.

Hendrickje looks in through the door and, seeing that all the witnesses have left, crosses to where Rembrandt sits dejected and rests a hand on his shoulder. He places his hand on hers and looks into her face. If the notary notices this show of affection he says nothing.

Rembrandt takes out the letter he has received that morning. 'You see this? Another summons to appear before the Marital Court. She is incorrigible, she demands more and more. How is she to be stopped?'

Hendrickje looks towards the notary who leans forward, his hands resting on the table. 'You must go and defend yourself.'

'I have already been more than generous.' Rembrandt subsides back into his chair.

The notary pulls on his cloak and, standing by the door, gives his parting advice, 'You have already been fined for non-attendance. Next you will be summoned for contempt. You do not improve your case by this defiance. You admit that you let her take the items of jewellery from the house.'

'I made it clear they were a loan; they were in trust. She had the use of them in private, but what does it matter? She had no right to pawn them. She knows it and so do I. Do I have any other course of action?'

'It may be the only way to resolve this dispute. You may have to make her a better offer, but at least in the Marital Court the Dircx woman will have to accept the decision; after all it is she who has brought the case. Take my advice, go.'

## 24

Everyone stands as the commissioners enter, climb the two steps onto a raised dais, and take their places behind a table covered by a heavy, oriental carpet from where they look down on the proceedings.

Once again Geertje faces her adversary, this time across the floor of the Marital Court in the Oude Kerk: the church that holds the remains of Saskia, his first wife, the woman she replaced.

All three commissioners are dressed in sombre black and wearing hats as befits a court whose duty is to uphold the moral values of the State. With them is the notary who drew up the original agreement and a lawyer who will question the two parties and the various witnesses.

Geertje is dressed plainly and her hair is held under a cap. She had debated whether to appear in a poverty-stricken manner, but decided her dignity and rank demanded a more straightforward approach. She is glad there is a fire in the room even if, at the same time, she is slightly over-awed by the atmosphere of gravitas enhanced by the high ceiling, tiled floor and tall, plain glass, leaded windows. Between them, in the gaps above the oak panelling topped with a simple wainscoting that surrounds the room, hang maps of the United Provinces and its possessions.

As for Rembrandt, he knows he must make a good impression on these men, convince them that he is innocent of the charges. He cannot afford the slur on his reputation if he is branded a reprobate. The commissioners are members of the class from which he draws his clients. Cornelis Abba is a brewer and sitting beside him is the burgomaster Hendrick Hooft. The third commissioner is a surgeon, Arnout Tholincx, married to one of the daughters of Dr Tulp whose portrait he had painted earlier in his career. Rembrandt's financial, as well as his personal, reputation is at stake.

Each party is allowed to set out their case. Geertje is first, she speaks directly to the lawyer choosing her words carefully. 'My husband was Abraham Claesz. He was in the navy: a ship's bugler. We were married when we were both very young. When he was killed in an accident I had to fend for myself so I came here to Amsterdam.'

The lawyer interrupts, 'Did you come to Amsterdam to find work?'

'I did, I was in service briefly, then I worked in an inn near to where I was born. I didn't like the work so I thought I would try my luck here in the city.'

One of the commissioners interrupts, 'You were working in an inn? Did you find that difficult?'

'Difficult: what do you mean, Sir?'

'Well, inns can be rough places. Men, especially sailors can be, how shall I say this, demanding: wanting certain kinds of favours.'

'No, there was nothing like that. No one demanded anything of me. I kept myself to myself and I had a husband then.'

'But when you came to the city, was it easy to find work?'

'Not at first.'

'What did you do?'

'I heard from a friend that there was work as an

artist's model.'

'So when you first came into Van Rijn's house you worked as a model.'

'I did, yes, but it was not my choice. Things were hard and I needed the money.'

'Would you say that being a model is a respectable profession?'

'I suppose so.'

'Did it involve removing your clothes?'

Rembrandt, who has been sitting impassively on the other side of the court room, is on his feet trying to interrupt. He is in something of a dilemma. He knows the commissioners are trying to discover what kind of woman they are dealing with, but he wants to defend his profession. 'Are you suggesting that there is something salacious or immoral about drawing from the nude?'

Geertje looks at the commissioners but they seem inclined to let Rembrandt continue.

'It is perfectly respectable to ask the models to pose naked. Drawing the human figure is the essence of my craft and has been for hundreds of years. How else are we to depict the ancient mythologies? I have to put my students through the rigorous discipline involved in representing the human form.'

Now the notary signals for Rembrandt to be quiet.

He turns away, muttering under his breath, 'Disegna, disegna, non perdere tempo.'

'What was that you said?' One of the commissioners asks, suspecting contempt of court.

Rembrandt rises to his feet again, 'I was simply quoting the advice of the great Michelangelo to his student Antonio.'

'And that was?'

'That he should draw every day, there was no time to lose.' He subsides into his chair, aware that he might have gone on too long.

The lawyer addresses Geertje again, 'Did some of the other models also work in areas like the Haarlemmerstraat and Haringpakkerssteeg?'

Geertje could sense the direction of the questions. 'Perhaps, I didn't ask. It was not my place. I was only there a few times before his wife asked me if I would help her when the baby was born.'

'She asked you?'

Geertje seems irritated by this question. 'Yes she did. She was very poorly.'

'She was pregnant and asked you to come to work in the house?'

'I had been in service before so I may have suggested to someone that I could be useful. But it was she who asked me to help while she nursed the baby.'

'I understand she died a few months after the birth and that you became responsible for the baby's care.'

'I had been helping around the house while she was ill and needed all her strength to care for their son. So it was natural that when she died he would ask me to help with Titus. As well as looking after his son, he wanted me to take over the running of the house.'

'So you became his housekeeper. And you claim that it was soon after that he began to make advances to you.'

'Yes, he did. He made much of me then, taught me better manners, to appreciate good things like food and wine, and to speak better.'

'But he didn't teach you to read?'

'No, he said it wasn't important, and in any case it wasn't right for someone like me to read. But I had to shoulder the burden of running the house; organising his life; so that he could work in peace. The house was very busy then, full of students. There were statues and paintings, stuffed animals, weapons, all manner of bric-a-brac that had to be dusted and polished.'

'Were there servants that you had to organise?'

'Yes, he gave me complete control.'

'And when you left, how had things changed?'

'Most of the servants had gone and I had to make do on what little money was left after he had frittered it away at the auctions. I took care of his son as if he were my own.' She glances across the room. 'I loved him then. He would be nothing without me.'

Rembrandt glares back as he tries to get the attention of the commissioners again. 'This is ridiculous: all lies. What does she know of love? It was all show: she never cared for me. What she calls love is not love but some kind of obsession.'

He turns to Geertje, wagging his finger in the air, 'It's a fantasy you have invented. Where is the proof? Where are your witnesses?'

He looks up at the commissioners, 'She has no claim on me or my house: it is mine. She took too much on herself always telling me what I could and could not do; what I should and should not buy; complaining about how I spent my money; money I earned with my talent, my labour. She was my servant with no rights in the matter.'

The lawyer signals for Rembrandt to be quiet and turns to Geertje. 'He made you a promise of marriage?'

'Yes, he said he would marry me. He gave me a wedding medallion. He made me feel I was safe there. I was a fool to think he ever loved me, but I believed him and shared his bed.'

Rembrandt can no longer contain his frustration and gesticulates wildly in the air. 'I took you in; treated you generously; I clothed and fed you. I thought you were kind and willing to learn, but you have betrayed my trust and pursue me with mad talk about promises of marriage. That medallion she speaks of it is a mere bauble, not even signed, so it means nothing.'

One of the commissioners appeals for calm. Rembrandt sits down disgruntled, muttering to himself.

The lawyer continues to question Geertje, running his finger down a document which is on the table in front of him. 'Tell me: did you make a will while you were still employed in his house?'

'Yes, last year, under his direction.'

'It was his suggestion?'

'Yes, he'd promised to marry me and that was part of the arrangement.'

The lawyer waves aside her answer. 'The question of marriage is not relevant, at the moment.'

'But surely —' Geertje begins to protest.

The lawyer ignores her. 'In this will you stated that on your death you bequeathed your possessions to his son, Titus van Rijn. Is that correct?'

'Yes.'

'And those possessions included some jewellery?'

'The jewels he gave me.'

'Must I listen to these lies?' Rembrandt interrupts again, 'How many times must I make this clear. I did not give her any jewellery or promise to marry her.'

Geertje looks towards the commissioners. 'He can shout all he likes. He did give me the jewels, and he made use of me.'

There is a hasty conference amongst the three commissioners, and then Rembrandt is asked to step forward.

It is Cornelis Abba who speaks for them. 'I should warn you that you must remain calm if you do not wish to have the court fine you for contempt.' There is a short pause before he goes on, 'Are we to understand that you put pressure on this woman to make a will in favour of your son?'

'I put no pressure on her. She was fond of the boy. She had cared for him since he was a baby. She offered to leave her possessions to him.'

'She claims these possessions include the jewellery?'

'No, no,' Rembrandt shakes his head, 'she did not have any jewellery to leave. I certainly did not give her any.'

'We have a copy of the will here before us. It states that after leaving her clothing to her mother, she bequeaths all other property, moveable and immovable securities and credit to your son Titus. You say this did not include the jewellery.'

Rembrandt hesitates. 'Does the document specify that they were part of her possessions? No, it does not.'

'So why did you allow her to take those items with her when she left? You also gave her an allowance.

Why? You were under no obligation to do so. Doesn't that indicate that she had been more than a servant and that the jewellery was hers?'

Rembrandt remembers the warning to remain calm but his voice has a steely edge. 'That had nothing to do with the will. It is true that when she left the house she took the jewellery with her, but we had an agreement that she would keep it safe and the allowance was a reward for doing so. But she is not to be trusted.'

Before he can go on, the lawyer turns to Geertje. He places another document on the table. 'You made your mark on this agreement and promised that you would not sell or pawn the jewellery. It was given to you for safe keeping, as part of the settlement, when you left the house.'

Geertje points at Rembrandt. 'He gave them to me. Those jewels are mine. As for that document; you know I can not read, so I must take your word for it.'

Cornelis Abba leans forward, across the table, this time to speak to Geertje, 'We have a statement from Geertgen Nannings, the barge skipper's wife and moneylender, that she advanced you money on the surety of certain jewels.'

'They were mine by right. He gave them to me.'

'You admit that you pawned three gold rings, one with a diamond cluster?'

'I had been badly treated. What if I did pawn them? I needed the money. It would not have been necessary if I had received the allowance he promised.'

'So you admit you were in breach of an agreement, which you had signed, when you pawned the jewellery in Edam. Then, when you were offered a new and better agreement, and promised money to recover them, you refused. How to you think that the conditions in the will can be met if you failed to redeem them and they were to pass out of your possession? How could his son Titus receive his inheritance?'

For a moment Geertje is confused and seems to be thinking hard. 'He has broken the agreement too. Ask him why I never received the money he promised? Even if I had, it would not meet my needs: it is only enough to rent a small room on the Rapenburg. That is not what I am accustomed to. I am forced to live in a hovel and receive a pittance, to watch every florin, and lose all those things that I could have expected after years of loyal service and the marriage he promised. All the things that accompany old age, love, honour, obedience and friends, they are now denied me and instead I have only poverty and abuse. You cannot imagine what courage it took to go to the moneylender in Edam. I hoped he wouldn't find out, but he did. He has spies everywhere. I cannot trust anyone. I have been cheated out of what is rightfully mine. He promised me marriage. He gave me the jewels. It is I who has been betrayed. His house is as much mine as his. I did not sign. I trusted him once, but never again. How am I to know that he has not altered that piece of paper? How do I know he will not rob me of what little I have left?' She looks venomously towards her accuser, 'Do you deny it?'

Rembrandt is on his feet again, shaking his fist. 'I do deny it. Rob you? You dare to accuse me of theft? When you left my house we agreed that the jewellery was yours to keep safe, not to loan or sell. Yet you pawned it into the hands of some dirty, unprincipled, villainous woman. That is as good as theft: so make no accusations against me.'

He turns his back on her and speaks to the commissioners, 'She wormed her way into my house behind my back, playing on my sick wife's fears. I kept her on after she died because my son was only a few months old and accustomed to her. I thought she would change into a loyal servant, but it was a terrible mistake. I felt sorry for her, I tried to improve her. I thought to show her another side of life so that she could rise above being a mere servant. But she was always recalcitrant and unwilling to make any effort. She is lying when she says I did not try to teach her to read and write. It was in my own interest that she should be useful because I had given her charge of the house. And what has been my reward for all this generosity? She became more and more obsessive, trying to run my life, acting the great lady, and then falsely accusing me of promising marriage. I had to dismiss her; she made my life intolerable. Now she comes to my house, stands in the street shouting curses and abuse at me, frightening my son and my housekeeper. She thinks that if she makes a public scandal she will get more money out of me.'

He turns quickly to face Geertje, jabbing his finger in front of her face, 'I made no promise of marriage. This is blackmail. You want to bleed me dry? Well you will not succeed. You are mad.'

Geertje steps back, colliding with a chair and almost

losing her balance. She recovers and gripping the arm of the chair shouts back at him, 'Mad! No, I am not mad. Whatever I have done, I do not deserve this. I curse the day I set foot in your house. I curse you and that whore who has replaced me in your bed. She does not know what is in store for her. This is all her doing. I curse myself for ever letting her enter the house. I gave her a place and this is how she repays me, by conspiring to have me thrown onto the street.'

'Curse me! Curse me? You dare to curse me?' Now Van Rijn's anger is fierce and implacable. 'This is intolerable. You defied me, me, Rembrandt, the city's greatest living painter. How dare you, how dare you?'

The lawyer rises to his feet and jumps down from the dais, concerned that blows will be exchanged. He takes Rembrandt by the arm and directs him to sit down but, as he moves to his seat, he looks back over his shoulder, 'She is not in her right mind. Do you wonder that I had to dismiss that woman? She made my life impossible.'

Geertje, in tears, appeals to the commissioners, 'And how did I defy him by wearing those jewels? The jewels he gave me.' She sinks to the ground in a melodramatic gesture and sobs quietly, 'After all I've done for him.'

## 25

So what did they make of all this, these commissioners? Three men of high repute are being asked to adjudicate between the two sides in a dispute. Their dilemma is to arrive at a compromise that will punish both the warring parties and serve as a warning to others to moderate their behaviour.

The economic depression and a fierce visitation of the plague, combined with an ill-fated naval battle with England, have made for a Calvinistic revival. Some are saying that God is angry with them. So the mood is for a robust prosecution of cases of notorious living; their religion demands it. But they must also be fair and be seen to be so; it demands that too.

Hendrick Hooft leafs through the pile of documents. 'One thing is clear from what we have heard today: these two people dislike each other intensely. They are at war. It is difficult to see how their two versions can be reconciled. The painter's evidence is straightforward enough: he simply denies everything.' He turns a page, 'He has not slept with the woman, nor has he offered her marriage, and he did not give her any jewellery.' He leans back in his chair, looking grave. 'According to his wife's will they were not his to give. So why did he allow Geertje Dircx to wear them in his house, and give them into her safe keeping when she left? Why keep the woman in your household if she is unwilling to obey your orders?'

There is a short silence before Cornelis Abba adds another question, 'And why give her an allowance after her insolence?' Before the others can respond he answers for them, 'Perhaps she is telling the truth and it is he who is the liar? The fact that he may be a genius does not excuse his behaviour. It all makes sense if he did promise to marry her, and was sleeping with her, then he would reward her with the jewellery.' He leans back and places the tips of his fingers on the papers in front of him. 'But even if we believe her, and I think we must, it is no excuse for breaking a solemn agreement. She had no right to sell or pawn the jewellery.'

Hendrick Hooft agrees, 'That seems clear enough. We can only assume his lust was greater than his common sense; not a rare occurrence. Perhaps he thought he could keep putting her off, but hadn't reckoned with her ambition to become his wife. Here is a young widow who finds herself in a position she could only have dreamt about: working for one of the city's most famous men, with status, good food, clothes, and in charge of a big house with servants to order about.'

Cornelis Abba adds, 'Was she so obsessed with the idea that she didn't consider it a threat to employ a younger, prettier woman in the house?' He pauses, 'But even if that were so and we accept she committed sins of the flesh, then so did he. They are both at fault and she has been badly used.'

'We are faced with a dilemma.' Arnout Tholincx takes off his hat, scratches his head, adjusts his spectacles and strokes his beard. 'There are those in our society who believe the future fortune of our commonwealth rests on our observance of moral cleanliness so we have to uphold certain standards. On the other hand, can we allow this breach of promise case to succeed even if we believe she is in the right? She may be more sinned against than sinning but there is no precedent for masters to be forced to compensate or, worse still, marry their servants simply for committing an act of fornication. Are we prepared to set such a precedent?' He looks at his fellow commissioners: 'I for one, am not.'

Hooft agrees, 'No, we cannot allow her to succeed. I think there is something suspicious about this woman Dircx. Is it not strange that the painter's wife became pregnant several times during their marriage and yet, although Dircx lived in his house for six years, she did not do so once? Either fornication did not take place or there is something wrong with her. I suspect she may be unbalanced or incompetent.'

'So are we agreed?' Cornelis Abba speaks for all three, 'We will not accept the charge of breach of promise but I think we must award her some compensation.'

'Exactly. I think we can ignore the statement of Hendrickje Stoffels. She is no more to be trusted than the Dircx woman. She has a lot to gain if her rival is out of the way. Van Rijn has already offered the money to redeem the jewellery so we should hold him to that, and I think we also insist he increase the allowance.'

The others nod in agreement. 'Two hundred guilders a year. Would that be fair?'

They decide that it would and the judgement is handed down. For Geertje, it is a small victory, she has won the moral argument and improved her situation, or so she thinks. She is tired and confused. All she wants is peace and quiet.

As for Rembrandt, he is furious. He had expected complete vindication, yet now he is saddled with an even greater financial burden; one he can ill afford and with no guarantee that the jewellery will be returned. True, he's not being asked to marry the woman but she still has the pawn ticket and he isn't placing any trust in her. He is out for revenge.

## 26

The night that I discovered I was not as essential to the household as I had thought was the same night that Rembrandt hatched the plot to have Geertje put away in the Spinhuis. After all my years in his house I realised that my future must lie elsewhere, perhaps outside Amsterdam. I suppose I should have known that it would happen eventually, and it was probably all for the best. I didn't like all this emotional turmoil or the tense atmosphere that pervaded the house. Van Rijn had changed: he was more taciturn and spent a lot of time on his own in the big workshop. On the surface, of course, everything appeared to be going well. He was still receiving commissions, but tastes were changing and although we still had students, as time passed, there were fewer of them. Money was short and there was a good deal of ill will among the local traders.

I was never part of his conspiracy. I didn't like what he was planning. I thought it unworthy of such a great man, but what could I do? I was even more shocked when Hendrickje went along with it. She should have been the one to persuade him that what he planned was evil. But she did nothing. I suppose she felt compromised and it would be best if she agreed to his scheme. After all, she had a lot to lose. I'm sure she would defend herself by saying she had his best interests at heart, and what they both really wanted was an end to all this vexation.

The court had ordered him to provide Geertje with the means to redeem the jewellery and she had given authority to Pieter Dircx, her brother, to collect the money and pay off the barge skipper's wife.

I was in my room one evening when I heard someone pounding on the front door. I ran down the stairs to find Hendrickje standing on the stool in the entrance hall with Titus in her arms and Rembrandt beside them. They were peeping out to see who was standing at the top of the steps outside.

'There are two men,' she whispered. 'One of them is Geertje's brother, but I don't recognise the other one. Shall I let them in?'

'Yes, you had better or they'll beat the door down. Leave them to me. Everything is prepared?' He stood in the centre of the room ready to receive them. 'He's probably as big a fool as his sister.'

'Come in, come in, welcome,' Rembrandt greeted his visitors and ushered them into the grand saal where the fire had been lit and candles blazed in the centre of the table loaded with food and drink.

I followed them in. He had asked me to be there in case of trouble. I was pretty sure nothing would happen but you could never be certain. After all, here were two tough looking men sent to collect a debt and with the authority of the court behind them.

'I can tell that you are seamen.'

If Dircx was impressed by this observation he didn't show it. In any case before he could reply Rembrandt went on, 'I used to live down by the docks and I noticed the rolling gait of the sailors. Please sit down. I know we have business to discuss but let me offer you some refreshment first.'

Pieter Dircx was a tall, rangy man who didn't seem nervous or out of place as he stood with his back to the fire. The other man turned out to be his cousin Pieter Jansz. Rembrandt made a feeble joke about not knowing which Pieter he should address but if he was worried that these seamen were going to intimidate him physically he needn't have been. It was obvious to me that Pieter Dircx wasn't as stupid as his sister and had his own agenda.

Pieter Jansz spoke first, 'Don't try throwing us a barrel. We are here to collect the money you owe to his sister, your former housekeeper.'

Rembrandt ignored him. 'Perhaps you will take a glass, some bread, cheese and we have some fine smoked ham? Hendrickje pour our guests some ale. Come, come sit down, we are all civilised people here.'

The two men remained standing looking at each other. Finally, Rembrandt held a chair for each of them and, exchanging knowing smiles, they sat down.

I realised that an elaborate pantomime had been planned for Pieter Dircx and his companion's benefit. The fact that they had been brought into this room with its furniture, sculptures and walls hung with paintings and mirrors was aimed at convincing them that Rembrandt was a man of substance with powerful friends. Later, I realised that there was also a more sinister agenda. He wanted to make sure that Geertje was put away for a long time where she could do no more harm.

A few minutes later, Cornelia Jans, the butcher's wife arrived at the house and joined us. I had never liked the Jans woman. She was mean-spirited, always toadying around, and if she was there something unpleasant was being hatched.

We all sat around the table while Hendrickje hovered behind the two Pieters making sure their glasses were always full.

'I should never have lent your sister those items of jewellery.' Rembrandt turned to Pieter Dircx, 'I told her they were a loan, not a gift, but it seems that she was not capable of understanding the difference, even though I made it as clear as I could. I credited her with more intelligence. You, on the other hand I'm sure, can see that I acted in all innocence.' He took a mouthful of wine, swilled the liquid around his mouth, and then swallowed. 'It was a mistake that I fully acknowledge.' He paused, looked into his glass, before speaking to Dircx again, 'I blame myself. I did not realise that a simple misunderstanding would result in all this trouble and pain, for all of us, and especially you.'

'My sister is a simple soul and no scholar,' Dircx said, 'and all this finery is not what she is used to. Maybe it turned her head.' He drained his glass, wiped his mouth with the back of his hand and got to his feet. Then he walked slowly around the room peering at the paintings and scrutinising the furniture, while the rest of us watched. After a few minutes he returned to his chair but didn't sit down. Instead, he planted his feet firmly apart, as if he were standing on the deck of a swaying ship, reached inside his jerkin and took out a thin bundle of documents bound together with twine. 'I have something here that might interest you.' He removed the twine and held out a thin, legal looking document. 'This paper gives me the authority to collect my sister's allowance: two hundred guilders. And in here,' he held out an envelope, 'is the docket to redeem the jewels from Edam. That's another two hundred.'

'Please, please sit down.' Rembrandt signalled to Hendrickje to refill Dircx's glass. 'This must be putting you to a lot of trouble. I assume your sister is paying you for this favour?'

'She did mention something about a small commission but I doubt I'll see a single guilder. So, as we were on our way here,' he indicated Pieter Jansz, 'we gave it some thought and reckoned we'd ask you if you'd like to make us a better offer.' He sat down and laid the document on the table.

Rembrandt did not reply immediately but reached for the writ. 'May I see that? Hendrickje help our guests to more food.' He opened the document and glanced through it, then looked up towards Cornelia Jans and nodded his head. He passed the paper and watched as she spread it in front of her.

For a few moments she studied it, and then pushed it back across the table to Dircx. She leant forward pointing to a paragraph. 'It says here that you have the authority to redeem the jewellery from Geertgen Nannings but I can't see where it says you have to return it to your sister. You've been here less than half an hour and although you've come up with this story about a commission, we still don't know what you intend to do. You could keep the jewellery for yourself.'

Pieter Dircx did not reply immediately. 'Certainly I could,' he said. 'It gives me legal possession of it.' He took another long pull of his ale. Apart from the crackling of the logs on the fire, there was another long silence.

'You do understand that the court found in my favour in all the important aspects of the case,' said Rembrandt, at last.

Pieter Jansz disagreed, 'Geertje told us they found in her favour.'

'No, no she is mistaken.' Rembrandt turned to Cornelia Jans for support. 'She pawned the jewellery, didn't she? A clear breach of the agreement she had signed.'

'You could say it was a form of treachery,' added Cornelia Jans.

'I'm getting tired of all this.' Pieter Jansz was on his feet having already consumed several glasses of ale. 'Why are we wasting our time with this tight-fisted reprobate?' He glared at Rembrandt. 'It doesn't matter what you say, the court has ruled that you must hand over the money. Geertje doesn't trust you and neither do I. The notary told us she was almost hysterical when she took out this writ. She cannot bear to be in the same room as you. Just give us the four hundred and we will leave.'

'Let's not rush things.' Pieter Dircx signalled to his cousin to be quiet. 'After all the trouble he has taken, I don't think he wants the jewellery returned to Geertje.' He looked at Rembrandt. 'Is that right? Perhaps you have a better idea and, as we are due back at sea in a few days, if you want my cooperation you must act now.'

For a few moments Rembrandt was caught off guard and at a loss for words. 'Do I understand you? Surely you are not offering to betray your sister?'

'He is either offering to betray her or blackmail you!' Said Cornelia Jans.

'I am not really concerned about you or my sister.' Dircx leant back in his chair. 'She was in this house for six years but I was never invited in. You know she is not a generous woman, never has been; always careful with money. And you,' he turned towards Rembrandt, 'with all these pictures, all this fine furniture, you seem to be a wealthy man. But she claims that you are pretty much bankrupt. Can that be true?'

'I too, am losing patience,' said Rembrandt ignoring the accusation. 'Your sister stole my property and pawned it. I want to be sure she cannot get her hands on it again.'

'You should have paid her the money you'd promised.'

'This was all gone over in the court. These things take time. I was about to pay her when I discovered what she'd done. I do not pretend that the items of jewellery are not important to me. They belonged to my wife and I wish to keep them in the family.' He placed a leather pouch on the table. 'But no more of that, I need to know that the jewels are safe, that they cannot be disposed of in any way. If the pawn broker were to sell them, it would be a disaster. Let us say I give you the money to redeem the jewels: two hundred guilders.' He pushed the bag across the table. 'There it is, but I need to be sure that I can trust you; that you will not do what your sister did. Can you find a safe place for them?'

'I could help.' Cornelia Jans has been primed for this moment. 'I could look after them; they would be safe with me.'

Pieter Dircx picked up the money bag and weighed it in his hand. He looked puzzled, as if he felt he was being outmanoeuvred. 'I'm not sure. I'm away at sea a lot of the time, and what if I do agree? What guarantees do I have that there's anything in it for me?'

Rembrandt is once more in charge. 'I knew we would come to an agreement,' he smiled. 'So I added a few guilders to the two hundred, to pay the pawnbroker and a little extra for your trouble. I'm afraid that's all the money I have at the moment. I was not planning to give you your sister's allowance as well as the money to redeem the jewels tonight but, of course when I do, I will pay you generously for your cooperation. I have some important commissions in hand so have no fear on that score. I can easily raise the money.'

Dircx carefully bound the two documents together again and put them back inside his jerkin. 'I'm not sure about all this. I don't want the law after me.'

Rembrandt sought to reassure him. 'You will have no problems with the law. As soon as you return from Edam and I know the jewellery is safe I will pay you Geertje's allowance: the other two hundred guilders. Even if she proves awkward about the jewellery you can point out that you have not returned it to me but it's been put in a safe place. You are holding it in trust and more importantly she will no longer be paying interest.' He points to Cornelia Jans, 'It might be advisable not to mention my good friend here: they didn't always see eye to eye. Even if Geertje does refuse you the money she has promised, you can deduct it from her allowance so you will not be out of pocket.'

'Geertje has a foul temper,' added Pieter Jansz.

Rembrandt turns to look at Hendrickje. 'We have seen evidence of that here in this house and it does raise another problem. I am afraid she may turn violent. Something must be done to make sure she can do no more harm. I cannot have her shouting abuse and frightening my son.'

Pieter Dircx looks at Rembrandt. 'What's this about shouting abuse? I know nothing about that.'

'Of course not, why should you. But it's there in the court records. I don't suppose she told you that she used to accost Hendrickje and my son Titus whenever they left the house?'

Cornelia Jans joined in, 'I saw her standing in the market square screaming all sorts of terrible things.'

'Tell me, what was she like before she came to Amsterdam?' Rembrandt asks Dircx.

'I had very little to do with her. I was away to sea as soon as I was able. She had the reputation of being a bit flighty. I suppose she was no better than she should be. She wanted what most women want I suppose, a husband.'

'What was he like?'

'Her husband? He was a ship's bugler, and a drunk.' Dircx had mellowed a good deal by now, accepting more ale, and so had the butcher's wife.

Hendrickje and I were the only ones still sober.

Dircx went on, 'He was killed in an accident at sea. Probably fell over the side, drunk.'

'Tell me,' Rembrandt leant towards Dircx 'do you think your sister is in her right mind?'

'What exactly do you mean?'

'Her mental state troubles me. This fantasy about marriage; and pawning the jewels: these are hardly the actions of a rational person. I have a suggestion about how we might help her. I think it would be in Geertje's best interests if we could get a certificate declaring her incompetent.'

Dircx looked puzzled. 'Incompetent? I'm not sure I could do that.'

'But it's a mere formality. She has already given you the right to act on her behalf. And this would just be a warning from the court to prevent her from doing anything she might regret. It will mean she cannot interfere with what you decide to do. And, just in case there are any further expenses involved, I will pay you for your troubles.'

'What do I have to do?'

'Make a simple declaration before the Burgomaster telling him what you have just told us. You might emphasise the bit about her temper and being flighty, as you put it. You say she is not well, not competent to make important decisions, that sort of thing. Cornelia will go with you, she knows about the shouting and abusive behaviour, so she can back you up. You can do it tomorrow and then collect the jewellery from this woman in Edam. Give them to Cornelia for safe keeping and there will be nothing Geertje can do. Nothing at all. And we can all get on with our lives again. What could be fairer than that?'

Dircx opened the bag of money and very deliberately counted it. He slid a couple of coins across the table to his cousin. 'You see, I told you things would turn out for the best.'

'There is just one more thing,' Rembrandt said getting to his feet. 'I do not expect you to swear an oath, but I think we should drink to our little agreement.'

It was at this point that I could keep quiet no longer, 'I would rather you didn't include me in your plan,' I said.

He looked straight at me, 'I should have known you would not approve. But no matter, you will be leaving my house soon: there is no longer a place for you here. I think a move to somewhere like Delft would be a good idea, don't you? Property is cheaper there and you will have less competition. No doubt you can make much of the fact that you spent some years working with me, the country's leading painter.'

As I left the room, I looked back. Geertje's brother was sitting like Judas, with his back to me. As they raised their glasses in a toast, I saw the light from the flickering candles and the glow from the fire throw huge, sinister shadows onto the wall behind them.

## 27

The sight of a horse on the skyline, leaning into its harness pulling an invisible load might puzzle an observer standing in a distant field. But on closer inspection the solution would soon be found in the canal lying behind the high bank on which the horse and its rider moved. The banks had been raised so high with silt dredged from the canal that the land surrounding it was below the level of the water. Passing boats were all but invisible, except for the occasional mast and the plodding horse set against the bright expanse of sky.

The tow barge to Gouda is crowded. Stacked on the deck in the prow of the boat are wooden, slatted crates containing chickens, crooning to themselves and fluffing out their feathers to keep cool. A goat and a calf are tethered in another crate; their bleating ignored by the human cargo. The chatter of the passengers also masks the quiet slop of the water against the canal bank as the boat slides by. An awning has been rigged to give some shade. The young boy astride the horse dozes under his hat while it plods on philosophically, hoping that he will wake and flick away the flies that buzz around its head.

Sitting apart, in the stern of the boat, are two women: Cornelia Jans the butcher's wife from Amsterdam, the other Geertje Dircx, the former housekeeper to the painter Rembrandt. Although the Jans woman carries no obvious symbol of authority it is clear that she is in charge. The demeanour of her companion shows evidence of her inferior position as she sits with a small portmanteau on the wooden deck between her feet. Jans seems willing to engage in conversation with her fellow travellers whilst her charge seems sullen, less sociable, preferring her own thoughts and council. So, apart from the odd desultory remark, nothing passes between them.

There appears to be no direct antipathy between them, it is just that Geertje seems beaten down by circumstance, as if some large burden has been unexpectedly placed on her shoulders that she must reluctantly carry. She may resent it, indeed as we shall see, she does resent it, but for the time being she can see no way of casting it off. Something has gone wrong and now she is suffering the consequences, but she is sure that it is not herself who is in the wrong. She is resigned to her fate for the time being, seeing no alternative until she has sifted the evidence. Then, if she comes to a new understanding and can lay the blame elsewhere, the process of revenge and retribution can begin. Until then she must obey the judgement upon her.

It is late when they arrive at Gouda. The sun, sinking low towards the horizon, casts long slender shadows across the cobbled quay as they disembark. Their travelling companions disperse into the streets and alleys, leaving the two women standing alone waiting for the barge captain and the boy to loose the horse and attend to the safe mooring of the boat. This done, Jans asks directions of the captain, shading her eyes against the sun, which is now so low in the sky that even the broad brim of her hat cannot protect her from the glare. The man points out the way and watches with curiosity as the two women set off.

By the time they arrive at their final destination the light is almost gone. But even the warm twilight cannot soften the imposing, but austere stone façade of a building that might once have been a convent. It is certainly a distinctive building but without ostentation. The main entrance is through a stone archway with large, wooden, double doors to allow for the passage of wagons and coaches. Set into the right hand door is a wicket gate with, at eye level, a narrow, sliding panel covering a metal grill so that those inside can inspect those outside discretely and in complete safety.

Cornelia Jans pulls on the rope hanging from a pulley in the wall and from somewhere inside there is the clink of a cracked bell. The two women wait for some time in the gathering gloom before the grill slides back and a face peers out. Cornelia Jans holds a document up for inspection. The grill snaps shut, the wicket gate creaks open and the two women are admitted into a large, cobbled yard enclosed on all sides by three-storey buildings. But to the newcomer, the most striking feature of the place is the smell. Geertje recognises it: the smell of lye. A common enough substance used for washing clothes and scrubbing floors, not unpleasant in small quantities and the right place but here it pervades everything. It seems to her that it clings to her clothes, her skin, and she fancies she can even taste it on the warm night air.

The superintendent is a robust, big-boned woman, dressed in severe black so that she seems part of the shadows. She wears a cap of the same colour, covering her greying hair. Her face is not designed to smile but her profession and the need to appear in public require that she adopt a look of kindness and pleasantry. But she is not a kind woman and it is clear to Geertje that Cornelia Jans has money to offer or they would certainly still be waiting in the street outside. This is a terrible place.

It is dark by now, as Geertje waits nervously in the yard, while the other two women disappear into a small office close by the main gate. Here, the superintendent inspects the documents Cornelia Jans has brought, more money changes hands but this time receipts are provided so everything is in order. Their business concluded, Cornelia Jans and the superintendent emerge into the yard where a few lamps have been lit. After a brief goodbye, and her job done, Mrs Jans steps back quickly through the gate into the outside world and is gone. Her charge is left in the safekeeping of the superintendent who, with a firm hand on her back, ushers her briskly away adding these words with well-practiced sincerity.

'Do not be afraid. You are in good hands here. It is not my place to extract vengeance for any wrong you may have done. Nothing could be further from my mind. No, my aim is to make you good, to show you the spiritual and moral rewards of hard work. If I sometimes have to be stern, it is part of my job, but deep down I have a kind heart. There will be none of your airs and graces here my dear, here we are all equal. You are detained at the discretion of the magistrates. My report on your behaviour will be what decides how long you stay. So my advice is to keep on the right side of me and, if you do, we shall manage very nicely.'

# 28

I still wake up trembling with rage, remembering some command, some insolence. His, 'do this', 'do that', his dominance, his, 'submit to me'. But I will not submit, not even after these long years, when I am worn out with suffering, still I will not submit. His cruelty gnaws at my soul and I hate him, how could I not? He has forgotten all the kindnesses I did him, the love I gave him has turned to loathing. He has become my enemy: betrayed me and given me plenty of time for my hatred to grow.

Those who use the word 'hate' carelessly can have no idea what they really mean. To hate the look or smell of something does not compare with truly hating a person. Someone who hates another takes a perverse delight in making mischief, it becomes the very spring of their thoughts and actions. They throw aside the trappings of civilisation; the wild beast resumes its sway and utters a cry of joy at being restored to freedom and lawlessness. It is horrible to be in the same room as someone who despises you and whom you despise. Even someone who has once been your lover; seeing the venom in their eyes; knowing that they are now your implacable enemy; bent on your destruction and that you are powerless before them.

I know that feeling, it is a bitter memory. I alone was the focus of his hostility and everyone, on that day in that room, agreed with him. They believed him and thought I was the liar. I was in the wrong, simply because of who and what I was, the housekeeper who had betrayed her master. And he was in the right simply because he was what he was: the famous painter Rembrandt van Rijn. If we had changed places it would have made no difference except that we should have known how much we loathed each other.

And what did I do to deserve this scorn; this hatred? Why was I being punished so? Not for inefficiency in running his house; not for neglecting or stealing the affection of his son. And certainly not for refusing to bow to his will when he wanted the comfort and satisfaction of my body. No, far from it, it is for not being his precious Saskia, for not being able to give him another child. I tried to interest him in the running the house. When Saskia was alive she had taken care of those kinds of things, leaving him free to do his work. I tried to do the same, but in those days there had been a cook and several servants. By the end of my time, and because of his erratic behaviour, most of the staff had left and the work was shared between me and the Stoffels girl.

Saskia was my rival even from beyond the grave. She died when their son was only a few months old and he was given into my care. Having no children of my own I accepted gladly, so to discover that the child's mind had been poisoned against me was another cruel blow.

And what would he have been without me? Nothing! It was me who took over the running of his house; looking after his furniture; cooking his food; cleaning his clothes and sheltering him from the irritation of life outside his studio. He was happy to make me his authority in the house. Didn't he give me the keys to lock up at night and make sure everything was safe and secure? In those early days, I believed that subjection to his will was my duty just as it had been for his wife.

But Saskia had been his first, and now I know to my cost, his only love. He has paintings of her as a young woman. She was no great beauty except, of course, to him. To him she was perfect and in his memory she has remained perfect. Just as I have become the embodiment of wickedness, to be humiliated, expunged from his memory and from his life.

And such a liar, with his fine words and fancy clothes, his grand house full of furniture and pictures. So many pictures, hanging in every room, a wonderful collection, or so he was always telling me. And he went on collecting: never missed a sale. Stuff was pouring into Amsterdam from all over the world and he had to prove he was the equal of any man. He wasn't able to relax, his will dominated everything. His trips to the auction house always led to a drama. He would come back with a cart load of stuff; junk most of it, as far as I could tell.

At first, I saw it as an indulgence. It was not my place to object. I was his servant but then, as things went from bad to worse, I tried to protest. Where was I to put it? What about the cost? He would splutter and shout, tell me I didn't understand him, didn't understand anything. How dare I accuse him of wasting money on junk? He needed it all, everything he bought was necessary. Towards the end, I felt I could vanish through the floor and he wouldn't notice. He wanted me to disappear, like an insect that he could sweep away with a swish of his hand. I had dared to defy him;

would not bend to his will and he could not allow that. I should never have made my mark on that damned paper. He cheated me, robbed me of what was rightfully mine.

What was I supposed to do when I was taken back to the house on the Breestraat? The house I had come to believe would be my home for the rest of my days. To be in a room with a man who could not bear to be near me, who my very presence made angry, a man who is a liar, a bully and a cheat.

It hadn't always been like that. When I first came into his house, things were very different. Saskia was still alive, although I could see she was dying. She was heavily pregnant but with that transparent, not-long-for-this-world look. The child was lucky to survive. I knew then he would need a nurse and housekeeper which was why I suggested myself for the job.

He lied to his precious Saskia, as well. His lies probably helped kill her, that and his extravagance. Why? I will never understand. He could have told her the truth; it would have made no difference, she would have forgiven him anything. As far as she was concerned he could do no wrong.

He was a good liar. He convinced me, made me believe his fame was secure, unassailable and permanent, above passing fashions. He told me his talent was inexhaustible; his fame already woven into the warp and weft of the country's history. His greatest gift was his command over his emotions, those unruly spirits that lay outside the door of his workshop, and his ability to harness them to his purpose, to make them fall under his hand, only to enter when bidden. In those days, he had not a shadow of doubt or self-reproach: well now he has, and I rejoice at the thought. How will he control his emotions now he's bankrupt, broke, out on his arse with only that young whore Hendrickje and her bastard daughter for company? And she isn't so young anymore, no longer the trim little tart she was when I first took her in.

And how have I been paid for my generosity? I've cried out time and time again for revenge, and now at last it's mine. I'll get back at them now for all those years in that stinking hell in Gouda. He made out I was mad and immoral, but it wasn't anything to do with morals. He tried to treat me like one of his stupid paintings, to be manipulated, used to his advantage, but I refused and was locked away with whores, thieves and riff raff for company, just because I defied him. I no longer trust any man. I have been betrayed too often. Even my own brother betrayed me: a stupid man, a very stupid man! My own brother and those who believed him all plotted to get me imprisoned. They were so credulous, bowing and scraping to the man who called himself Amsterdam's greatest painter.

It is no compensation to remember that the commissioners at the Marital Court must have believed me. After all, they made him increase the paltry allowance he gave me. But they didn't know him: they believed that because he was one of them he would honour the agreement. I knew that he would never agree to anything that did not give him exactly what he wanted. I never thought Van Rijn would honour the agreement. I gave my brother legal authority to collect the money and redeem the jewels. You would have thought I could trust my own brother and being a sailor and used to rough company he would be able to get me my money. But I hadn't reckoned with the blandishments and flattery Van Rijn would use to get his way and have me condemned to the Spinhuis.

I should have resisted, but I was so weary of the whole business. Although how he persuaded them to lie I'll never know. There must have been something in it for them, money most likely. They thought that they were doing him a favour, with his puffed-up manners and grand house: a house he never paid for. But he was still full of confidence, self-importance, so sure of himself. He claimed to be heartbroken when his wife died. But was he, I wonder? Some said his paintings changed. I wouldn't know: that part of him was always a mystery to me. All I do know is that the money began to dry up. Perhaps he did change in his head, but not in his breeches. He was up for fucking before too much time had passed. It was not even a decent interval as far as I was concerned. True, he's had his disappointments: he'd buried three children before he buried his wife. But it wasn't long before he wanted me as his mistress. He made that plain enough; her side of the bed was barely cold before he dragged me into it. I tried hard to resist, but he promised me marriage as soon as enough time had passed. How was I to know he couldn't marry again because of some financial arrangement that had been agreed when he married Saskia?

He said she had been his soul mate and that she had

understood and sympathised with his every need. Now she was dead, and he needed, craved the comfort, the physical intimacy of another and I was to be that other. He had a mucky mind too, showing me his collection of drawings from the antique. From the antique my arse, they were all curly cocks and cunts. He said they were copied from Greek vases. I don't know anything about Greek vases but some of those sexual antics would defy even the most acrobatic Dutchman, and he was no acrobat. Mind you, it didn't stop him trying. Once, he took me for a walk in the countryside, fucked me in a field in broad daylight with a man scything hay just the other side of the hedge! Not that I cared, I thought he would marry me. He said he would, I should have been more suspicious. We never lived like man and wife; we always had our separate rooms. At first he would take any opportunity, inviting me into his workshop when no one else was about. Sometimes, during the night, on his way to look at his paintings, he'd come padding along the corridor to visit me. I'm sure other people in the house knew what was going on but no one would help me when I went to court, he made sure of that.

At first he was pleased with the way I looked after the boy. I took care of the house and the domestic arrangements, made sure it was always clean and warm. That wasn't easy; it was a big house and there were all those students racketing about the place and they had to be looked after.

I didn't understand his paintings; they were a mystery to me. But I never interfered with his work, except once, when I suggested he did something more saleable, but that threw him into such a rage I never mentioned it again. I thought he appreciated what I did for him and if I'd fallen pregnant perhaps things would have been different. He wanted more children I could tell that, but I hadn't managed it with my husband and I couldn't for him. But he did say he'd marry me. I swear to that. Didn't he give me a wedding medallion? But the cunning bastard didn't have it engraved.

He couldn't be bothered with domestic details so it was me who took on the Stoffels girl. I did it as a favour to a friend, a sergeant in the military, one of his brothers had known my husband. Hendrickje was 18, so when he asked me to find a place for her in the house and we needed a maid I thought it was the perfect solution. She was from a military background like me. I liked the idea that we would have some things in common. She must have been used to rough talk and behaviour. I certainly was and I'd once been in the same situation, looking for work in a strange city. She must have known the ways of the military and to pretend to be all innocence was ridiculous. It was all a sham but he swallowed it; her false airs and graces. Perhaps he knew it too. If he did, he didn't care. She was after him from the start and he didn't fight her off. I realise that now, now it's too late.

She was another liar: swearing on oath that I'd made promises, signed papers, when I can't even read or write. I admit I made my mark but they could have written anything or changed it later by adding things. How would I have known? Besides, I was desperate: I would have signed anything. It was a bad time for me, being dismissed from his house like that, when it had been my home for all those years. When I moved in it was a dream come true, such a fine house with servants. And I made myself useful while his wife was alive. I knew he'd need someone to take over when she died so I made sure I was ready to manage things.

Women like me have a hard time, so can you blame me for wanting to better myself? I was from the provinces, which was how I knew about the two Trijns. I worked briefly for one of them, a self-righteous busybody, her husband was still alive then. Her friend, I quite liked. She was a hard-nosed harridan but at least she had a sense of humour. At the end, I suppose I was just grateful that they were both honest. I left Edam and worked in an inn in Hoorn, after that I went to my brother. He was a ship's carpenter in Waterland. It was there that I met my husband Abraham. He was a bugler in the navy and away a lot of the time. Then, after he died, I was on my own again. I'd never been to Amsterdam but everyone said I'd find employment there. It wasn't easy and the only work I could find was modelling for artists. Most of the women who worked there had fallen on hard times, some were servants who had lost their jobs others, like me, had lost their husbands; some even had children to support. It's true that a few were fairly easy with their virtue, but not me. They made out I'd been immoral before I went to his house: it wasn't true. If it was true why did his wife take me on as a nurse for her baby? That's how I came to live in his house.

Things changed pretty quickly when the Stoffels girl arrived. My efforts to keep things tidy and clean became a fault. He accused me of moving things so he couldn't find them, that I rearranged his collection: all that armour, stuffed birds, old paintings and prints, bits of statues, all sorts of bric-a-brac. And he kept on adding to it, even when he was in debt he'd still come back from the saleroom with more clutter. He couldn't resist buying things. If either of us was mad or immoral it was him, but I was the one who finished up in the Spinhuis.

I wish that I had not gone so meekly with that Cornelia Jans woman, another of his lackeys, a woman with no moral scruples of any kind. I wouldn't be surprised if she wasn't another of his sexual conquests. She wouldn't have taken much persuading; she was in it for the money, the status, the chance to rub shoulders with the great artist, but mostly the money. They had got an order that I should be locked up 'for the sake of my soul' the magistrates said, what could I do but submit? It was only when I had time to think that I realised what had been done to me and thought to protest, then it was too late.

They made a great thing about the jewellery I pawned: the jewels he gave me, jewels that I'd worn before, sometimes I'd been naked except for a pearl necklace. That used to excite him. He'd to say it was so that he could see how they looked against my skin: how a Goddess would have worn them, but it always ended in the same way: me under him or him behind me. My reward was the jewels; they were mine that is what he told me. It was only when he wanted to be rid of me that he had the cheek to swear they were only on loan. But if that was true why persuade me to leave them to Titus in my will. I didn't object. I thought he meant to keep me close, to marry me. So I why should I mind if, after my death, they were to be returned to his son? Now I realise what a clever move that was. He knew he had no right to give them to me. If I'd known I would never have put my cross on that, so called, agreement. I have no children of my own. I'd cared for Titus since he was a baby and I'd become very fond of the boy. I had no quarrel with him and besides I didn't sell them, I just borrowed money against their value. I'd paid for them with my body. How much would it have cost if he'd gone whoring along the Geldersekade? He gave me that marriage medallion. He told me he would have it engraved with my name. But he lied: he had no intention of marrying me. He owed too much money.

All I ever wanted was a reasonable reward for the years of service I'd given before I was thrown onto the street. I'd get no other place with the bad character he'd given me. All I could afford was a squalid little place on the Rapenburg. So what if I did have the odd gentleman caller, I had to live. I never saw any of the 160 guilders a year he'd promised and in any case it was nowhere near enough for my needs. I was used to a bigger place, his place, by rights my place too.

I know I'm not that bright, not as bright as him and that little tart. She can read and write but I'm not completely stupid. I pawned the jewels in Edam to a barge skipper's wife: three rings; one with a diamond cluster. I was desperate and getting into debt. I thought he'd never know. He went mad when he found out. How he did, I'll never know. He must have spies everywhere. In my defence, I made a complaint to the commissioners for marital affairs about the way he'd treated me. I told them that he promised to marry me and that we had often slept together as man and wife. He didn't even turn up to the hearing: too important a man to be bothered with the likes of me; the woman he'd chucked out; the woman he wanted out of his bed; out of his house and out of his life. I thought him not turning up was proof I was telling the truth but all they did was to fine him three guilders, three miserable guilders, and they had the cheek to tell me they'd heard it all before.

Perhaps I shouldn't have gone to court. True they made him give me more money, but I never saw any of it, it just made him more vindictive and cruel. He swore that he'd never slept with me and that was why I didn't get pregnant. He got people to lie, to say I'd always been immoral and was unstable so he could have me locked up.

So what if I did break my promise and defy him? He broke his promise to me and to the court. He was never going to give me my yearly allowance he was on the way to being bankrupt.

He made that Stoffels woman lie, saying I'd understood the papers I'd signed, but how could she know? She wasn't there, wasn't even in the room. He must have told her what to say. I did make my mark but I didn't really understand. Anyway, what does it matter, she wasn't there so how could she swear to anything?

They persuaded me to go back to the house to make a new agreement on the understanding that I'd get more money, but it turned out that all he was offering was 200 guilders to redeem the jewels. The 160 guilders a year wasn't going to change and I had to promise not to make any more demands. But 160 guilders wasn't enough. I'd got used to better things and he owed it to me that I should live reasonably. What if I got sick? He said he would help me but I didn't believe him. He would have done nothing, I'm sure of that. I know I shouldn't have lost my temper like that, but he was such a bully, denying he'd ever slept with me, damning me to prove it.

When I was shown the papers committing me to the Spinhuis in Gouda, it completely took the wind out of my sails. I never expected him to go that far. I was so taken aback; I almost believed what they said: that I was incompetent and there was something wrong in my head. He had witnesses and affidavits so I went like a lamb to the slaughter. I had taken so many knocks to my pride and self-respect I began to think I deserved to be punished. That didn't last long.

We are all too casual about what happens to others. I'd never given a thought to what went on in a Spinhuis. I always thought they were a necessary evil, that there are people who needed to be reminded of their responsibilities, to be shown the error of their ways and to receive the appropriate punishment to turn them into better citizens, but the Spinhuis does none of those things. The work is hard and the food meagre. We existed on a kind of gruel made, it seemed to me, from the sweepings of the oat mill floor mixed with water. There was some black bread, peas and beans.

Perhaps their founders did have a moral purpose when they set them up but I suspect it was more an act of vengeance and to clear the streets of people they'd rather not be reminded of.

I was faced with the stark choice. I knew his hatred was implacable. Perhaps I could have managed on the money he'd promised, but I didn't think he would ever pay me and I would be out on the streets. Was I expected to make a living from taking in laundry and sewing? It was not possible: I was used to better things.

I met women in the Spinhuis, women like me who had been uprooted and evicted from their place of work, often from the houses of the wealthy. They had tried and failed to avoid penury so had taken to the streets just to survive. Some had worked in brothels which gave them a precarious living, but it was a terrible life, brutal and degrading. I would rather be in the Spinhuis than that. Many had been punished more than once: scarred from venereal disease, flogged and banished to remoter parts of the country. The foreign girls, some Danish and German, were sent away to their own countries, but even there they were not accepted and so came back to the city illegally, to be caught and punished again.

Another one of my nightmares is the sound of the pounding of cloth and the clatter of spinning wheels when we were made to spin yarn. It was backbreaking work and if we slacked or fell behind we were beaten. Washing cloth was a terrible task: first it was soaked in stone troughs using lye, everything and everyone in the place stank of the stuff, and then we would beat, pummel and rinse it until it came out sweet and clean.

They collected our piss, using it to soak the cloth all night, then we had to rub it to remove any stains. Often we had to do it over and over again so that at the end of the day our hands were numb and raw. If that wasn't punishment enough, there were the endless prayers, sermons and readings from the scriptures to scour the filth from our minds and bodies so that we might say; at last, we are shriven of all our sins.

There were days when the public could pay to come in and see us. There were times when the whores who were there for correction and redemption were allowed to wear makeup and the same erotic clothing with hats and feathers that they'd worn when plying their trade in the streets outside. On those days men paid to come inside and see them, and they pleasured each other through the bars. It was disgusting. I was thankful that I was there because I was mad and not because I was immoral.

The guardians said it was allowed because it meant the women would realise how low they'd fallen and how shameful their behaviour was. But that was nonsense. It was as if the brothels and music halls had been brought inside with women being paid to give pleasure to men, and some of those men were the guardians of the place. The women learned nothing except that they were being punished by a hypocritical and corrupt society.

As for me, I hoped that what I heard being preached in the Spinhuis was true. That all the pain and humiliation I have borne has redeemed me and that he, Rembrandt van Rijn the great painter, is doomed to rot in hell in place of me.

## 29

The first time they meet: the painter and the philosopher, it is by chance in the salon of the Gilded Sun, a grand house on the Singel, a house maintained on the profits of diamonds and death. They move amongst the subtle scents of rosewater and Moroccan leather, nibble almonds, dried figs and sip Spanish wine from tall glasses. The tables are covered with exuberant carpets from the East, Persia and India and although we might describe this room in romantic terms, the reason for their meeting is more down-to-earth and practical. It is just as well that we are not concerned here with the morality of Alphonso Lopez, the owner of this dazzling display. In Calvinist Amsterdam this room would be seen, not as a sign of wealth and success but, as the mark of Cain: not the scent of the exotic, more the stench of decadence and self-indulgence. Gem dealer and procurer of weapons, Lopez lists among his clients the French prelate, Cardinal Richelieu.

Our painter is older now, but his dark eyes are as quick and enquiring as ever. He is studying a painting. He is still amazed by Raphael's portrait of 'Baldassare Castiglione'. Perhaps recalling the time when, at the height of his fame, he had tried to buy it only to be outbid by Lopez whose wall it now decorates. He is also fascinated by another wonderful painting that passed through Amsterdam's saleroom: Titian's 'Portrait of a Gentleman' but that too had been beyond his means. As his eyes take in the room, he can only envy the exquisite Indian and oriental miniatures that far surpass his own collection. He has some consolation: he is represented in this Pantheon with a painting that Lopez bought from him some years ago: 'Hunter with a Dead Bittern'.

He is here to seek help from Lopez in a dispute with another rich Jewish merchant. The spring tide produced a wall of water that breached the St Anthony's dyke, flooding several villages. The water rushed up to the end of the Breestraat but, by what seemed a miracle, the lock held. However, the force of the wave disturbed the foundations of some of the houses in the street, including that of Daniel Pinto, a Levant trader and the artist's next door neighbour.

He speaks in a low voice, hoping not to be overheard by the third man in the room who is reading intently. The painter explains to Lopez that he and Pinto share a party wall and both houses need repairs. They had agreed to divide the cost of the labour with each paying for their own materials. However, the work has taken longer than expected and what began as an amicable agreement has now turned sour.

'Pinto tells me that he has been invoiced for wood that you have used.' Lopez suggests.

The painter shrugs his shoulders, 'That is between him and the timber merchant. I know nothing of any such irregularities. He cannot claim the money from me.'

Lopez takes an almond delicately between his fingers and very deliberately places it into his mouth. During these few seconds, he eyes the painter with curiosity. If he is to negotiate a treaty between the two men, where should his loyalty lie? Should it be with a fellow Jewish trader, or this

Mennonite Dutchman, who it is rumoured, is on the verge of bankruptcy? And yet, the man appears to be successful; his house is full of students; important people come and go, and he is still buying at the auctions. Lopez needs to probe deeper to discover just how much of a problem the payment for the timber will cause. He must also weigh in the balance that he is dealing with a man generally regarded as a genius, the country's greatest living painter. But there is also this business with the ex-housekeeper. It is common knowledge that she won a judgement against him in the Chamber of Marital Affairs, although now the woman has been committed to the Spinhuis in Gouda. And there are rumours that may be or may not be justified, of underhand dealings.

'Tell me?' Lopez asks, 'Do you have much work at the moment?'

'Yes, more than enough. But what am I to do? The repairs to the house have dragged on and I find it difficult to work with all the noise and disturbance.'

'Could you pay Pinto if he takes you to court?'

'Yes, I could pay him but why should I? If his house requires more materials what am I to do? This is why I am here, to ask you to intervene on my behalf, to advise Pinto that there is no point in a protracted court case which he will lose. We have both had arguments with the timber merchant, but I know nothing of these extra invoices he claims to have received. Perhaps, instead of going to court, he might accept a painting or two as compensation?'

'I will see what I can do, but I am not hopeful. The war with England is not going well and the plague is on the prowl.' Lopez gestures towards the third man, who having carefully closed the book he has been studying, crosses the room to join them.

When we last met this young man he was still a curious child in the Vloorienberg. Now, in his early twenties, he is handsome with a bright, friendly face and well-shaped figure. He has the olive complexion of the Portuguese Jew, with long, dark hair and deep languid eyes. He appears self-possessed, even arrogant. We might guess that he is a successful businessman, but he is clearly not concerned about expensive, extravagant or ostentatious dress, except in one particular: he has fine silver buckles on his shoes.

The painter eyes the young man with curiosity. He has heard rumours about dissention in the Jewish community. Tongues wag, fingers point, eyes are averted, heads turn away as they pass in the street: that is to be expected. All religions are quarrelsome, but the rumours surrounding this young man are more serious. He is daring to question the very foundation of their belief.

'Pinto will want more than paintings to settle the matter.' Lopez ends the interview abruptly. 'And now you must excuse us.' He takes the young man by the arm. 'My friend Baruch Spinoza also has problems with his neighbours, but they are of a more serious nature than a dispute about some baulks of timber.'

When Lopez and the young man go into an adjoining room leaving the painter alone, he crosses to the book where it lies on the table. The text is in Arabic and he examines it intently, listening carefully for any change in the tone of the muffled conversation coming from the other room. Using the tip of one finger to lift the cover delicately, he turns the pages, stopping at an illustration of an amulet engraved with an elaborate pattern. An idea has been forming in his head and this little image might be the clue he needs to bring it to completion.

He closes the book but, as he turns to leave, he catches a glimpse of his image in a tall mirror. The room is also reflected, reminding him of the disparity in wealth between Lopez and himself. And he has lied. He could not pay Pinto and with the noise and disturbance of the building work, he has not produced a painting for months. He suspects that behind the dispute over the timber, his neighbour is playing a long game: hoping one day to gain possession of his house. This appeal for help is a desperate attempt to save something from the wreck of his finances. The face in the mirror is lined and careworn, the figure thickening, curly grey locks pushed beneath a beret. The clothes, sober but expensive, have seen better days. He has the look of the world weary patrician, solid and permanent. Then he sees, with a start, there beside his reflection, that other figure again, standing in his shadow. Who is this other self? Can he be trusted? Has he, without his knowledge, made a pact with some dark force? Has he demanded too much from his talent, a talent he knew to be extraordinary even in those first tentative attempts back in Leiden? Has he been wrong to seek a deeper understanding of human nature through his art? His once proud boast, that he could control his emotions, use them to his own ends, has proved to be an illusion, a sad joke. His ability to paint portraits that not only mirror outward appearances but reveal the character and emotions that lie beneath the surface doesn't seem to apply to this reflected self, standing on the far side of the glass. The self that he has charted for 30 years and whose form he thought he knew best has betrayed him. And the price has been high: his wife, children and now, when at last he has found someone whom he can rely on to help him through this dark time, the hideous spectre of his past wrong doings rises up before him, blocking his path, and his very livelihood is to be snatched away.

He moves to take one last look at his painting. It stands up pretty well in this illustrious company. He had once entertained the hope that Lopez would buy from him again, but now he sees little chance of it. He isn't painting like this anymore, nor does he want to, but what of Lopez's young compatriot? No, he thought not. He might be a mystery to himself but he could still read others and that young man was not seeking anything in the material word. He was after a deeper truth, perhaps looking to escape from the solid reality of the world around him? If so, he would be disappointed. Experience had taught the painter that there was a constant tension within a creative life. On the one hand there was the attempt to get away from the mundane into an imaginary world, and on the other, the practical self that kept reminding this dreamer of the dire consequences of ignoring the matter at hand. Should he warn him about the treacherous nature of the world of the imagination? No. He knew there would be no treaty for him with Pinto and no compromise with his peers for the young man with the silver buckles.

## 30

I was invited to the Gilded Sun because I was asking questions: awkward questions which the Jewish community in Amsterdam was not prepared to answer. Alphonso Lopez, a friend of my family and a powerful man in the city, had been persuaded to try to convince me that I should moderate my ideas. Here in Amsterdam, where we are free to practice our religion, there is division and debate, sometimes even hostility, within the community. Some in the Jewish community are concerned that those Sephardic Jews who survived their long exile in Spain have become sceptical and lax. Their critics are mostly Ashkenazi who came to the city from the Eastern Europe. They want to set an example: to retain and re-establish the old orthodoxy. I have been asking, who are they to decide which of the old ways are correct?

In my anxiety, I arrived early. Lopez was talking to a man I recognised as the painter Rembrandt. He invited me in and asked me to occupy myself for a few minutes. From their conversation it appeared that Lopez was being asked to be an intermediary in another dispute. I have heard lots of rumours about this artist, how extravagant he is and with an overreaching ambition. They spoke quietly but from what I could hear of their conversation it seemed to be more domestic; to do with invoices and building materials. I soon lost interest and was more taken with the fine collection of books and manuscripts. I was impressed to find a beautiful copy of the Book of Splendour, the classic text of the cabbala. It is a book that has had an important influence on Jewish spirituality, but which contains many fanciful elements that I cannot accept.

When they had finished their conversation Lopez took me into an adjoining room, also richly endowed with fine paintings and furniture. He motioned for me to be seated then took out an elaborately enamelled watch. He examined it carefully as if to indicate that his time was precious, but I suspect in reality it was to give him time to gather his thoughts. He clicked it shut with a flourish and returned it to his pocket.

'Can I offer you a pipe?' He said, which I took to be another sign of his nervousness in broaching a difficult subject. 'I have some fine, pure tobacco from America.' He produced a delicately carved, ivory box and, when I accepted, he filled a pipe for me, offered me a light then settled himself in a chair.

'I find myself in a difficult position. It is not long since your father's death.' He paused, as if searching for the right words, 'As you know, we were good friends so I feel it my duty to tell you about the disquiet among our community around some of the ideas you have been expressing. You seem to be heading into dangerous waters. There is the threat that you will be declared an Apostate and be cast out from the synagogue. I cannot insist, but in memory of your father and the good of our community here in Amsterdam, I strongly advise you to cease these activities immediately.'

I realised at this point that Lopez was not proposing a compromise but capitulation. He expected me to acquiesce to his demands, but as I was not prepared to give way. I decided to defend myself.

'Perhaps I might try to explain?' I began.

Lopez seemed reluctant but spread his hands and nodded.

'I am grateful for your concern and I am aware of the whispers against me. Perhaps it is a blessing that my father is dead, at least my fate will no longer hurt him in any way. What do you suggest I do? You are a man who moves amongst the rich and the powerful, you know that progress relies on scientific and philosophical enquiry. You remember that my father wanted me to become a Rabbi. He told me that a father has a duty to teach his son the Torah, to find him a wife and get him a trade. I think he could have added that, in this city, he would be wise to teach him to swim!' I looked at him to see if he had understood, but he did not respond. 'The education he gave me and the culture that surrounds me have led me to become more interested in secular and liberal ideas.'

'It is Rabbi Morteira and Rabbi Abohab, your teachers, who are calling for your ex-communication.'

'But, both you and my father have experienced the result of religious intolerance. It is the reason we are living in this city. Surely you believe that we should have full freedom of thought and religious practice, as long as we conform to the laws of the land?'

Lopez got to his feet and paced across the room, then turned to face me again. 'Perhaps, but you must see that some of your ideas are an anathema to our community in Amsterdam. We are welcome here and live in freedom as Jews so we can begin to rediscover our cultural heritage. But we must reassure the city fathers that we believe in the same God, that we both trace our roots back to the same founding father, Abraham.'

'But, what is our culture? I am not sure what you mean by "rediscover our cultural heritage". What does it mean to be Jewish? Is it a matter of creed, of culture, of family or of blood? Many of our people converted to Christianity'

'Of course, but we had to survive: the Inquisition was seeking to destroy us. As long as we married within the community the fact that some of our rituals and festivals went unobserved was not important. We had to walk a fine line between self-preservation and oblivion. But what you would have us do is deracinate ourselves, cut ourselves off from our past, from our history. We cannot accept that God is only a philosophical construct and that the soul dies with the body. These ideas you talk about are blasphemy and will not be tolerated. I must warn you that should you persist in your course you will be cast out and cursed as Joshua cursed Jericho.' Lopez had worked himself into quite a state.

I waited some time before I replied, very deliberately, 'I believe it is time we ceased to confuse the experience of being an immigrant with the experience of being Jewish. I am sorry, but I am not able to give you these assurances. I cannot in all conscience agree to the wishes of the Synagogue. I cannot remain silent.'

'But do you deny the supernatural character of the miracles?'

'I do, yes. I find all around me that science is discovering things that cast doubt on the truth of the scriptures. It is now proved beyond doubt that it is not the sun which circles the earth but the earth which circles the sun.'

This assertion seemed to hit Lopez like a blow. 'Do not voice such ideas in my house!' He said angrily, glancing about the room as if frightened that we might be overheard. 'This is dangerous talk and blasphemous. The Catholic church has condemned such ideas as heretical. Even here, they are only discussed in private.' He went to the door as if to check that no one was listening, but seemed to change his mind and turned to me again, 'And the Torah: do you not believe that it is divinely inspired?'

Once again, I had to deny him the answer he required, 'No, I believe it was written by men, several men in fact, who came later than Moshe Rabbeinu. I cannot believe something just because I am told to believe it. In all my years of study, I find that matters of conscience, despite being debated for many centuries, are still disputed and are therefore open to doubt. All the so-called facts that I have been taught are still being questioned. There is always ambivalence, no clear conclusion, yet it is forbidden to probe deeper. We are told to believe in the word of God as written. I have studied the Bible in Hebrew and Greek trying to fit words and script together so as to recapture a clear voice that speaks out. But in spite of my best efforts I have come to the conclusion that its only value is as an historical document. What is important is the moral message. I am against all religions that are life denying, that regard this life as only a preparation for a life to come. Religion, as most people conceive it, is a form of superstition, fermenting intolerance and unhelpful as a basis for a good life, our primary aim should be joyous living in the here and now.'

'But that will encourage scepticism and laxity. The Rabbis are set against the very idea. Your father was a warden of the Synagogue and the Jewish school. You and your brother have taken over the family business and made it a success. You are both respected members of our community. Can you not see that all this will change if you do not retract these ideas? Why cannot you submit and accept, with patience and gratitude, what God has given you?'

'I wish I could oblige you. I am only too aware of what might be the consequences of my actions. But do you not see, the fact that you wish me to withdraw is evidence for my case. We can no longer invoke supernatural causes or magic for our existence. We should stand in awe of nature with a deep sense of wonder. Not as a motive for submissive religious worship but for love and admiration of God and nature. I have found nothing that is written that allows for solutions to our present problems, especially when science and our rational minds point us in a different direction. There is nothing that sanctions intolerance within Judaism and Christianity or between them. Only by understanding ourselves can we be free.'

'Then you will be banished,' he said emphatically. 'Doomed to roam amongst the brutal beliefs that lie outside the walls that surround our faith.' Having accepted that he had failed in his attempt to make me change my mind, he seemed to relish his role as the one chosen to deliver this dire warning, embellishing it by deploying a symbolic landscape. 'It will be wild and chaotic out there; a labyrinth of tracks and channels through which, at first glance, there seems a common thread, a shared stream, but it is all a snare and a delusion. In reality so much depends on which track you follow, which fork you take, how you negotiate the twists and turns along the way. Outside the faith you will have no tradition to guide you, no one from whom to seek advice and counsel and this will be crucial if you are to survive and prosper in this world and the next.'

And so I left him there amongst the wealth and luxury that God had given him, things that few men would find difficult to accept. I made my way home, back to the Vloorienberg, knowing that I was amongst that few and, despite all of Lopez's dire warnings, my course lay clearly ahead of me. I had come to believe that the need for a deity is a matter of culture and upbringing. Perfectly sensible people can disagree about whether there is a God or not. And, to be sure, there are people in the population who have neither the intelligence nor the inclination to form an intellectual belief of their own. For these people religion gives a worthy example to follow. But surely, when the followers of one religion seek to deny the values of another it is because they are uncertain of the ground on which their beliefs are based. They can countenance no close examination because they suspect it will be found wanting.

Lopez had failed to convince me to change my course of action and I had some inkling that he would also fail in his attempts to mediate for the painter. His loyalty to his religion, to his race, would not allow him to be wholly impartial in any dispute.

# 31

The second meeting of the painter and the philosopher was also a chance event, although the philosopher might object to the concept of life being ruled by chance.

The painter had often walked out with Saskia, his young wife, beyond the city walls, along the deeply rutted dyke roads to the southeast of the city, where thatched cottages, farms and villages, with the occasional clump of trees, clustered together like small islands beneath the expansive sky and the boats and the nets hanging out to dry are a reminder that this land was once under the sea.

Sometimes they had taken a boat out to the Omval, a popular place for courting couples, with its fine inn, away from the prying eyes of the clergy. On occasion he'd hired a wagon, dressed up and gone with friends for a picnic.

When, after her death, he had come out to the countryside with his mistress Geertje his motives had been darker. It was lust and a desire for sexual adventure that had driven him far from the house and the bed he had shared with Saskia: rutting under the open skies, on the hard ground, amongst the barley: but now he feels it was also in full view of God.

The affair had ended when his frustration and anger had reached such a pitch that he had struck her. It was meant only as a tap with his open hand as if admonishing a child, but the look of defiance she had shown and his overwhelming desire for gratification had combined into a potent poison. She was challenging his authority, in his own house, but he felt it was his right and he would have his way. Hadn't he given her a home, raised her above the lowly station she had been born too? She had been willing enough in the early days, even encouraging his advances. Why after all those years had she become so perverse, obstinate and sulky? He had forced himself upon her. She had fought fiercely but in the end he had subdued her. Afterwards he had stormed out into the night, his thoughts whirling chaotically around like dice in a gambler's fist. He followed where his legs led him, his shadow passing from door to door of the ale houses and brothels along the Geldersekade. Damning himself for a fool, his inner voice chanting, 'it's finished; it's finished'. Was this his punishment? To be haunted forever by regret and remorse, cringing at this involuntary memory, which like an unruly fool, would not be silenced.

Now, he stopped under the bright sun and clenched his fists, trying to muster these scattered, anguished thoughts together, cursing himself for his stupidity. What had he seen in the woman? Why had he allowed his baser instincts to get the better of him? It was no consolation that she has been locked away in Gouda for five years. Soon she would be free. Free to torment him again, free to cause trouble. How could he make certain she stayed out of the way?

He breathed deeply trying to still his racing heart. He had with him paper, pen, ink and his imagination in his knapsack, even an etching plate prepared with tallow ground through which he could scratch the wiry lines to act as the scaffold for his drawing; the drawing he will bite in acid on his return to the studio in his house; the house he will soon lose to his creditors. He must put that out of his mind for today.

He had been working all morning and was now making his way towards a country inn that stood separated from the canal by a high bank, with the tall masts of sailboats peering over.

As he got nearer, he was surprised to see the young man he had encountered in the grand house on the Singel. He was leaning back on a bench in the yard of the inn, his eyes closed, enjoying the sun on his face, oblivious to the world around him. A thin drift of smoke curled upwards from the long clay pipe that hung from his mouth. The painter noted the sketchbook lying beside the pewter pot of beer on the table. So he fancies himself an artist. Was making images another sign of his rebellion?

The painter sat down a short distance away and ordered beer. He was in two minds: whether to remain in his solitary state, or pursue the idea that here might be a possible client. He had several Jewish patrons and there was the sketchbook suggesting an interest in art. This young man was, after all, still a member of a successful trading company involved in worldly affairs so perhaps he might just be persuaded to buy something, if only a drawing or an etching. It just so happened he had made a drawing of a windmill standing on the bank of a dyke, part of the cities defensive walls, that very morning. It was known locally as 'the little stink mill' because it processed leather with cod liver oil. Adjacent to it stood a cottage and, although he had drawn it as picturesque and tumbledown, he knew this mill was relatively new. Not the perfect pastoral landscape perhaps but he had balanced the buildings against the high, open sky. Now it just needed a couple of figures in the distance to give it scale.

The two men sat apart for some minutes, the philosopher continuing to enjoy the sun on his face and the painter making a quick sketch of his head and shoulders. And at the same time an idea for a painting insinuated itself into his imagination: between glances at his subject he continued to sip his beer.

Finally, the philosopher opened his eyes and reached for his tankard. At first, he seemed unaware of the other's presence and, having taken a mouthful leant back, closed his eyes and sucked on his pipe: but it had gone out. As he got to his feet to go inside the tavern to rekindle the tobacco, he nodded politely in the painter's direction. When he returned, he collected his beer and moved to sit opposite him. The pipe smoke drifted across the painter's face carrying with it the mingled scents of prunes and tobacco.

'I trust your meeting with Lopez was successful?'

Slightly taken aback by this direct question, the painter drank slowly so as to give himself time to frame a reply. He did not relish a conversation in which he might have to reveal his straightened circumstances. The façade of success that he was struggling to maintain was beginning to crumble, but it would not do to provide more evidence or ammunition to his creditors. He had not entirely dismissed the idea of a sale and there was the thought that this young man was also at odds with the established order. He had to admit that he was intrigued to know more about his ideas.

'I am hopeful that it will lead to a successful outcome,' he replied, trying not to commit himself but added, so as to turn the conversation away from his own preoccupations, 'What about your problem? Lopez suggested that it was serious.'

The philosopher drew on his pipe and gave the painter a careful look before he responded, 'Serious, perhaps, but for whom? Some members of the Jewish community do indeed regard my views as unorthodox.'

Both men sat silently for some moments, each waiting for the other to speak.

The first to break the silence was the philosopher, 'Did you know that I once visited your house when you lived in the Vloorienberg?'

The painter lifted his head and a look of deep sadness passed briefly across his face, 'It's a long time since I lived on the Binnen Amstel.'

'I was only six years old. Your wife, at least I think it was your wife, gave me a cake.'

The painter smiled wistfully. 'That was indeed a long time ago. And if anyone gave you cake it would have been my dear Saskia. Many things have happened since then.'

The two men sat in silence; the philosopher with his pipe, and the painter with his thoughts.

It was the painter who spoke first, 'Would it be indiscreet to enquire exactly what this disagreement between you and your community is about, and whether you think that Lopez can sort it out?'

The younger man gave the painter a serious look as if gauging his level of sympathy before replying, 'Would you say that you and I are both outsiders and that we share the problems that come with that condition?'

The painter seemed perplexed by the question and asked by way of a reply, 'Do your ideas about being an outsider put you at odds with your community?'

The philosopher smiled at him and continued, 'I sympathise with other outsiders: regardless of their religion, place of birth, or other marks of identity. For me, as a Jew and, I think for you as an artist, it is important to be an individual, with the individual's loneliness, responsibility and also, I think, a willingness to take risks. But my deepest concern is justice, for myself and others like me: outsiders.'

'And your father's generation sees things differently?'

His companion drew on his pipe. 'Yes quite differently. For them, to be a Jew is to belong to a separate and unique group, loyal to one another and to their history. They believe they have a collective memory that differs from all others. The individual must ultimately sacrifice himself to the group and be more concerned with the power this gives to protect and allow them to negotiate alliances with those who are even more powerful.'

The painter did not reply but examined the young man seated across the table. He is sympathetic to his ideas, in as much as he understands them. He does not regard himself as an outsider: on the contrary all his life he has striven to become an integral member of the culture that surrounds him, an indispensable part of its hierarchy, to share in its wealth. If he was now being excluded from society it was simply because the standards by which he lived remained the same whilst the values of the society around him shifted.

His silence was taken as encouragement and the young man continued, 'It makes things difficult because I wish to avoid any scandal and I believe my ideas threaten no one. On the contrary, I hope they offer a solution to the conflict of how Jews should live in a Christian society. I do not think we should be burdened with a sense of guilt. The problem for me is not who I am, but more importantly whose values and qualities do I wish to adopt as my own?'

'I know a little of the history of your race. I have a few Jewish friends and clients. Many of the Jews in Amsterdam are Sephardim. They tell me their ancestors came from Asia Minor.'

'Yes, my family believe that too. They claim to have their origins in Sefarad, the Hebrew name for Sardis. It had been an important cultural centre for as long as anyone can remember. Then, six hundred years before Christ was born, they moved to Spain and Portugal with the Romans.'

'More than two thousand years ago. That is a long history.'

'A very long history, one not easily ignored. But you see that is part of the problem: an obsession with the past. When they arrived with the Romans they didn't speak Hebrew but Latin and the remnants of Aramaic. That remained the case until the Muslims conquered the peninsular.'

'What happened then?'

'Nothing. For the most part the Arab leader Abd al-Rahman treated the Jews and Christians benignly and they absorbed Arabic culture, creating an even more complex linguistic situation. The daily spoken language of the Jews, both learned and vernacular, became Arabic, but they wrote in a kind of Judeo Arabic composed of Hebrew characters, except for poetry which was written, but not spoken, in Hebrew. So there developed a strange amalgam of Hebrew and classical Arabic writing that became a literary as well as a sacred language.'

'And I suppose that lasted until the Muslims were expelled from Spain?'

'Exactly, and then a modified Latin called Castilian became the main language of Christian Spain and the Sephardic Jews living there. When we Jews were forced out and came to Amsterdam, we had to learn Dutch. So if a culture relies on custom and language for its identity what remains of Jewish identity?'

There was a silence between the two men until a young girl appeared from the inn and they both asked for more ale.

Their glasses refilled, the painter asked the philosopher, 'And what of your own history, where do you fit into this complex web of events?'

'My family lived in Portugal for generations: eventually they were forced to convert to Christianity; they became what the Spanish called "Marrano".'

'I don't quite understand. If they became Christians, why did the Spanish continue to persecute them?'

'Because many kept their faith secretly and even if they were not discovered the Inquisition never trusted them. They claimed that although the Marranos accepted the divinity of God, they denied the divinity of Christ and, at best, regarded him as the last of the great Jewish prophets.'

'As, I believe, do the Moors.'

'Indeed, that is the case and it is not the only similarity. My family went first to France and then to Amsterdam where, as you know, my father became a successful merchant importing olive oil and dried fruit from Portugal. I was born and educated here but my first language is Spanish. I also understand Arabic and Hebrew.' The young man paused to sip his ale then went on, 'Do you read Latin?'

The painter replied warily, 'Yes, I learnt Latin in school, but it is a long time since I read anything of a serious nature.'

'But you must know of the work of Monsieur Descartes?'

'No, no, I have heard that his ideas are discussed in private but I am not privy to those conversations. From what little I have gleaned he treads on dangerous ground and so, I imagine, do you if you are prepared to examine his ideas.'

'More dangerous than that,' the young man replied smiling mischievously, 'I am learning Latin so as to read and understand more of the ideas that are being debated throughout Europe.'

'You are interested in those ideas?'

'But of course, any rational, thinking person should be interested in the ideas of his time. What I find fascinating is not that we exist, but that the nature of our existence is becoming intelligible and comprehensible to reason. We need to remove obstacles to clear rational thinking. Emotions cloud our reason and lead to groundless fears and hatreds which then lead to destructive practices. There is a tension between religion and the natural sciences, ideas about the soul, the inexplicable mystery. People find spiritual and intellectual nourishment in belief. They want it to be there. The paradox is that these things need to be open to verification, to proof. According to Descartes: what one might call "me" is actually two things: one intellectual with no physical extension, and the other, the body, a physical presence.'

The look of bemusement on the painter's face did not deter the young philosopher who answered the unvoiced question, 'I can conceive of a mind without a body but I cannot conceive of a body without a mind.'

'And do you subscribe to this idea?'

This question was ignored.

'Descartes believes that the body and the mind are completely separate. He has even made a drawing of the eye which shows a little man sitting looking at images on a screen.'

'Some artists use such a device. It is called a camera obscura. But what does it imply?'

'It implies that you can have an objective view of the world in which your mind is completely absent. Up until now, it has been possible to think of the material realm as separate from the spiritual, so that religion could tell us about matters of the spirit and the natural philosophers could investigate the material universe, treat it as a piece of machinery trying to understand the mechanism, the laws that govern it, the principles of the material world, without impugning any of the eternal truths of religion. Now many of these eternal truths are being challenged and theologians are becoming concerned to defend and preserve them. Galileo Galilei tells us that in order to get to the essence of things we should ignore our experiential world, the world of colour, taste and feeling, and examine instead the measurable qualities like space, position, size, and quantity of motion. He is proposing an analysis that takes us away from common sensory experience.'

'Does Descartes agree with this analysis?' The painter asked his voice heavy with irony.

'Yes and no. He has tried to give a philosophical justification as to why this is the correct way to proceed. He agrees that science should be based on measurement. He believes that all matter can be explained on scientific and mathematical principles by breaking it down into smaller and smaller elements that can be seen to be causing larger phenomena. His problem is including the human soul or mind as part of this picture.'

There was a long pause while the painter wonders how, if at all, he is expected to participate in this absurd discourse.

But it seems that it is not required, the philosopher continues now in full flow, 'I believe Descartes is confused. There are other approaches: Pierre Gassendi, for instance, favours the empirical approach to understanding the world. Using the senses but verifying observations with scientific rigour.' He leaned forward, lifted his tankard to his lips and drank deeply.

The painter sat entranced. There was something compelling about the other man's enthusiasm. Here they were, both on the edge of disaster, and yet this young man was calm and defiant, seemingly willing to compromise, yet surely knowing that the conditions attached to any such compromise would be an anathema to his accusers.

Putting his ale on the table between them, the philosopher leaned back, dangled his arm over the bench and blew smoke into the air.

The painter waited until the young man swung forward and fixed him with a serious gaze, 'The problem, as I see it, is that Descartes believes that you can only measure surfaces, only see surfaces, he believes the spirit is there behind them but you can't measure it. But how can you argue logically that the spirit is there if it cannot be seen or measured. No, he is trying to reconcile his sense of self with an acceptance of God as Creator. But, it seems to me that he proves God exists by exhaustion. He tries to establish the existence of a deity by consciousness: and the authority of consciousness, by the existence of a deity. That is to reason in a circle and, I think, a flaw in his argument.'

The painter remained baffled by this discourse, except for a feeling of irritation, and a wish to return the conversation to a more mundane level.

But the philosopher was suddenly enthusiastic. 'Let me set you a puzzle: the Moors in Spain had a long history of philosophy, one of their great thinkers was a Persian, Ibn Sina. He lived at the beginning of the eleventh century and is better known as a physician. But he had a thought experiment that I think you will find interesting.' The philosopher smiled at the painter, leaned back and let the sun fall full on his face as if trying to recapture the heat of his lost ancestral south. Then he opened his eyes and said, 'Imagine a man falling through a void; there is no sound; he cannot taste or smell anything and he is blindfolded so he can see nothing. He is fixed in such a position that no part of his body touches another. The question then occurs: what can this man know of his own existence?'

They sat in silence for some minutes, the painter trying to gather his thoughts before he gave an answer. There had been an idea forming at the back of his mind since this conversation began and he wanted to articulate it as clearly as he could. 'I cannot solve your riddle. I am not even sure that there is a solution. I can only speak for myself. I doubt that reality is a unified thing or that the language we speak can describe it effectively. I think there is truth in myth, poetry and, dare I say it, in painting. I prove my existence by what I do, not what I think. Sometimes, I believe I am only the things I make. I am compelled to make my ideas visible because they are useless if they remain simply images in my head. I understand time and space through what I see around me. Events that follow each other give me my understanding of time and I comprehend the world through the sensations in my body. I must use my intellect and physical skills to make them into a reality: a painting. To be a poet or an artist is to try to discern things deeply. No quality must escape: it is like a hand playing on a finely tuned instrument of emotion, knowledge passes instantaneously into feeling and feeling flashes back as new knowledge.' The painter looked keenly into the young man's eyes, 'It is a condition that only comes in fits and is difficult to conjure up at will.'

There is no immediate answer from the young man. He draws on his pipe, ponders for a moment as if adding this observation to his stock of knowledge, then slowly releases the smoke into the air. 'So your skill resides in your ability to think with your heart and to feel with your head. What you say raises interesting questions. If existence is simply consciousness, our identity would be the sequence of impressions recorded and stored in the memory. Perhaps we are caught in a trap? Perhaps there is nothing in the mind that was not first in the senses? Our comprehension of the world reaches us through our bodies, but even when it is functioning properly, it does not perceive the world directly, and cannot always differentiate internal from external stimuli. Perhaps consciousness can only be explored from within.'

This time the painter remained silent. Is he expected to unravel this conundrum too? 'So what do you believe?' He asked.

There was another long pause before the young man replied, 'I am not sure. I can no longer believe in a Creator God, distinct from the world he creates. It seems to me that there is only the one substance: everything is nature, it was not created by God it is God!'

'That goes against common sense. I can only conceive God and nature as distinct things, one created by the other.'

'Do you claim God to be infinite?'

The painter hesitated, sensing a trap, 'Yes, I suppose I do.'

'Then how can there be anything that isn't God. If the world is separate from God then God has boundaries, limits, and so cannot be infinite. If God is infinite he must co-exist everywhere. If two things share all the same qualities and are identical, then really they are the same thing. I am beginning to think that human beings and nature are all part of only one substance and that it is universal. There can be no separation between the spiritual and the material world. Like Descartes, I do believe that certain ideas in philosophy or the natural sciences are axiomatic and that other truths can be inferred or drawn from them.'

'I wish you luck. My experience is that the world is chaotic and not open to the kind of logic you suggest. I find I must be as practical as possible.' He got to his feet, downed the last drops of his beer and then slung his bag over his shoulder, 'Let's hope the rain stays away from the city until we are safely home.'

The two men set off together to walk along the raised bank that guides the canal back towards their destination, its towers and steeples spread before them with the sea glistening above. The air had become heavy with the threat of a thunderstorm and on the horizon oily black clouds tramped across the sky on shafts of slanting rain as simultaneously the sun drew moisture from the sea. They walked in single file until the path widened and they could walk side by side.

Rembrandt is still curious about the future plans of

his companion, 'Now tell me, what of your business?'

'Now that my father is dead, I am not disposed to work with the family much longer. In any case, my sister Rebekah is trying to block my share of the inheritance due to me from my father's estate.'

'What will you do?'

'I shall challenge her in court to establish my claim.' Rembrandt is puzzled. 'Why?' He asks, 'If you do not intend to carry on the business and, from what you tell me, you prefer a simple lifestyle, why challenge her? I do not understand.'

Spinoza stopped and turning towards Rembrandt answered, 'It's a matter of principle because, even if I win, I shall renounce my claim. I want to demonstrate why I cannot remain loyal to a community whose values I no longer share.'

'Tell me,' the painter asked, 'will the consequences be serious if you hold to your course?'

'There will be consequences certainly, but how serious I do not know. There is the threat of excommunication.'

'Really? Is it as serious as that?'

'Yes, but there is nothing they can make me do that I would not willingly undertake for myself.'

'But how do you propose to live?'

'There are those who have some sympathy with my views and have already asked me to teach.' He resumed the walk towards the city. 'There is also a steady demand for spectacles, microscopes and even telescopes. I shall apply my skills to grinding lenses. I seem to have some aptitude for it.' He cast a sideways glance at the painter, 'I could perhaps interest you in some lenses; many men of your age need help with their eyesight.'

The painter smiled conspiratorially, 'I already have some, but I think my failing eyesight has its advantages. I find that if I work without any help from spectacles, my work is broader, freer. I am not constrained to attempt too much detail. I work in a kind of blur that I resolve to my satisfaction and usually I find, when I see it more clearly, what I have done suits my needs.'

'And your clients: do they approve of this new aesthetic?'

The painter shrugged his shoulders, 'There are those who can follow where I lead, in the same way that there will be those who can follow you. But I fear that they will be few in number.'

'But your reputation: that counts for something, surely?'

'My reputation?' The painter paused, trying to decide whether he should share his inner thoughts with this young man. 'At the time you say you visited my house on the Binnen Amstel, I believed I was the best painter living in this country. I had no doubts about it.'

'And were you wrong in your belief?'

The painter stopped and looked hard at the young man beside him, 'No, no: it was true then and I believe it is still true today.'

'And are there others who still believe in your work?'

The painter has to decide what level of trust he can place in the other's discretion. 'Of course, but it has been at such a great cost. And I am no longer sure the price has been worth paying. My wife and three of my children are dead and buried. Now I am to be dragged into bankruptcy.'

The two men left the countryside behind them and arrived at the city's outskirts. The storm seemed to have passed. They shook hands and prepared to part but before they did, and because he saw no possibility of their meeting again, the painter asked one more question, 'There is something else, something I should like to know about your philosophy. The question it raises for me: why do people like you, intelligent men, ask such riddles and then spend their lives trying to solve them? What relationship does it have to the world we live in, the here and now? What need have I for your philosophy or clever ideas?'

The philosopher was thoughtful for a few moments, 'I am still young, but it seems to me that most experiences in my life have been vain and futile. All the things I feared were neither good nor bad except as my mind was affected by them. I intend to enquire as to whether there is anything that is truly good because my reason, unlike your imagination, tells me that my situation is not accidental but necessary. What we can know for certain will be useful to us. The more I understand, the more I am convinced of the illusion of freedom in this life. It seems to me that we cannot know beforehand what good or bad we are capable of: what a body or a mind can do in every situation. So this leads me to think that we should pursue what is best for our own nature. To think of good as an unpredictable combination of forces, different for each of us. Not something fixed, no specific moral system, not properly a morality at all. It cannot be found in the pursuit of transcendental reward, or in conformity to a set of rules. We should seek to match what is good in ourselves with other good things in the world: follow our own nature and become capable of conceiving many things: walk in gardens, see plays, eat pleasantly and, whenever possible, do work that is meaningful to us.'

They shook hands warmly before going their separate ways. The painter watched as the young man made his way back towards the city. He suspected they would never meet again, but he could draw some comfort from what had passed between them. Although, for him, what mattered most was an understanding he has lately come to: that man cannot attain perfection in this world. He is weak and sinful and only redeemed through imagination and creativity. However fervently they: the artists, the philosophers, the Christians or the Jews might act in the drama of their lives, only time would tell whether the play was a tragedy or a farce.

He took out the drawing he had made of the young man: he could make use of that, at least.

# 32

The widows Trijn are well known throughout the town of Edam. Every Sunday the two are to be seen in church dressed in true Calvinist manner: long, black dresses, white bonnets and lace collars. At other times they wear the more practical, but still sober dress favoured in the north of Holland with a high neck, long sleeves, fitted bodice and gathered skirt. Sometimes, when working, they put on a plain pinafore over this ensemble. They go together to the market, sit outside in the sun making lace, and work on their shared plot of land growing vegetables and flowers. They have been close friends since childhood but, although they spend much time together, they value their independence enough to maintain separate households.

In spite of this closeness, there passed between them an almost permanent stream of abuse and invective, each pointing out the faults of the other to anyone who cared to listen, as if they were testing their friendship to breaking point. Paradoxically, they are also fiercely loyal to one another. No one else is permitted to utter a word of reproach or criticism about either of them without running the risk of receiving a lecture on the other's unrivalled and excellent qualities.

Trijn Outger has a rotund appearance and bustles about like a fat bee. She is excessively house-proud and follows a strict routine. For Trijn Outger, there are two Bibles: one, the Holy book translated by Calvin on which she bases her religious faith, the other, 'The Skilled and Responsible Householder' is almost as holy but belongs more to this life. Hard work and involvement with the world are what Trijn Outger believes in, not withdrawal and flight from them. She considers herself an expert on the subject of marital and domestic values: deference to her late husband as lord of the household had been one thing, but that was conditional on his obligation to confide the governance of the house into his wife's charge, and to abstain from all conduct that would bring house and family into disgrace. She made sure that he never violated that covenant. It is common knowledge in the town that her obsession with order and cleanliness had driven him to an early grave. She firmly believes she is one of God's Elect, chosen at the moment of Creation to be saved and destined for Heaven when she dies. With this privilege come responsibilities: she regards herself as a model employer, feeding her servants decently but denying them coffee or tea as these are known to lead to bad habits, preferring instead a regular ration of ale. She pays them modestly and gives them small gifts at Christmas and birthdays. She discourages gossip although she expects to be kept informed at all times of the local goings on. She will have no undue familiarity between her male and female servants and keeps a close personal eye on their work, requiring certain tasks be done at the proper time. She makes sure they do not waste anything. Neither meat nor cheese dare go mouldy in Trijn Outger's household; butter does not go rancid nor bread become stale. The hall and the front steps are scrubbed first thing every morning, the brick pavement outside brushed and washed at the same time, even in winter when it is dark and the water freezes on the ground. One day a week is set aside for scrubbing and scouring, two afternoons for dusting and polishing, and she checks assiduously that the dishes and pans are washed after each meal and that linen is folded to her exact specifications. Every summer the house is cleared so that carpets can be beaten and spiders' webs and other insect infestations purged from the building. For Trijn Outger cleanliness is Godliness.

Of the two, Trijn Jacobsdr is the more impressive in appearance: a tall, thin, austere-looking woman with large hands that now, as an adult, she regards as an asset. As a child she hadn't noticed them, or rather had been too busy washing, cleaning and scouring to notice. She is not so certain about her place in the celestial hereafter. It sometimes seems to her that it is a rather perverse concept. Just because God knows everything that has and will happen, has, in fact, planned the whole of Creation from start to finish in every detail, He must already know the fate of every living thing in the world. It follows from this that He must have decided who is to be saved right from the beginning and no matter how hard you try to obey His Commandments if you aren't amongst the Elect you are doomed to the eternal fires of Hell. It causes her some disquiet and not a few sleepless nights.

She is hard-working, conscientious, honest and loyal, qualities she shared with her late husband the slaughterer. When they were first married she had accompanied him on his journeys out into the countryside, beyond the town to the farms where his business took place, sometimes for several days at a time. Even when they had young children, and it was more difficult, she still made the occasional outing in the summer, jogging along beside him on his cart. She has retained his knife as a reminder of those days. He had been no beauty, but then neither was she, yet he had a delicacy about him that was attractive. Killing animals could have made him cruel and indifferent to suffering but, in fact, it had had quite the reverse effect. He would talk softly to his victim, cajoling and coaxing before he struck. He was quick and strong: an ox lifted by its forelegs and split from top to bottom, its entrails spilling out in a steaming mass in less time than it takes to tell. Together they made a formidable pair, their marriage a true partnership. He had left her with a pair of healthy sons to carry on the business. She allowed herself two indulgences: smoking and spitting, but only outside, never in the house.

Trijn Jacobsdr was not by nature house-proud, and saw little point in employing the number of servants required to maintain this perfectionist routine. As for Trijn Outger, she was prepared to overlook some of her friend's weaknesses, but this more relaxed approach to housekeeping was a permanent affront. Once she had mounted a campaign to purge her of these slovenly ways. This involved arriving at her friend's house unannounced to check that everything was as it should be. Short and stumpy though she was, she had demanded a chair to stand on so she could reach up and run her finger along the architrave above the door, examining it for evidence of dirt. She had checked under the beds for sluts' fluff, peered behind pictures and slapped cushions for any suspicion of dust.

She threatened to repeat the exercise at some future date but there was a flaw in her strategy. Being such a creature of habit these unexpected visits could only take place at certain times of the day, times that Trijn Jacobsdr was fully aware of. So in order to thwart her friend she took to setting off early to meet her on the way or, better still, arriving at her house before she had set out.

This cat and mouse game caused much amusement to their neighbours as the two women tried to outwit each other. Trijn Outger, realising the strategy of Trijn Jacobsdr, varied her route so as to avoid encountering her and, having succeeded, banged at her door until the servants allowed her in. This impudence annoyed Trijn Jacobsdr so much that she told the maid to refuse Trijn Outger entry, under any circumstances, unless she was present. The result of this was that one winter's morning they both rose before dawn, Trijn Jacobsdr set off to thwart her friend's arrival while Trijn Outger travelled by the most devious route to catch her friend at home. Each was forced to tramp through the streets in the dark and freezing rain. A truce was called.

This affectionate rivalry was well known in the town and stories true and apocryphal abounded about their adventures. The fence post was a favourite: the two Trijns needed to erect a fence on their vegetable plot and decided it was well within their compass to do it themselves. After much discussion about the placing of the posts and how deep they should go, the conversation moved onto the danger posed to the one holding the post from the one wielding the hammer. Finally, it was agreed that Trijn Outger, being the shorter of the two, should steady the post while Trijn Jacobsdr drove it into the ground. She had, amongst her possessions a heavy hammer, another relic from the days when her husband was alive, and it was this instrument that she proposed to use. She assured her friend there was no danger, her arm was strong and her aim was true. Swinging the hammer carefully, she struck. It promptly bounced off the top of the post and gave Trijn Outger a heavy blow on her upper arm. The cry of pain was heard over a wide area and those who ran to help were left in no doubt about how she had been subjected to a deliberate attack at the hands of her unfeeling friend. Trijn Jacobsdr protested her innocence, insisting the other Trijn had moved the post just at the moment she struck. In any case, it had been only a glancing blow, a mere trifle and not worth all the fuss. In spite of this she was made to see the seriousness of her offence and spent a great deal of time scuttling about to find potions, lotions and poultices to soothe the pain and repair the damage. It was only when she suggested inviting an apothecary who was expert in the application of leeches that Trijn Outger began to recover.

The situation was reversed when they set about nailing a hook to the wall of Trijn Jacobsdr's kitchen. This time, the shorter of the two swung the hammer while her friend held the hook in place. The nail was driven home without incident and they stepped back to admire their handiwork. It was only when Trijn Jacobsdr attempted to hang a cloth on the hook that they discovered it was pointing downwards. Who to blame? Guilt was never established or admitted by either side, each accusing the other of incompetence on every conceivable occasion.

In spite of, or perhaps because of, these and similar incidents they gained a reputation for being a source of wisdom and experience to be relied on to see both sides of any argument and they adjudicated and settled disputes between neighbours, many times.

## 33

It was a warm day and the two women were sitting outside the house of Trijn Outger making lace and arguing as usual. What exactly was the subject of their disagreement? Each would have been hard pressed to recall, it was simply an excuse to revisit old enmities, to fight another battle and enjoy one other's company.

'Excuse me?'

The two women looked up, shielding their eyes from the sun, surprised to be interrupted by this complete stranger. Neither stood up but waited expectantly for the woman to state her business.

She introduced herself as Cornelia Jans. 'I'm making some enquiries about a woman called Geertje Dircx, whom I believe one of you employed some years ago?'

The two Trijns cast cautious glances at each other. Rumours had been circulating that someone was snooping around the town ferreting out gossip about the time before Geertje had left for Amsterdam.

Trijn Outger spoke first. 'What do you want to know?'

'Was it you, who she worked for?'

'She was in my employ briefly,' Trijn Outger said, carefully placing her work on the bench beside her. 'But that was more than ten years ago, when her husband was still alive.' She turned to her friend. 'Do you remember her?'

'I do, and her husband. He was in the navy, a good-looking man as I recall but feckless, and a prey to drink and bad company. She was lucky he died when he did or she might have fallen into bad habits too.'

'Why did she leave?' Asked Cornelia Jans.

'You should ask her,' Trijn Jacobsdr responded sarcastically, pointing to her friend.

She returned her look, and answered with an irritated edge to her voice, 'You know very well why,' she said. 'Her work was barely satisfactory, not really up to the standards I require. I simply suggested she looked for employment elsewhere. We were on perfectly good terms when she left.'

Trijn Jacobsdr smiled, 'That's not true.'

'Yes it is.'

'No it's not.' Trijn Jacobsdr turned to Cornelia Jans. 'The reason Geertje left was that she made a rather unflattering remark about her to me.' She indicated Trijn Outger, and then added playfully, 'It was so funny I told her what Geertje had said. That was a mistake because she's got no sense of humour and she dismissed Geertje immediately.'

'Don't be so ridiculous, that had nothing to do with it.'

'Yes it had.'

'I knew you'd blame me.'

'Of course I blame you, it was your fault.' She turned to Cornelia Jans. 'She's never seen the funny side of anything.'

'And you haven't seen her since?' interrupted Cornelia Jans.

'Well yes, we have,' said Trijn Outger disregarding her friend. 'She came here about five years ago. She called on me to pay her respects and to tell me how well she had done in Amsterdam. She was housekeeper to some famous painter. She even talked of marriage. So you see, there was no ill will on either side.'

Trijn Jacobsdr would have none of this. 'She actually came to see me, you just happened to be in my house at the time.'

Before Trijn Outger could add anything, Cornelia Jans went on, 'And how did you find her?'

'What do you mean?' It was Trijn Outger's turn to speak.

'Did she tell you why she had come back here, to Edam?'

'She didn't say, but she was from these parts so perhaps she was visiting relations or had some business here.'

'You didn't know she came here to pawn some jewellery she had stolen?'

The two women conferred in hurried whispers.

'We knew nothing of this,' pronounced Trijn Jacobsdr, mystified.

'You don't know that she was found out and since then has been locked away in the Gouda Spinhuis, held for reform without time limit?'

'Are you really suggesting that she was a thief? Our memories of her are quite different.'

Cornelia Jans went on, 'Her brother Pieter swore before the burgomaster in Amsterdam that she was morally corrupt and unstable before she left for Amsterdam.'

Trijn Jacobsdr was particularly incensed, 'Then he is a liar and if he were here I'd tell him so.'

'He's away at sea right now so you can't,' said Cornelia Jans. 'But why should he lie? When Van Rijn dismissed Geertje he gave her a generous allowance and she signed papers giving her brother power of attorney to collect it for her. He has no reason to lie.'

'So why are you are here? Is it to get information so he can make sure she stays locked up?' Trijn Outger demanded.

'He is certain that it is she who lied about what she did before she moved to Amsterdam. She betrayed him, stole some jewellery and broke a legal agreement. Now, as she still refuses to repent, he thinks she should not be released.'

'So this Van Rijn fellow is the one she told us was the best painter in the Province, is he?' Trijn Outger continued, 'Well, we'd never heard of him then and we haven't heard of him since, have we?' She turned to her friend, 'He thinks his fame allows him to act as if he is God, as if he knows the Almighty's Will and Purpose. Well not in my religion, it doesn't.'

Trijn Jacobsdr agreed, though for different reasons. 'Yes, who does he think he is sending you, a mere skivvy, to persuade us to slander Geertje and say she was mad or immoral when we know nothing of the sort? The cheek of it! Does he really think his reputation and wealth will overawe us? The very idea! We'll show him what loyalty and integrity really mean. Let me tell you Mrs Jans, or whatever you call yourself, that you will get no help from us. Now be off before I set the dogs on you!'

By this time a small crowd had gathered and Cornelia Jans, deciding that the interview was over, backed away hastily and retreated up the street.

There followed a rare moment when both women were stunned into silence, but not for long. Trijn Jacobsdr was the first to recover, 'Painters! Who needs them? They are just artisans like us! There isn't much that you can throw away from an animal carcass, but there are some useless bits and, as far as I'm concerned, artists come into the same category. What makes them so important? It's a mystery to me. As far as I'm concerned, it is the practical that is beautiful; the blade that keeps its edge; the cloth that keeps its shape; a jug that pours well, and my bonnet that sits tight in the strongest winds. I can appreciate bits of decoration on the jug or the bonnet, or at least the skill that put them there, but as for all those grand paintings, I don't see the point of them. They are an affront to the plain, simple life that the good Christian should seek. The sorts of pictures I appreciate are about people enjoying themselves and having a good time.'

Trijn Outger sighed and raised her eyes towards Heaven. This attitude was another cross she had to bear. Trijn Jacobsdr's taste in art was so terribly vulgar: inn scenes with rowdy people puking and pissing. She on the other hand had pretensions to a more sophisticated taste. Although her religion condemned any ostentatious display of wealth and power, she saw no reason not to allow small-scale images of the life around her as long as they promoted a more refined taste. Indeed, it seemed to Trijn Outger that a celebration of the simple pleasures enjoyed by simple people could be in no way offensive to God. After all, hadn't they, the people of the Low Countries, like the people of the Old Testament led by Moses, parted the waves, tamed the sea and created the land? She had paintings in her house: still lifes and landscapes that she thought added lustre to her place in the local social hierarchy.

She had little appreciation of their artistic qualities, her criteria for excellence being based solely on subject matter and price.

'That's all very well but I'm not concerned about his profession. God is sovereign and our sole authority should be the Scriptures. This painter seems to have trodden that authority underfoot. Clearly, the man is deeply enmeshed in sin. But what about Geertje, what is her place in this web of intrigue?'

'Don't be too hard on her. Whatever she has done she does not deserve to be locked up any longer. Her mistake was to put her trust in that painter, a man who preys on the vanity of others.'

Trijn Outger agreed, 'I knew something was wrong when she came to see us all those years ago. Yes, even then, and you know I'm never wrong in such matters: it was bound to end badly. She was a little too sure of herself for my liking; saying that he would marry her; she was too easily taken in.'

'Clearly the man has no scruples. I shouldn't be surprised if there was another woman involved. You can't throw away all those years of service just because your trousers are straining at the sight of a younger woman.'

Trijn Outger gave her friend a withering look, 'Trust you to see the lewd and blasphemous side of things,' she said. 'But you cannot deny she lied to us: it was all a fantasy. It seems the truth was, he had no intention of marrying her, and had already kicked her out onto the street. But why did she sign those papers agreeing to his terms when we both know the silly woman can't even read?'

'And we weren't to know she had possession of some jewellery and had come here to pawn it,' Trijn Jacobsdr said. 'If she'd been honest with us and told us what she was planning to do we could have helped her.'

'Helped her? You mean, we would have told her not to be so stupid.'

'Perhaps so, but still she has got courage. She was stranded there in Amsterdam, but she managed to survive.'

'She's cunning too,' Trijn Outger said darkly. 'What I would like to know is: was she wholly innocent? Or has she, as I suspect, been mingling with the unrighteous and brought this punishment on herself? That Jans woman might be right. There were rumours back then about some of the things she did to survive, not all of them very flattering.'

'I don't much care for gossip,' added Trijn Jacobsdr. 'I know she's not clever but she's not wicked.'

'Nor is she's completely stupid either, but it seems she has been tricked by a man she trusted. In fact she's been betrayed at every level. Promises have been made but broken; undertakings agreed then not honoured; relatives whom she should have been able to trust have let her down; friends bribed to betray her; the list is endless and at the centre of all this intrigue is that painter, always that painter. A man of some standing, it seems, but a slippery customer, not to be trusted.'

'He must be a sly one, to persuade all these people to lie for him. Even getting Geertje's brother to testify against her. Money must have changed hands.' Trijn Jacobsdr was thoughtful, 'I never trusted Pieter Dircx. What made Geertje think he'd help her? Perhaps she thought that, being a rough type, if she gave him the authority to collect her money he would frighten the painter into handing it over?'

'For once I think you might be right. I would never have trusted him either,' said Trijn Outger. 'Satan is always on the lookout for souls to corrupt and this painter is simply the Devil's cat's paw. Pieter Dircx is a fool: couldn't he see he was being used? Fancy selling his soul for few trinkets: he'll get nothing out of this but a lot of trouble. The fact that he's been away at sea for some time makes no difference. We're not about to wait for him to come home and try to lie his way out of this mess. We must help poor Geertje. I know what is right and I shall see it done.'

'That's all very well but what are we to do?'

'We must gather more information. We must write some letters first, to the magistrates in Gouda, to get them to look at Geertje's case again.'

'What about the power of attorney she gave to that treacherous brother of hers?'

'She must revoke it immediately.'

'And who will do that?'

'What do you mean?' Trijn Outger asked.

'Well, it's all very well writing letters but Geertje can't read so don't you think one of us should go to see her, to tell her to dismiss her brother. She must not despair. We will get her released. But who will go to Gouda and who will write the letters?'

'I shall certainly write the letters,' said Trijn Outger. 'I don't think we can risk you writing any letters.'

'What do you mean?' Trijn Jacobsdr was exasperated

at this slight on her writing ability. 'I used to help my husband with his business.'

'Come now, you know you could never see the point of book learning when you were a girl. You decided the life you were going to lead didn't need such clever things like reading and writing until you discovered how useful it could be. And then, I admit, you did learn to do simple sums and sign your name, but comes a crisis and you still come running to me.'

She thought carefully. She had never strayed outside the safety of the town and had no intention of going to Gouda or anywhere else but felt it wouldn't do to let her friend know. She must employ a subtle tactic. 'I should also be the one to go and visit Geertje. After all, I'm the one with the brains.'

Trijn Jacobsdr seized her chance. She didn't want to seem to be taking the initiative but she would like to travel and wanted her friend to suggest it. 'I agree, but won't it be difficult? You know you don't like to leave the house, not at this time of the year, when there's so much to be done. I don't suppose you would like me to take care of it for you, would you? I promise not to mess things up.'

'Certainly not. No, I wouldn't trust you. You're hopeless at that kind of thing. I'd never have a moment's peace.'

'But surely you can rely on your servants, can't you? Or would you be worried they'd cut corners and let a few spiders sneak back into the house or moths hide in your linen cupboard while you're away?'

'It's a risk I might have to take,' Trijn Outger replied in a tone which she hoped showed that she had not yet decided.

'Well don't say I didn't offer to keep an eye on them for you.'

This time Trijn Outger replied more emphatically, 'I've told you I wouldn't trust you to do even that simple task.'

'Well in that case wouldn't it be better if you stayed here to supervise them?'

'I don't like to agree with you,' Trijn Outger saw her opportunity, 'but perhaps this time you're right. It's a pity, but I really don't think I can go. However, I don't think you should go either: you're not to be trusted.'

Trijn Jacobsdr, sensing victory, ignored this slur on her character. 'Well there's no one else, so it will have to be me. We both know it would be pointless you going. You can't cross a bridge without me and how on earth would you deal with all the rascals, vagabonds, pimps and prostitutes who roam the countryside? At least I did some travelling in the old days and if it makes you happier you can make a list of all the things I will need to do and the questions I should ask.'

'That, I think, is the sensible solution,' said Trijn Outger placated now that each of them has got what she wanted.

'So that's agreed: you do the letter writing while I go to Gouda? There is one other thing,' Trijn Jacobsdr is delighted to be going travelling but wants to include Amsterdam on her itinerary. She has never been to such a big city before, 'I don't like to be underhand in my dealings with anyone, so perhaps on my way to Gouda I should visit the artist and inform him of our intentions.'

Trijn Outger was not so sure about this course of action. 'Do you think that is wise? It would mean going to

Amsterdam. I don't want you to go and ruin our plans. You can be a proper fool sometimes. Think of all the sin and temptation you will find there: you will need to be careful. He's probably one of those disgusting men who are always trying to enter you from behind or to have carnal intercourse on the Sabbath.' She thought carefully, 'But I suppose I can take comfort in the fact that you will probably be safe. You are old and ugly so you're unlikely to be attractive even to this reprobate. I wonder sometimes why you are not ashamed to look so antique.'

Having got what she wanted, Trijn Jacobsdr was prepared to ignore another insult. 'Good, so you have no objection. We cannot turn back. I had better meet the man face to face. If I could persuade him to see reason, cease this persecution and not punish poor Geertje any more it would save a lot of trouble. Famous painter indeed: we'll soon see about that.'

## 34

From the shore, there appear to be two boats joined at the waterline both dismasted at the gunwales. Above and below them squats the fog with not even a ripple daring to raise itself on the mirrored surface of the water. Two figures sit in the stern, smoking. The drift of smoke from their long, clay pipes matching the smoke from the galley chimney as it labours upwards to join the mist above. As the sun rises, the estuary throws off its nightly attire and the mist, like a phantom, slips away in every direction leaving only the dew to hang upon the rigging. With luck the warmth will send a breeze; until then they must wait: part of the boat; part of the stillness; part of the seascape, the only sound the moisture dripping from the rigging, plip-plopping onto the deck.

One of the figures is none other than Trijn Jacobsdr, deep in thought, waiting for the coffee to brew, having the night before, taken a drop too much gin when they'd moored behind a high bank, and supped at the nearby inn. She spits over the side. The other character is a tall, lean, bearded man with a strip of cloth wrapped around his head to keep his unkempt hair in place. He has on a leather waistcoat over a coarse calico shirt, his trousers caught up at the knees. He is barefoot, his piratical appearance embellished by gold earrings, framing his weather-beaten face. When he is ashore he walks with a casual roll, the result of spending most of his time on water. He is the skipper of the boat trading along the coast of the Zuiderzee between

Hoorn and Amsterdam and occasionally, when he has the cargo, to England.

He is simply the best sailor she knows, able to bring his boat single handed up to the jetty in any kind of wind and just as it comes alongside leave the tiller and step ashore, as nonchalant as you like. One minute he is sailing the boat, the next he is striding away along the quay leaving it moored, bobbing gently behind him, like a sea bird taking off, leaving one element and entering another, equally at home in both.

He had known Geertje in the old days when her husband, the bugler, was still alive, so he was as shocked as any of them that she should be locked up in Gouda. When Trijn Jacobsdr asked if he took passengers, he agreed to take her to Amsterdam, and to arrange for her onward journey by tow barge.

Now the sun was up, the sail and rigging began to steam. Trijn spat over the side and got to her feet as the ripple of a breeze ruffled the still waters. Where was the boy with the coffee?

Later, she sat with her back against the taffrail as the boat slipped quietly along, defying the few remaining rags of mist, watching as the skipper guided the boat and the boy attended to the sail.

This trip to Amsterdam is a great undertaking for Trijn Jacobsdr: she's never been to such a big place before. Trijn Outger had never been to Amsterdam either but had felt it her duty to instruct her friend on the sinful ways of the city and to warn her, in great detail, of all the temptations she would find there. Trijn Jacobsdr had submitted to all this impassively. She finds little difficultly in remembering the things to ask. Being someone without book learning she has, of necessity, developed a capacity to memorise things. As for the lecture on the sinful nature of the city, she has every intention of surrendering to some of the temptations of the place. After all, could there be any harm in taking a drop of gin and smoking some good tobacco? And as for the pimps, pick-pockets, rascals and thieves: just let them try. She is the widow of a slaughterer and would be more than a match for any of them. She spits over the side again.

# 35

My friend Trijn was right about the stink of sin in the city; it mingled with the smell of fish, mud and the stench of the whale oil factory. When we eventually arrived in Amsterdam, even though it was early in the day, we were faced with a whole crowd of pimps and harlots lying in wait for the sailors. They gathered around the lanes and cuttings leading from the docks and along the streets lined with bars and musicos. There seemed to be hundreds of these women plying their trade.

I found the painter's house close to this area, in a street of respectable houses and, from the outside, it looked well kept. It was a big house built on four floors with a stone doorway, a cellar and attics. The steps leading up to the front door were scrubbed, the pavement outside swept clean. I kept watch for a little while, observing the comings and goings of what I assumed were his students. There were other more important people as well, judging by the hang of their clothes.

I was prepared to believe this new woman: his housekeeper was just another victim of the painter's lust. Most probably, she too had been deceived, had promises made to her and been lied to in the same way that Geertje had been, to make her complicit in his misdeeds. My experience of men has not left me with a very high opinion of their behaviour. In my view most men are weak and ineffective and now that women are becoming more emancipated, their other faults are also being revealed. Many are liars and cheats, so I decided to deal with the painter on that basis. What I needed was proof that his current mistress, Hendrickje Stoffels, had been persuaded to lie, and that now her master was unwilling, or as I suspected, was unable to meet the maintenance payment he had promised in court.

It took me a little time to pluck up the courage to confront him but I had come all this way. When I was satisfied that he was at home, I went up the steps to the door and knocked. A maid answered, but when I asked to see her master I was told he was at work in his studio and could not be disturbed, so I asked to see the housekeeper. The maid still seemed reluctant so I insisted more forcibly and, as a result, was invited to wait in the hall while she sought her out. With a few minutes to myself, I took a good look around. By the window, looking onto the street was a step stool, so someone could peek out to see whoever was calling without being seen. It was an old trick and a good idea if you wanted to avoid awkward visitors, but it made me think something was wrong. I have an eye for that kind of thing. There were six chairs, four with leather backs and seats. Also on display were a couple of small statues of naked children. I noticed marks on the walls where furniture had been taken away, pictures removed and others rearranged to hide the gaps. I liked a few of those that were left, some small landscapes and a couple of inn scenes, but all the evidence pointed to the fact that money was short.

Eventually, a young woman appeared: slim with dark hair and carrying a baby in her arms. She introduced herself as Hendrickje Stoffels, the housekeeper. Behind her was a young boy about 12 years old with auburn curls. He seemed a little apprehensive but intent on seeing what was happening. I repeated my request to see the master of the house but received the same reply.

'Yes, the master is here but he is working and cannot be disturbed.'

'And when will he be free? It is most important that I see him. I have come a long way.'

'I don't know when he'll be free. Who are you? What do you want to see him about? He is a very busy man. You will have to come back some other day and take your turn like everyone else and hope that he will see you.'

It seemed to me that this young woman needed a lesson in good manners and to know who she was dealing with. I told her who I was. 'I think you can guess why I am here,' I said. 'I am an old friend of Geertje Dircx's and I have come all the way from Edam to put right the wickedness you have done to her. Your master has behaved badly and I am determined to put things right. Aren't you ashamed of yourself, conniving with this man, when he is acting out of sheer malice?' 'I don't know what you mean?' She said, 'I am only in charge of the house. My job is to make sure he has peace and quiet in order to do his work.'

'You knew Geertje,' I told her. 'You know she served him well, and yet you stood by while he cast her aside just because she sought to get what she believed to be hers by right. She has already been five years in the Spinhuis - five years! Isn't that punishment enough? Hasn't she paid for any wrong she might have done? Now he is set on further cruelty. How can you bear to be a part of all that? Does it mean nothing to you? To defend a man who swore an oath with evil intent, and now you have born him a child, damning yourself to the eternal fires of Hell. Do you intend to perjure yourself again?'

The boy stood beside the young woman with tears in his eyes. She put her arm around him, spoke quietly in his ear, and he left us and went slowly up the stairs.

'That was Titus, his only surviving son.' She pointed after the boy, 'You know his father has buried his mother and three of their children.'

She held the child out to me.

'And this is Cornelia our new little daughter. The children are his pride and joy.'

I didn't doubt her sincerity, but it was all lost on me. I was having none of it and I told her so. 'It is obvious that you are well versed in the art of putting people off, but it won't do, not with me. I've seen it all before. Far cleverer people than you have tried to get the better of me. For the sake of the boy and your child, I would prefer a private meeting but, if I have to, I will confront him on the street or in the market, wherever I find him. He won't be able to leave the house. And don't think I will be put off. I will be back again and again until he does see me. Your master, this painter, is the son of a miller isn't he? They're usually alright but he's obviously one who's gone to the bad. Geertje will be released, I shall see to that, and you and your master had better get used to the idea. She has right and justice on her side, whereas you have only debts and disgrace for your reward.'

I could see that, although she had been taken aback

by my outburst, she wasn't to be easily won over. I decided it was better to leave, but not before telling her she'd not seen the last of me. I had the satisfaction of knowing that the painter would be told of my visit and that, as I wasn't after money, he might be more willing to see me. I have taken some hard knocks in my life and had to learn the hard way. I've come across all sorts of people who were in the habit of lying and cheating. Some, who you would have thought were too stupid and had no imagination of any kind, could come up with the most fanciful reasons why they couldn't pay what they owed, expecting me to believe the most incredible lies. I've known people invent a whole world of uncles, cousins, aunts who owed them money; illnesses they couldn't foresee; circumstances beyond their control; half-truths; downright lies and deception. My husband was a man who killed animals for a living and you'd have thought that he'd have no time for people who wouldn't pay their bills, but he was also kind and forgiving, easily taken in. Eventually I had to take over the money side of the business. I can't really remember a time after that when he disagreed with me. Our customers began to realise that it wasn't wise to try to cheat and they paid up promptly. With the farmers it was fine, he knew them and they knew him, there was a shared sense of fair play; honesty was the common culture. But in the towns it was different, you had to be more careful and besides there were all those foreigners flooding into the country. It's all very well being tolerant, but it can go too far. A lot of people were getting rich and they weren't all Dutch.

Later, when I got chatting to a few of the local shopkeepers I found my suspicions about his financial state were correct. Some of them tried to be discreet. He had been a good customer and they hoped he would be again. I also found out he was having trouble with his next door neighbour, a rich Jew. I don't trust Jews myself, and I also discovered he owed this one money over some business to do with repairs to the house. I thought I might use the information to get him to admit he'd lied. But I was going to have to watch myself: I was beginning to feel sorry for this new mistress. What a mess she was in, as well as money troubles, she'd born him a child, perjured herself, and been condemned by the Church authorities for immoral behaviour.

I decided to be a bit devious. I realised I couldn't confront him in the street. He was still a man of some importance, with influential friends and I was only a slaughter's widow from a small provincial town. On the other hand, as I was later to discover, many of his friends were beginning to abandon him, realising he was sliding towards bankruptcy. Still, I was sure he'd claim that everything he'd done was legal; that he'd broken no laws. In any case public humiliation might make him even more stubborn and I needed him to withdraw his objection to Geertje being released. I hoped he would realise that as he hadn't kept up the payments to the Spinhuis, Geertje was now one of his creditors; he owed her money, so it would be in his own interest to drop the charges against her.

I went to the house again, very early the next morning, almost before it was light. Even so, the maid, who was scrubbing the front steps, said there was no one at home and refused to let me through the door. I knew she was lying because, as I went back down the steps, I glanced over my shoulder and saw the little boy's face at the hall window. It was only a fleeting glimpse but my eyesight isn't that bad. I stood for a few minutes on the steps but, when the students began to arrive, I retreated and waited out of sight a little way down the street. I didn't have to wait too long because sure enough, Stoffels and the boy came out and looked quickly up and down the street before they set off. I hung back, keeping out of sight and wondering if I wasn't the only one they were trying to avoid. I supposed the woman was taking the boy to school because he carried a bag and a little later she came back alone.

I had decided that, if I was going to confront him in the privacy of his own home, I needed the cooperation of the young woman. I didn't want to frighten the boy but I thought it would do no harm to use the woman's protective instincts towards him to my advantage.

The next day I made sure I arrived as they were leaving the house. I stopped them in the street just as the students began to arrive, threatening a row. As I had hoped, to avoid embarrassment, she took me into the house. The only flaw in my plan was that this time, the painter really wasn't there. Apparently he'd gone off very early to the saleroom.

When we got inside, the woman did something which I had could not have foreseen. She must have thought she'd make an attempt to win me over, or at least make me more sympathetic. She placed the boy on the stool telling him to keep watch for his father. Then she indicated that I follow her up the stairs. She seemed very anxious, acting as if I was a clandestine lover she was smuggling up to her boudoir.

She stopped at the top of the stairs. 'We must be quick,' she said. 'He might return at any moment.' She opened a door and waved me through before closing it behind us. I wondered why she had brought me here, fearing it might be a trap, and that she was going to accuse me of some kind of crime.

I found myself in what I assumed must be his workshop. I looked around feeling a little overawed. The room was like the chaotic cave of some robber: drawings stacked in piles; boxes stuffed with clothes and rich materials in heaps on the floor. There was barely room to stand. But now I understood what was going on, they were packing. Was he planning to move or more likely being forced to sell off some of his possessions? As I stood there wondering how to respond, the woman moved some boxes aside so she could get to where a number of paintings were stacked side by side covered with a cloth.

'I don't expect someone like you to understand how important his work is to him, and some of his friends say, not only for him but for the whole country,' she said drawing back the cloth.

I was puzzled, wondering if this was another ploy to gain my sympathy.

She took hold of a painting on a wooden panel where it leant crookedly against the other pictures and dragged it clear, propping it up so I could see it better.

To be sure it did give me a shock, but I soon recovered myself, it was a painting of an ox: dead, headless, butchered and bloody, strung up to a beam.

Stoffels didn't say anything, just stood there beside the picture, her eyes pleading with me to see what she could see. But it was no use, if it had been bigger, I might have taken it for the real thing: a real carcass. Why would anyone want a picture of a dead ox in their parlour? It was absurd, comic: fancy asking a slaughter's widow to be impressed by a painting of a flayed ox? I've seen too many of the real thing. I'm not about to spend good money on something like that, and I can't think of many who would. No wonder he was going bankrupt. But, as she stood there, looking at me with those sad eyes, I realised that this young woman had something I lacked, something that Geertje had lacked too. She was no better educated than me but she seemed to understand what he was about, had some sense of why it was so important. I couldn't see it myself but obviously she could.

She must have realised I wasn't to be taken in and, gently let the painting fall back against the pile; she indicated that we should return downstairs. But it was too late, there were footsteps on the stairs and suddenly he was there, standing in the doorway, holding the boy by the hand. The little lad was trying to hold back his tears, to be brave, but crying all the same, tears running down his cheeks.

'Why isn't he in school?'

Close to, the painter was smaller than I had imagined, older too.

When he saw me, he let go of the boy, 'Who in Hell's name are you?' He demanded, 'What are you doing here?'

He came towards me and I wondered what he was going to do. The young woman took his arm to restrain him. He was furious; so angry he almost couldn't speak. She began to explain who I was and why I was there and this seemed to release his tongue.

'I thought I told you to keep her out,' he said, giving her a menacing look, before he turned on me and, for a brief moment, I thought he might strike me. If he had I would have hit him back.

'How dare you come into my house, frighten my son, and threaten Hendrickje with this ridiculous story claiming she committed perjury? It was all settled years ago.'

'You may not have broken any man made laws but you've broken Christian and moral laws. You know Geertje can't read, so the document you made her sign is meaningless. You confused her until she was afraid she'd get nothing. You wore her down till she was too tired to go on arguing and she'd have agreed to anything.'

'Hah,' he snorted contemptuously. 'She knew exactly what she was doing. She thought she could blackmail me in front of my guests.'

'Is that why you are so vindictive; why you hate her so much? It is your arrogance and pride that are wounded. Is that why you cannot forgive her?'

He kicked out at the piles of brocades lying at his feet. 'I will never forgive her. She is dishonest and immoral.'

'And who are you to accuse anyone of dishonesty and immorality? You, a man who uses smooth words and bribery, who made promises to get her into your bed, promises that were empty and worthless.'

'I'll hear no more. She betrayed me.'

All this time the young mistress was clinging to his arm. 'Please be quiet you will wake the baby.'

I was beginning to get angry myself, 'You promised to marry her!' I pointed at the young woman, 'Did you tell this poor creature the same pack of lies? Have you made her a party to your deceit? Have you promised to marry her, as well?'

'No, I have not and I made no such promise to the Dircx woman either. She went on and on about marriage, driving me to distraction. She can say what she likes: I did not at any time offer to marry her. She made my life impossible. She defied my orders, moved my things, told me what I should or should not paint. She was insufferable: gossiping and spreading rumours. I have students to teach, clients to see. I must have time to do my work. I need peace and quiet not endless demands about domestic and petty details, but she would pester me all the time.'

He turned away towards the door, leaving the young woman holding the boy's hand amongst the litter of fabrics.

But I was not about to let the conversation end here, 'Geertje told me you thought she was an excellent nurse and housekeeper. Was that nothing to you?'

He spun round waving his arms in the air, 'And so she was at first, but I see now that it was part of her scheme to get hold of my money. She took advantage of my loneliness and my need to have someone to care for my son. I needed help, not trouble. She is a sly, cunning and ruthless woman. I was a fool not to have seen it earlier but, as soon as I realised what she was up to, I got rid of her. She could have settled for being my housekeeper. Wasn't I generous towards her? Didn't I give her command of the servants and the running of the house? She was well cared for and could have remained here.'

'What? And live under the same roof as you, the man who had cast her aside and was bedding a new mistress?'

'Leave Hendrickje out of this: I've told you, that woman was too demanding. Things change. She wanted more of my time and attention than I could give.'

'Yet you gave her your dead wife's jewellery!'

'I tell you, I did not give her any jewellery. The jewels were not mine to give. They belong to my son. She was to have the use of them during her lifetime: it was all written down. She had no right to pawn them,' he said with more exasperation than anger. 'God knows I was generous to her. I gave her a home, fed her, and gave her all manner of privileges but she made my life impossible. I was glad to see her go.'

I sensed a slight advantage and pressed on, 'You expected Geertje to understand your vile ways, to step aside and watch you sleep with another woman, and to sympathise with your needs; to sacrifice herself on the altar of your art; for your honour; your fame; your fortune.'

Suddenly he seemed deflated, 'Didn't I offer her money for the rest of her life? I would have given her more if she'd needed it.'

'At your discretion, you would have used your so called "gifts" as weapons to keep her quiet and compliant.'

He stepped forward wagging his finger, 'Of course at my discretion. I didn't trust her; I made her a more than generous offer when I could have done nothing. I agreed to the allowance and she came back and demanded more. I agreed to give her more and still she wasn't satisfied. There would have been no end to it. She would have come back again and again.'

The young woman was hanging onto his sleeve sobbing bitterly, but it was too late for me to stop now, 'You should have married her. That would have been the honourable thing to do.'

'Marry her! Marry her? Are you mad? Is that what you want? You want me to marry a mad woman?' He pointed to the painting where it still leant uncovered against the others, 'Like that? To flay me alive, mutilate me and make me a martyr? I despise the woman: she wronged my dead wife and me. She is a bloodsucker. Do you take me for such a fool? You talk of honour. I could have thrown her onto the streets, penniless. That's what most men would have done.'

I was tired of this tirade. I stood firm with my arms crossed. 'And now she is one of your creditors and you cannot pay. You are bankrupt and it is you who will soon be in prison.'

He pushed his face close to mine, glaring up at me. 'You dare to threaten me! Get out of my house you interfering old woman. My reputation still stands for something. I do not need to bow to the petty threats of someone like you. I shall write to the magistrate at Gouda and we shall see who has the most influence. I think you will find my standing is worth something even there.'

It was at this point, I decided to leave. I had done my best. I had wanted Geertje to be allowed out in peace, not to have to fight every inch of the way. But as I set off down the street, I was reluctant to admit it, but Trijn Outger had been right. My visit had only made him more intransigent and I would have to act quickly before he had time to make it even more difficult to get Geertje released. Just at that moment, I heard the sound of someone running and turned just as the young woman caught up with me.

'Please ask Geertje to forgive me,' she said breathlessly, rocking backwards and forwards in her distress. 'I cannot desert him, not now. He is the father of my child and Titus needs me, more than ever. I've begged him to let things go, not pursue this quarrel to the bitter end and poison his life. We are on a course for disaster but he seems unable to find a way out. There will be a sale this autumn of all his goods and we are going to lose the house. He's just come back from making the arrangements for the move to a smaller place in a cheaper district. So you see, your threats are useless.' She took me by the arm, 'But you must hurry. He is, at this very moment, writing to the magistrates in Gouda demanding they refuse to hear Geertje's plea to be released. He is determined to find the money to keep her there, just how, I do not know.' She turned and ran back towards the house.

# 36

I wanted to help him. The situation was impossible, intolerable. At first I wasn't sure what I should do. I had no idea how much encouragement he had given Geertje. More than he would admit to me, I was sure of that. But even if he had encouraged her, she should have known there was no future in it. I mean, as far as marriage was concerned, I always did, I was just grateful for my place.

What he wanted was a housekeeper and someone to care for his son. He wanted more children too, although I didn't know that when I first came to his house. Most of all he needed someone to protect him from the everyday irritations of life; the running of the house; disciplining the servants; organising the students. Although there were very few other servants and hardly any students by the time I took over. Making sure the house was kept clean and tidy; cooking the food; paying the bills, and keeping the creditors at bay too, as he retreated into what he called his 'grand style'. He would fly into a rage if anyone dared to mention the work of his rivals, saying he wanted nothing to do with their smooth finish and empty rhetoric.

He told me that when he was younger, and just starting out, he had been certain that his way of working was correct. All he had to do was hone his intuition to a fine point. He had learned from the masters in Italy and Spain and he knew he was going in the right direction. He hadn't known why, couldn't explain it, he just knew. He'd followed his instincts, and the facility that he'd had since he was a boy, and these had been his guide. Luckily for him, as a young man making his way, this facility had been in tune with his time, the prevailing taste, there had been a certain confidence and he'd been part of it.

When Saskia died it was as though everything he'd worked for was lost. The direction of his painting began to change. Something dictated the way his work developed and he felt compelled to follow where it led. I asked him if he had tried to resist, but he told me he had not protested, did not, could not, thwart this inner voice. It had sent him off on this new path even though he sensed that the way would be difficult and, in the material sense, unrewarding. There would be those who would follow, but many would not. Some had put it down to arrogance and a wilful disregard of taste and convention. He couldn't argue to the contrary because he didn't have the words. He was becoming more and more taciturn, and not sure whether his genius was leading him towards a deeper understanding of what lay behind the surface appearance of the world. It forced him to believe that somewhere, in the ancient myths and stories in the Bible, there lay a more profound truth about reality and man's true nature.

I was flattered that he told me these things, but he had found little sympathy for such ideas amongst other painters. It was into this emotional mix that Geertje had been plunged when she came into the house. She had arrived, seemingly straightforward and competent, not a stupid woman, but with no appreciation of his work, and seeing no reason why she should make the effort. He was partly to blame as I later came to understand. He told her it was mostly a trade, a craft which he had mastered to make money and could apply to any subject. He didn't tell her that it also demanded a sense of spontaneity, an intangible something beyond what was immediately visible. So when he asked me to help extricate him from the domestic mess he had got himself into I felt I must try.

I guessed that there was more to what Geertje did for him than simple housekeeping. I'm not that naïve, but I wasn't thinking of taking over from Geertje. She had given me my place and I was grateful. I should have realised that it might cause problems, but I was flattered by his attentions and tried to make sure nothing else happened. I was pleased to think I was attractive to such a famous man, a man whose artistic skills had been admired by all of Amsterdam. Now his talent was overshadowed by newer values and fashions with which he was out of sympathy. He needed more time for thinking and philosophy.

When he asked me to confirm that Geertje had agreed to the conditions contained in the document presented to her at the house that October, I didn't see it as my place to deny him. Although, I hadn't actually seen her make her mark: if he said she'd agreed, what reason did I have to doubt him? Geertje later maintained that I put him up to it, so that I could take her place, but it wasn't true. I did talk to him about how he could extricate himself from the mess, but I only made sensible suggestions. He was the one to decide, not me. It was his house and his writ ran there, not mine. I was only the servant. Later we became closer but that was because he needed someone like me to give him some stability. His genius was fragile, and he relied on me for support. Is it a crime to want to help someone in their darkest hour, to help them through a difficult time in their lives? Some might say he used me. Perhaps he did, but if what I did is thought to be a crime, I was a willing partner.

I took risks myself. When I became pregnant, I was accused of practicing whoredom and denied communion. I was cast out from the Church, but my rewards were our daughter Cornelia, named after his mother, and my increasingly close relationship with him. Certainly I felt sorry for Geertje, and did my best to get him to be generous. But she was bitter and wilful and he had to be protected from her or else she would have destroyed him. And the fact of my bearing his child proved one thing: she had accused him of being impotent, because he had failed to get her pregnant. He said it was because they had never slept together. My pregnancy proved he was telling the truth because if they had been sharing a bed how could it be that she remained childless?

It seemed as though we needed allies in our dispute with Geertje. She thought she had right on her side, which of course she did, or at least I thought so at the beginning. After all, she had cared for Titus since his mother died. It was true that women had gained more freedom, but it had its limits. The men still ran most things and the Church was not about to change its ways. I had no wish to take over Geertje's place as housekeeper or any other services she rendered. They were not my concern.

Of course he always had clients, those who stuck with him into his new style, but there were fewer of them. For some, his reputation was enough, and they trusted his judgement. I knew there was another sort of truth that drove him on. It was as if he were two people: one was the craftsman, who knew about paint and canvas, composition and what effects could be achieved; the other was the one who was always on at him to improve, to get closer to his inner self, the one who could understand what he had said in paint. He told me all this at the beginning, although I didn't really understand until much later.

And it would have only got worse because the more Geertje complained and made demands, the more he retreated into his workshop and into his inner-self, the self that no one could get at.

Once, there had been a time, when he would work regular hours and had a rich social life, a time before my time, when his workshop was the place he retreated to, a place of refuge, but at least a place where he could be found and sometimes persuaded to come out. He had his times, his routines, his cycles and his seasons but that began to change after Saskia's death. He still disappeared into his workshop, but it became more of a sanctuary, where he could disappear into himself. Poor Geertje, she couldn't understand this at all. It seemed that only I was able to get through to him. He came to need me. I didn't want to be drawn into this emotional turmoil, but what could I do? Geertje's behaviour only made thing worse and so she had to leave.

## 37

So that was how I spent my short time in Amsterdam. I had hoped to see a little more of the city before I left, but I had pressing matters to attend to. The captain had arranged for me to take the tow barge to Gouda, perhaps the same boat that had taken Geertje there five years before. My way took me through Haarlem so I made the precaution of visiting a notary and swearing a deposition against the painter, setting down how he had threatened me and verbally abused me, waved his fists in the air: altogether an exhibition of unreasonable behaviour and armed with that I continued my journey to Gouda.

I found the Spinhuis easily enough, although the people from whom I asked direction gave me some curious looks. It was as if they were surprised that a respectable looking woman like me should be seen visiting such a place. From the outside it had the look of an austere convent with a large front door set in an arch made of brick with a stone surround. At the apex of the arch was the statue of a woman holding a flail with, on either side, two naked men held in chains. It made me shudder to see it.

As I came near, the wicket gate set in the front door opened and several women came out onto the street. They were dressed in rough calico smocks and carried baskets full of rolled-up cloth. They formed a line under the supervision of a large, rough-looking woman then trudged off towards some open fields a little way towards the edge of the town. A couple of the women seemed in good spirits: I suppose they were pleased to be out in the bright sunshine and chatted amiably with the custodian, but there was one who walked alone hanging back from the rest. There was something familiar in her appearance. Just as I approached her, the guardian, seeing me looking closely, took her roughly by the shoulder, cuffed her on the head, and pushed her along after the others. I stifled an urge to protest but decided it was best to bide my time.

I took lodgings for the night and the next day made my way back to the Spinhuis. To my surprise there was a queue of men outside the entrance. When I enquired what was happening I was told that there was a local festival and on such occasions the public could pay to go inside and watch the inmates at work. So, much to my annoyance, I had to pay for the privilege of visiting Geertje, which only added to my dislike of the place and all those associated with it. I found a guardian, who I recognised as the same woman I had seen bullying one of the inmates the previous day. She was surly and tried to put me off by saying they were busy and asking why I had not made an appointment. She told me I must come back another day, but seeing that I was becoming angry, she decided it best to summon the superintendent.

While I waited, I took in my surroundings. The place stank of lye: vicious stuff that I knew well. We used it for washing out the slaughterhouse, but at least we could open the doors and let in the air. Here, it was so strong you could taste it. And there was another smell mingled with it that I couldn't at first identify: except that it was disgusting.

Strung from posts across the yard were lines of washing, drying in the warm sunlight. There were some women dressed in the same rough calico I had seen the day before, busying themselves, taking down and folding sheets. I was surprised to see another group of women, whom I assumed were also inmates, wearing ordinary clothes. There was even a group wearing gaudy dresses with feathered hats and painted faces looking just like the harlots I had seen in Amsterdam. They seemed very free and easy, leaning against the walls, taking in the sun, smoking and chatting to the members of the public who wandered around.

I thought about the conditions in the place. I am all in favour of punishment for serious crimes, but I also think that the punishment should be part of a process of correction and redemption. I was not at all sure what was happening here. It was difficult to tell who were the most immoral, the inmates or their custodians. Finally, the superintendent put in an appearance. I saw through her at once: a vulgar, graceless woman with a supercilious manner, a bully with a domineering and cruel character, probably given the job for that very reason. I wasn't fooled by her display of concern for the wellbeing of her charges. Her first response to my request was to be obstructive.

'What do you want? You haven't been before, have you? It's the first time I've laid eyes on you. What's your business with this woman? Why the sudden interest? Has someone left her money?'

'I need to see Geertje Dircx on a legal matter,' I insisted.

'I don't suppose you would recognise her, would you?' She said, 'She might be in the building somewhere or out on the bleaching ground. I can't be exactly sure where she is, or for that matter who she is.'

'You mean to tell me you don't know the names of the women in your charge?'

'No, not their real names: all those who come here are treated the same. We shave their head and dress them alike. They are all given new names, too. It takes away the sin of pride to be just another of the women in here. Most of them were never christened anyway so what does it matter? We give them names in alphabetical order so I will need to know when she came in, so I can look back at the records.' She paused and looked at me, 'That might take me some time and cause me inconvenience especially today, as we are so busy. Of course if you would like to make a contribution to the expense of running this place, to buy some little creature comforts for my girls, that might help to speed things along.'

I was taken aback by this effrontery. 'Are you suggesting I pay a bribe?' I said. 'How dare you insult me by such a suggestion, this is really too much. May I remind you that I paid good money to come in here and I will have no truck with any kind of villainous behaviour.'

Luckily for me, I had the correct papers with me and could give her the exact date. Finally, she realised that there was no gainsaying me and set off for the office to get the information she needed to identify Geertje. She warned me beforehand that under no circumstances should I enter any of the buildings and that I conduct my interview on a bench outside in the courtyard.

I sat there waiting for what seemed an interminable length of time until finally, in a fury, I went and sought her out again. I found her, as unconcerned as ever, sitting behind a desk with another woman; one of her gang of guardians. Once again, she tried to put me off with a lot of bluster and procrastination, repeating that they were too busy because the public were about the place.

'Hold your tongue,' I said.

'I beg your pardon?' She said, 'Do you mean me?'

'Yes you. Shut your mouth. I am here to see my friend is released, so I should be obliged if you would stop your prattling and excuses and bring her to me, and be quick about it.' It gave me some pleasure to see the consternation on her face as she sent the other woman scurrying away to reappear a few minutes later with a thick ledger, which she thumped down on the desk.

'Five years, she's been here, you say. That's a long stretch. Most of them are only here for about half that time. Is someone paying for her to be kept in?' The superintendent, who was still sitting by the desk, gave me a dark look as she turned over the pages. 'Here she is Geertje Dircx - she became Margarita, Maggie we call her.'

'You'll be lucky to get a word out of that one,' the other woman said. 'She has spoken hardly a word since she came here. Except to say she's innocent. But they all say that.'

'She has no visitors?'

'No.' The superintendent added, 'But don't look surprised. After all, you've never been to see her before have you? And you say you are her friend? Wait outside in the yard and I'll go and find her.'

She took me into the yard, now empty of the visitors who had all gone inside, leaving only a few women still attending to the washing.

'She doesn't know everything.' The guardian said indicating the superintendent as she disappeared into one of the buildings, 'Maggie did have a visitor once. But that was when she was first here. A painter fellow from Delft, I think. He told us he used to work in the same house where she was employed. He only came the once, never again.'

A few minutes later the superintendent returned followed by the thin waif of a woman who I recognised as the one who I had seen abused, the previous day. I had thought there was something familiar about her, but could this really be Geertje? I couldn't be sure. True, I hadn't seen her for many years, but if it was her she had changed almost beyond recognition. What once had been a handsome woman with a firm figure was now a thin and emaciated ghost. Her skin was sallow with livid red patches, her hair grey and lank and her poor hands raw and calloused. She had once been quite a lively character, now she looked a broken woman.

'I'll leave you to your talk.' The superintendent said, 'Mind my instructions, and stay outside in the sun.' She pointed to the drab creature standing, head bowed, behind her. 'It will do her good.'

'Who are you?' The woman asked, as soon as the superintendent was out of earshot. 'I've never seen you before.' She had a nervous twitch in her face and, as she spoke, she kept looking around to see who was close by and if we could be overheard.

'Don't you remember me, Geertje?' I tried to reassure her, 'I'm Trijn Jacobsdr from Edam. You remember the two Trijns, me and Mrs Outger who you worked for before you went to Amsterdam.'

She seemed not to hear me and was still looking around. Finally, she drew from her apron a grey piece of cloth, and then quickly, with one more furtive glance, revealed a lump of some nondescript substance.

At first I thought it must be soap but then she broke off a piece and showed it to me.

'This is what we get to eat, our daily bread, for which we must give thanks to the Lord.'

I held out my hand. 'If you give it to me Geertje, I will get rid of it and bring you something more wholesome.'

But instead of handing it over, she gave me a horrified look and clutched the bread to her bosom. 'Who are you? Have you come to steal my food?'

She pushed me away before shoving the revolting thing back into her apron. She ran her fingers through her hair and then thrust them close to my nose.

'Can you smell it? I stink of this place. Can you taste it, the stench of it? I breathe that filth; drink it, even my shit stinks of it: it makes me vomit.'

I finally managed to get her hands away from my face. 'Please Geertje, try to be calm. I'm here to help you, to get you out of here.'

'No, no, you can't,' she whispered. 'Can you keep a secret, I'm not who you think I am, my name is Margarita.'

She looked around furtively again as if she really was

as mad as Rembrandt claimed.

'I don't know why you keep calling me Geertje? It's all her fault, it was that Dircx woman. She was the one who sinned, but I'm the one being punished.'

What was I to say? I tried to reassure her again. 'You must believe me. Whatever sins you committed in the past, have been more than paid for. You have been punished enough.'

She seemed to be rambling again. 'Sometimes we get a piece of rotten meat, but that's only so that they can deny it to us if we break the rules and they are easily broken. The work is hard and they beat us.' She turned on me again. 'What do you want with me? Be careful, or I'll call the guard.'

'Geertje listen to me.' I tried again.

'My name is Margarita.'

'Alright then, Margarita, I've been to see the man who put you here and he wants you kept locked up until you die. He's trying to get more evidence against you, but now you have some power over him. The money he promised has not been paid. He is bankrupt and you are one of his creditors.'

She clung to my arm again, looking fearfully about as if her torturer might be somewhere close.

'Who have you been to see? Van Rijn? Don't trust him. Don't trust anyone, I don't. Even my own brother betrayed me. I've done with love. I've turned my heart to stone.' Her face became suffused with anger. 'If there was any justice in the world that monster would be here begging my forgiveness on his knees.' She looked around again. 'Can we really make trouble for him?'

I wanted to end the conversation and get away, but she was leaning close to me gripping my arm. The reek of lye and the smell, which I now realised, was pease porridge, made my stomach turn.

She went on, 'I'd like that. Could we make everyone see that it is really him who is the criminal?' She grinned through her broken teeth, and then she was rambling again. 'Where am I? What have I done? What shall I do? What pain eats through me?'

I tried to comfort her, while at the same time trying to loosen her hold on my arm. 'You need wait no longer; I can get you out of here. He has another in his bed now, isn't that bad enough? What else do you need after all he's done? He is unrepentant I saw the cruelty in his eyes. No pity, no grief; he didn't even pretend. I did not see him soften for a moment, he doesn't care. He will hurt you more if he can. Let's find some pleasure in being a trouble to him.'

'Yes I do hate him, how could I not? He forgot all the kindnesses that I did him, the love I might have given him turned to hatred. He betrayed me and I have had plenty of time for my anger to grow. He has made me his enemy.'

I tried once more to explain what we should do. 'He leaves you with no choice. You must move quickly, strike first. You must rescind the power of attorney you gave to your brother. He must have collected your allowance but kept it for himself. He has already given the jewels back into Rembrandt's hands.'

'You don't understand there's a worse pain. My heart, my cowardly heart, still takes his side. I feel that I am still his, even if secretly. After all this time, all his cruelty, why did he torture me? There are no mirrors in here but even if there were I couldn't bear to look at myself, I'm afraid to see the state I'm in.'

She gripped my arm again and looked fearfully about. I tried to stiffen her resolve, 'Don't be a coward. How can you pity him still? Will you pardon him? You can't revoke all this rage. What does he care about you? Your revenge is now so close.'

'I tremble just to think...revenge!' She went on incoherent and rambling again, 'Let him die. He's not alive to me. The traitor triumphs, mocks and scorns my hurt. He thinks he'll see this storm dissolve in tears. So will the end of all my love be death?' Suddenly she was rational again, 'You can act for me?'

'Yes, he thinks he will triumph. He shouted at me too when I told him what I planned. He thinks he'll see this storm blow over and scorned my attempts to help you. But if he expects us to waver and be weak he hasn't reckoned with me. If he imagines that he'll stop these blows, he's very much mistaken. He judges you by your past kindness, but I'll make sure he'll take a different view this time. You hate him now and you can punish him, if only in a small way.'

'I got no thanks for the love I gave him, all the shame is mine all the fame his. I wish that he had endured as much pain as I have.'

I was now quite desperate to get away but I tried to comfort her, 'You hate him and rightly so, but now you have some power over him. The money he promised has been used to pay for keeping you here, but he cannot pay any longer.' I told her again, 'He's bankrupt: you are one of his creditors. You can punish him, if only in a small way.'

All at once she seemed to change, as if the subject of her release was no longer of interest. She put her finger to her lips to indicate that I should be silent then pulled me to my feet and led me across the yard to one of the buildings. By now I was more and more anxious to escape and even though I knew she might be punished, I looked around for help but everyone seemed to have disappeared. Her grip, with her bony fingers on my arm, was so painful; I judged it best to follow.

She stopped beside a wooden shutter, set low in the wall, which she pushed open. Hidden behind it was a tiny opening obscured by cobwebs but I could see and hear what was going on. I looked down into a basement where some of the women, perhaps the most hardened whores, the ones who I had seen earlier wearing their finery including exotic hats and makeup, were now flaunting themselves before several men who had been allowed in to watch them through a barred partition. It was no real barrier for what these men wanted. The women lifted their skirts and waved their backsides for all to see and there was a lot of groping and groaning from both sides of the bars. It was quite disgusting and I was about to cry out for it to stop when Geertje pulled me away and hushed me to be silent in case she got into trouble.

When we were back sitting safely in the yard, she told me that the men paid to come into the place and this was sanctioned by the authorities. She said the shame involved in such activities was supposed to lead to self-improvement. Some of the money the supervisor received was paid over to the women so they could buy extra things and sometimes to pay their fines and be released. It was nonsense of course. I am not against people being punished for their crimes, sometimes severely. The Bible sanctions such action by society, but this kind of exhibition was monstrous. Geertje begged me not to say anything until she had been released. She told me that if they found out she had let me see what went on, even though it was supposed to be officially sanctioned, she would be punished. She already had a difficult time because she would have no part in any of these sordid activities. She was made to do the harder work and chastised for her lack of contrition over her sins.

As I was leaving, I told the warden that I was on my way to visit a lawyer and instruct him to apply to the magistrate for Geertje's release. I told her to treat Geertje kindly and be very careful not to be vindictive because I would be watching out for her.

# 38

It was just getting light when the small door set in the Spinhuis gate swung open. At first, there appeared to be no one inside but then, out of the gloom, stepped a slight, diminutive figure clutching a stick and a battered portmanteau. As soon as she was through the door it closed silently behind her. There was no one to meet her, only a lone rat meandering close to the wall unconcerned by her presence. For a few seconds, the woman stood alone, confused and muttering to herself, as though unable to decide which direction to take. Meanwhile, the rat disappeared under the gate that she had just stepped through.

She didn't seem to be expecting anyone but looked up and down the road apprehensively before deciding her direction. She set off towards the centre of the town, leaning heavily on the stick and clutching her bag close. The streets were just coming to life in the grey dawn and a few people were going about their business: setting up stalls in the market place; piling vegetables in heaps on the cobbles: potatoes, onions, cabbage. The fish and meat stalls were together on one side of the square under the portico of a public building. Occasionally, the woman stopped and, glancing stealthily around to make sure no one was watching, took a purse out of her bag, opened it and held it close to her eyes scrutinising the contents. Then, as if reassured, she slipped it back into her bag.

She arrived at the quayside and took a seat a little apart from the few other passengers who sat in the stern of the waiting barge. It was now full daylight and a horse was led out by a youth and harnessed. A few minutes later he was joined by a man who helped him mount before casting off the ropes and taking his place at the tiller. As soon as he was in position the youth clicked his tongue and gave his mount a flick with the whip and they set off just as rain began to fall.

# 39

What of the girl who has just left the room: Cornelia, his 14 year old daughter by Hendrickje, her mother and his mistress, dead these four years, one of the multitude plucked by the plague, the same pestilence that only a few months earlier had carried off Titus. His son, married and dead within months, never to see his daughter Titia enter the world: another tragedy to add to the pile.

It seemed that death was now his constant companion. The three women he had shared his life with were gone and of his five children only Cornelia remained. It was because of her that both he and Hendrickje had been condemned by the Church to everlasting damnation; the consequence of their carnal sin. He lent back in his chair and absentmindedly gazed into the mirror. He didn't believe in that cruel doctrine. It wasn't worthy of humanity or any God he might believe in.

Was it really two years since Cosimo de' Medici, Duke of Florence had stood in this very room? Perhaps not an event to compare with the illustrious visit of the Holy Roman Emperor to the workshop of Tiziano Vecelli in Florence: but there was some consolation in that the Duke had bought one of his self-portraits. It was a confirmation of his fame and reputation throughout Europe. It almost overcame his irritation at not being the only painter in Amsterdam that Cosimo de' Medici had honoured with his presence.

He smiled to himself. What had the young Duke made of him? Would he still think of him as Amsterdam's greatest artist now that he was living in this little house on the Rozengracht? He supposed he must; after all he had sought him out here in the Jordaan district, a poor, rough area of the city populated by small scale industries and inns. Of course, he couldn't be sure because his visitor hadn't stayed long and had looked a little disdainful too, keeping his handkerchief close to his nose.

And yet, and yet, if he was the best why was it that when the decorations for the New Town Hall were allocated, the commissions were shared among several painters, some of whom had been his students. He'd only been given one of them, the same as Leivens. When was that? It must be seven, eight years ago because Hendrickje was still with him.

He scratched himself vigorously. Could it be that he was a bit lousy? It was hard not to be, especially in the summer. The cold of the winter killed off most of the fleas but some clung on for the warmth of human contact and his blood. But then, someone was always after his blood.

He knew the authorities considered him an ill-mannered reprobate. Cornelia was living proof of his sinful ways. But for him, it didn't matter; he'd ceased to care about those things long ago.

The Town Hall commissions had been a big job and he had needed the money; there were hundreds of guilders at stake. He felt angry and insulted when they gave the original commission to Govert Flinck. After all, it should by right have been his and once he might have expected it would be. He should have known, perhaps did know, that what they were looking for was something smoother, more decorous, than the work he was making then and still was now in his old age.

So why not give it to Flinck? Apelles Flinck, as he was now known, another of the men who had served under him and was now making a fortune. Flinck could be relied on to produce clear, unambiguous histories; high minded but shallow; canvases full of elaborate costumes; ostentatious architecture; a pretentious, mannered, sanctimonious, ridiculous pantomime.

And it had killed him. Whether it was strain or plague, Flinck had died leaving only his sketches behind. The authorities had had to think quickly. They were in such a hurry to see the work completed that they were forced to spread it amongst several artists and, whether they liked it or not, they had to entrust a major piece to him.

He eased himself wearily out of his chair and rubbed his finger as he went over to the window. On the other side of the canal he could see the trees leaning out over the water, the weak sunshine scattering their shadows onto the brick buildings opposite.

They had given him 'The Conspiracy of the Batavians under Claudius Civilus': a massive painting, 20 feet wide and just as high in the centre of the lunette. He had been told to follow Flinck's sketches so it would match the paintings already in place. The city fathers felt they must keep faith with the original concept. But what about his concept? Flinck had once been one of his students for God's sake. He was the master and he had to be true to his own interpretation, to his own vision. Was it his fault if it was nothing like Flinck had planned?

The spring day had been bright and clear that morning but over to the east the sky was leaden, threatening a storm. He went back to his chair, furious again at the memory of the humiliation that he had suffered when the picture was first seen. They had the effrontery to demand he change it. Change it! Why? He had refused, of course. How could he agree to alter it? Why should he change anything? Wasn't he the greatest painter alive? It would have been a triumph if they had had the boldness and courage to trust to his vision. If they had read Tacitus, as he had, they would have known his account was accurate. But no! It didn't do to show your Republican hero and his fellow conspirators as a bunch of bandits, drunk, even if only on freedom, when they took the oath. Worse, he had used the paint in such a way as to echo the mood of the subject, applied coarsely with a palette knife.

He banged the arm of his chair angrily. What had happened? Why not another success to match the 'Company of Banning Cocq' all those years ago? Why should he fail this time? But, he told himself, he did know why. Of course he did. His way of painting had moved a long way since then, well beyond the comprehension of the dolts who were the city fathers. He broke off some bread and chewed methodically, manoeuvring it around in his mouth to avoid his rotten teeth. Then, in spite of himself, he broke into a smile remembering the baffled look on the faces of the committee when he had unveiled the painting.

His protests had been to no avail. They had sent it

back and the monster had lain rolled up in the corner of his studio for months. With the help of Titus he had spread the painting out on the floor and cut away the important parts. He'd reworked them, and then persuaded the art dealer Van Ludick, to whom he owed money, to take it as payment. Mutilating such a major painting had been anguishing but at least there had been some compensation.

Did he fear being forgotten more than he feared death? Lasting fame relied on the work of scholars who could promote some artists and consign others to oblivion. Perhaps he feared total anonymity more than death? Everyone wanted to be remembered; otherwise what was the point, not only for having lived but for having accomplished something during their lifetime. Was that what kept him going? Was it the belief that his work would leave some kind of inscription on the carapace of history: testimony to his existence? If his work endured, then those whose lives he had touched would be remembered too, even the mediocre would gain lustre from being associated with his name, for having passed through his studio.

The immortality of his clients and patrons rested with him. He would make them immortal, their hidden emotions, fears, ambitions, and arrogance just another ingredient in the mix to be translated into paint. He could make them manifest with a touch of the brush. Those subtle, almost imperceptible aspects of character that his sitters themselves might not recognise or admit to: they were there though, he saw it all. Hadn't they chosen him over other painters in the belief that, through him, they would be honoured and held in high esteem long after they had all departed this life?

There was always a bargain to be struck, a balance to achieve and now he was an old man it was more difficult, even though he knew his work to be infinitely better. Now the decision-making was more enigmatic and profound. In the days before Saskia's death he had had the bravura of youth, the confidence and facility to dare to challenge the conventions of the time. Now in old age he had left all that behind. The challenge now came from within. He would spend hours gazing at the canvas looking for the answer to some intractable conundrum.

There was another painting, unfinished, propped against the wall. It was at an early stage; a huge canvas covered with dark underpainting showing two figures in red with a third kneeling in front of them. It was the moment when the returning prodigal son and his father meet again. It was not finished because it remained a mystery to him. He had made an etching of the same subject when he was much younger and had based the figure of the father on his own father who was going blind, and once again he shown the prodigal's father with his eyes closed. The focal point of the painting was the hands resting on the son's shoulders as he knelt before his father to receive his blessing. He held out his own hands in front of him: there was a lifetime of skill and experience locked into those hands. He had a vague memory of a conversation, many years before, about the prodigal son's journey and the fact that the narrative symbolised the spiritual journey of humanity: specifically a circular journey that returned to its point of departure: birth to death.

So why did he paint? Was it for the money: certainly, except that there was less and less of it. Was it for the fame? That too, but had he really achieved anything or was it all a chimera; an insubstantial thing with no substance; no protection against the vagaries of taste. Sometimes, he wished he could stop. A wan smile crossed his face. He couldn't do that. It was what he was; what he did. What excuse had he to stop: only a dull fatigue. What else would he do with his time? Did he really suppose he could have lived the kind of mundane life that other people lived? No. He needed something that challenged him and nothing else would do. Even after all these years, when he'd proved to himself beyond any doubt that he was the best: it remained a challenge. So why did he doubt it, if he did doubt it? Or was it the man in the mirror: his constant companion for all the lonely years. This man he'd tried to paint in order to discover who he was. He'd dressed him in exotic clothing: disguised him as the lover; the warrior; prophet; and now as himself: an old man. But had he ever really seen him directly or had he only glimpsed him now and then out of the corner of his eye? He couldn't be sure. He seemed always to have been there, always to hand, like a ghost. Was it this other man who doubted? He looked hard into the mirror. Even with this portrait, tomorrow or the day after, he knew he would look at it again and find some fault, something not to his satisfaction. And off he would go again on the fruitless journey to unattainable perfection. He was exhausted; drained; frustrated and dissatisfied and yet he would go on.

# The End

## Acknowledgements

*Although the novel is constructed around real incidents and characters in Rembrandt's life the events described are entirely imaginary.*

*I have had the good fortune to see many of the paintings and prints mentioned in the book and have used catalogue notes and other reference books for research.*
*These include; Mauritshuis, The Hague; Rijksmuseum, Amsterdam; Ashmoleon Museum, Oxford; National Gallery, London; Gemäldegalerie, Berlin; Old Masters Picture Gallery, Dresden; Kunsthistorische Museum, Vienna; Frick Museum, New York; Museum of Fine Arts, Boston; The Art Institute of Chicago, and the State Hermitage Museum, St. Petersburg as well as many smaller museums and galleries.*

*Two books by Simon Schama: 'An Embarrassment of Riches' and 'Rembrandt's Eyes' have been invaluable reference points also the early biographies by Sandrart; Baldinucci, and Houbraken.*

*Any creative activity requires periods of self reflection and analysis; this is especially true of painting which has been the main preoccupation of my career. Writing also entails periods of isolation but it is a more collaborative process with editors, designers and publishers.*

*Jim Dales*